THE SHELTERING STONES SERIES

2

PRAIRIE FLOWERS

A NOVEL OF HISTORICAL FICTION

JOANN KLUSMEYER

innovo
PUBLISHING

Published by Innovo Publishing, LLC
www.innovopublishing.com
1-888-546-2111

Providing Full-Service Publishing Services for Christian Authors, Artists &
Ministries: Books, eBooks, Audiobooks, Music, Screenplays, Film & Curricula

THE SHELTERING STONES HISTORICAL FICTION SERIES FOR ADULTS

BOOK 2

PRAIRIE FLOWERS:
A Novel of Historical Fiction

ISBN: 978-1-61314-732-0

Cover Design & Interior Layout: Innovo Publishing, LLC

Printed in the United States of America
U.S. Printing History
First Edition: 2021

Has God called you to create a Christian book, ebook, audiobook, music album,
screenplay, film, or curricula? If so, visit the ChristianPublishingPortal.com to
learn how to accomplish your calling with excellence. Learn to do everything
yourself, or hire trusted Christian Experts from our Marketplace to help.

CONTENTS

CHAPTER 1

I t was in the year of 1896 that the best picture she could think of to describe her life's work was the few lines of verse written by a 13 year old student in her class.

> Look Up! A vast expanse of skies
> As blue as Scottish lassie's eyes.
> Around! Windswept trees and grass are seen,
> A necklace strip in shades of green.
> Look Down! Beside the footpath as you pass
> Are blossoms growing in the grass
> Like tiny chips of painted glass.
> By Miss Francine Canfield.

She stood in the stony shelter of the Prairie Academy and watched the four young girls who were concentrating on the sheets of paper before them.

Carmelita Wilson, age 13, tapped her pencil against her teeth in deep and careful thought. The teacher was watching, even as she was teaching math to the next class. Miss Josie Wheeler, the teacher, could always see two places at once and maybe three if she needed to.

The thirteen-year-old girl buried her dimpled chin into her hand and propped her elbow against the table. Time to get down to business.

The class of four girls had just spent the last month working on sentences, parts of speech, and capitalization, and now they were studying stories and narrations. A story... they all knew... had three parts: a situation, problem, and a solution. A narration was the chronological enumeration of events.

It was now near the end of their study year, and they were being tested. They would write a narration consisting of their own lives from birth until today. That would be the whole of their Grammar/English final test from the Academy. It was to be written in third person.

She began:

"Carmelita did not remember being born in New York, but her parents insisted that she had been. She kind of remembered being a tiny girl, carried on shoulders, and of being swung in a swing where other children played. Most of what she remembered was the time of looking at the big river."

The thirteen-year-old girl with the pencil was sorely tempted to say "I remembered..." but she knew she must not. This was not an autobiography, told in first person. It must be in third person... like she was writing about someone else. She wanted a shorter name for the little girl, so she decided to make it "Lita."

She continued, "Lita remembered the big river very clearly, the way it was the color of chocolate milk, and how it turned itself over and over and up and down, like the water that made boiled eggs. She remembered the river because it was so easy to see.

"It had seemed a long time ago that the family had moved from the house on the quiet street with the playground at the end of the block. She wished they had not moved, because everything was so different now. She had liked the playground.

"Now she lived in the tall house with two staircases up to the little room where she stayed with her brother Jeff and the baby, Darrell. She had her six-year-old birthday in that house.

"Her brother, Jeff, was nine years old, and he was a big boy who could go to the store to buy milk, bread, potatoes, and beans. Sometimes Lita got to go with him, and they could each spend a penny on candy sticks.

"The worst thing about the tall house was that they were all the time waiting. Papa and her two older brothers had gone across the river to run. Why did they do that? There was a nice place to run in the park where they lived before they moved. The playground was big, and people could run all the way around it. It was a puzzle to Lita, but they moved anyway.

"When Papa and the boys came back, everyone would leave the tall house and maybe move to a playground house again. But then they might have to go a long way in the wagon pulled by a horse. It depended on the place where Papa ran and if they were able to win the race. It was all terribly confusing.

"The only thing not confusing was the river of chocolate milk and the tiny ships that moved up and down on it. Lita could see it plainly from the window of the tall house, and if she blew her breath on the glass of the window, she could make marks with her fingers. She could make rounds and squares and count them. She could count all the way to twenty. Her big brother, Jeff, had helped her learn.

"Sometimes she wrote her ABC's, but there wasn't room on the window for them all, and the breath dried out before she got through.

"Mama hummed a lot and wandered around in the room. When baby Darrell was asleep, she watched out the window with Lita, and sometimes told stories.

"Lita's big brother Jefferson complained a lot because he couldn't go places and was tired of waiting, and Mama made him read books he had already read. Lita didn't care, though, because she liked the stories even if she knew how everything would turn out."

Sharing the table with Carmelita were three other girls: Rosalie, Francine, and Carlotta. The four had listened with open-mouthed horror at Miss Josie's words when she told them that part (actually, all) of their grammar test would be a 2,000 word narration of their lives, up to now. Everything would be true to the best of their memories.

They would attend to sentence structure, punctuation, paragraphs, capitalization, and paragraph indentation. All of these things would be on their certification test, so this was part of getting ready for it next year.

The teacher, Miss Josie, came and stood by the round table where the girls were at work. It usually paid off to have students remember they were being watched. As she looked at the girls, what she experienced was pure pride.

These girls had come into her class at ages barely 10 to almost 12 with scant formal education. Multiplication and division were a foreign language; the whole world consisted of New York, St. Louis, the Mississippi and Arkansas rivers and the Oklahoma Territory. History was made up of what they could remember of their short lifetimes, and their poetry was "Mary had a Little Lamb" and others like it.

For the last two years, these girls had crammed. No four girls had worked harder to press into their minds what they could before returning to their duties at home, as they were well aware of the family sacrifice that permitted them this treat. After all, how much education did a girl need... just to get married, cook, and have babies?

As in every one-room school, older students hardly learned a concept before they must assist in the teaching it to those behind them, and these girls had spent hours with the 5, 6, and 7 year olds. These hours helped to cement their own recently acquired knowledge.

Miss Josie smiled to herself wondering, with pride, if she herself could have done so well. There was Carmelita, called Mellie, with her red-blond curls tight around her face, her delicate bone structure (how could she hope to stand up to the work required of a pioneer woman in the Territory?), and dainty hands.

There was her complexion as pale as milk and her pink tinted lips and cheeks. Eyelashes pale as the fuzz on a dandelion puff and eyes as blue as the sky in October. Delicate chin possessing a deep dimple, identical to Josie's own. She was a beautiful girl and would only become more so. All of this wondrous beauty belonged to her own cousin, and any education that Josie could give her, Josie knew, would not have come to this girl if her own tragic circumstances had not brought her to the Territory.

On either side of Carmelita were the sisters, Rosalie and Francine Canfield, less than a year apart in ages. Both girls took their coloring from their Italian mother, but that was their only similarity. Rosalie, age 11, almost 12, was round faced and dimpled. Her fingers delicately pointed and her hands small. Tan complexion and abundant coal black hair in a dutch cut... short with bangs. A style requiring very little care after a quick comb.

She sister, Francine, was less than a year younger and two inches taller. Face slim, with dark brows growing straight across over her eyes and well pronounced. Cheekbones that would become more pronounced, and shining black hair that reached her shoulder blades. Today it was tied back with a strip of flowered fabric. Arms long and shapely and fingers smooth with blunted ends. Josie had heard that the blunt finger shape was called artist's hands. Well, time would tell. At this moment, Francine sat tall and straight and stared at her paper in intense concentration.

Last at the table was Carlotta. One could say that most of nature's bounty had been settled upon this eleven and a half year old. Her complexion was purely English, pale cream and deep rose. A sprinkling of tan freckles were on their way to fading out. Light brown brows in a classic arch and face shape as oval as a smooth almond kernel. A face that dimpled deeply when she smiled. From the time she could walk, Carlotta's beauty had turned eyes, and it was a certainty that the attention would only increase with her age. The girl, an only child, had been so carefully reared, that she had never considered herself prettier than any other and was forever alertly eager to please. She loved just being included.

Eighteen-year-old Josie had plans for these four. She had never considered herself a teacher but only a person favored with an education that was not usually given to girls and a desire to pass it on. Perhaps these girls would choose marriage and a home life, and that was good, but it should be of their own choosing and at a time they chose. On that, Josie was adamant. An option. They should have a choice. Most girls in the Territory in the late 1800's did not have, or expect to have, that choice.

Of the three commonly offered directions open to girls were kitchen help, sewing, or school teaching. Of the first two, Josie was not qualified to help, but the third was a definite possibility if these girls chose to avail themselves.

Josie had already procured a copy of the certification test for school teacher and learned that the state minimum hiring age was 14. She was determined to have these girls ready with certificate in hand if that was their choice.

She had issued 10 sheets of paper (more if they needed it) and an assignment to write a narration of at least 2,000 words covering the remembered experiences of their short life. This would require an in-depth memory search to fill that word requirement, and that, also, was part of the education. As her own teacher had told her, "The mind of a child was not a bucket to be filled, but a muscle to be stretched."

Not much stretching happened in the homes on the frontier, especially for girls. There was just too much work that descended upon everyone, all of it necessary just to exist.

Carmelita, of the strawberry blond curls, tapped her teeth with her pencil, touched her tongue to the lead, then applied it to the paper as a newly remembered experience inspired her.

"Mama must not have known at first that Papa was home because when he knocked at the door, she shivered and would not go to open the lock. Then Papa said, "Nettie? Are you in there?"Then Mama started to cry as she ran to open the door.

"Papa and the boys were grinning happily, but Lita had no idea what that meant. Would they be going to a house by the park, or to the wagon crossing over the chocolate milk river? No one asked her what she would rather do. If they had, she wouldn't have known what to answer.

"She had never been across the chocolate milk river, but it sounded as though that was where they would go.

"Something really bad could happen. That was when the little girl shivered with fright. How would they keep the chocolate milk from seeping into the wagon, and would the horses be able to swim when the milk boiled and turned itself over and over like it was full of ropes? She tried to ask someone, but no one seemed to care what she said. Even though she spoke plainly and said each word carefully.

"It was that very same day that everything in the room in the tall house was put into two wagons that had a tent over them like a little house. Papa, Mama, Lita, and the baby crawled into the tent house on the first wagon, and Junior, Douglas, and Jefferson got in the other one. Junior sat on the driver's seat and looked so small after watching Papa, but he knew what he was doing. So did Douglas, and he sat right up there beside Junior as their wagon moved along behind Papa's. Jefferson was standing up behind Douglas.

"Lita had been scared so long she was no longer frightened by thoughts of the Hot Chocolate river. If she drowned??? Well. She's just drown, but it would be with her family, and why would she want to live without her family? She looked out the back of the tent on the wagon and stared right into the faces of her brothers. They were laughing and talking, and her other brother, Jeff, was laughing and talking with them.

"So… if her brothers were not afraid, then she would not be afraid, either. She was still looking back when the wagon beneath her began to rumble and rock, and when she crawled to the front beside Papa and Mama, she saw that she was on a BIG, BIG boat and the Hot Chocolate was all around her.

"She grinned with relief and began to laugh with sheer happiness. Papa turned to look at her and asked what was funny. Lita stopped laughing long enough to say, "Papa! We aren't going to drown in the Hot Chocolate!"

"Papa said, "Hot Chocolate?" It was just like he didn't know what was in the river.

"Yes, Papa," she answered, pointing. "Just look out there. See all the Hot Chocolate boiling?"

"Then Papa said, 'Look out there, Mama. Doesn't that look like chocolate? This girl of ours is going to be a writer. Just you wait and see.'

"Mama was too busy to look. She was cleaning up where Baby Darrell upchucked. That was all right. Lita would tell her about it after a while.

"At night they all went to sleep beside the road. Next to them was another wagon, and people were sleeping in it. Lita wondered if they were going to the race to run like Papa, and the big boys had. She could have told them that it was no use to go because her Papa had already won the race.

"For breakfast, the family had huge bowls of oatmeal with yellow lakes of butter melting all over it. There was even brown sugar to sprinkle on top, but Baby Darrell didn't get any sugar. He only got butter. He wouldn't have gotten butter if Jeff had watched him like Mama said and grabbed his hand. He made a real mess with the butter. "

Miss Josie had told the girls they might stay after school for a while and write if they wanted to. She had also told them that the first copy... the rough draft, she called it... must be done at school while she could watch. They could make notes if they thought of something at home that they wanted to include, but it would be written at school.

Then, after they finished, they would be given brand new clean sheets of paper to copy their essay in their best penmanship. They could make any changes they wanted to make. Miss Josie told them she would also want the rough draft as well as the finished copy. It was all a part of the test.

She told them that these biographies, along with the memorization of the nine rules of capitalization would be their final test before taking the certification test that would enable them to be a teacher.

Rosalie Canfield, the almost 13-year-old girl, quick thinking and quick moving, had finished several pages filled with her sloping cursive words.

...“One of the nicest things was the gifts Grandma Nicolo gave the three children. Rosalie and Francine received such darling little chests, or maybe they were like suitcases. Inside the case, Rosalie came eye to eye with the most beautiful doll in the world. She wore a dress that was all pink lace, and there were pink crocheted stockings. She wore the most precious little shoes made of white felt and tied with a shiny white ribbon.

“A peek at Francine's case showed the same doll dressed in yellow.

“The girls' brother, Raymond, didn't get a suitcase. He got a box with a hinged lid. When he peeked in, he was too excited to talk, and he crawled to the back of the wagon hugging the box, and then opened it, so he could take everything out. From where she sat, Rosalie thought it was a lot of wooden animals and boy things that were painted in bright colors. He seemed to like them, and that was good. Maybe it would keep him from whining.

“Rosalie lifted out the doll, and beneath it there were six more dresses. They were made in all different colors with stockings to match, and there was another pair of shoes made of brown felt and a pair of boots made in black. There was a pink flowered night grown made in soft, fuzzy flannel, and it had a cute little nightcap knitted with pink yarn.

“The girl could see below the dresses that there was a blanket pieced like a real quilt, and when she lifted it out to wrap the doll, she saw that in the bottom of the case there were four picture books with stories and they all said 'For My Sweet Rosalie from Grandma Nicolo' written in pretty blue ink.

“Under the picture books were a color book and two boxes of crayons with six different colors in each box.

“Mama had watched as the girls looked at their presents, and she smiled as they squealed with excitement at each new thing. She said she was glad that the dolls were different and that none of the dresses were alike, so they wouldn't get mixed up, because it was going to be a long trip, and she didn't want any problems.

The girls weren't really sure where they were going. Mama tried to tell them, but they still didn't know. They only knew that

Papa was happy all the time, and in his loud voice he sang all the songs he knew. It was fun to see Papa so happy. He sat up on a high bench while he drove the horses, and Mama could sit beside him if she wanted, but she mostly didn't want to. When she didn't want to, the girls could take turns on the high bench, but they couldn't take all the gift toys with them if they did. Rosalie took the first turn and wrapped the doll in the quilt and left the rest of the suitcase full of gifts under the bench.

"There wasn't much to see. She saw one little hill after the other and watched the horses as they waded through one little stream after the other. Papa watched with her, and they saw a lot of birds, and Papa pointed out the different ones and told her their names. The birds wouldn't stay still so she could get a good look at them and know them later. Maybe they didn't want anyone to know them, all except the crows. Papa didn't have to tell her about the crows, because she already knew about them."

The children of the Prairie Academy had trooped out at the end of the day, and after a last look around, the helper, Miss Janine, rounded up her little brother, Tray, and headed home. It was amazing how much she could find to do to help out so she could earn the time it took for her brother to learn.

The four remaining girls nibbled cookies and scribbled on their paper. Francine sat straight and tall, her long fingers easily moving the pencil. She always insisted that the lead be sharp, so she was more often working with the whittling knife. She examined the point of the lead and deemed it satisfactory.

Her story was now three pages long, and she continued to write as her memory directed.

"Francine, often called Francy, took her doll from the little wooden box and set her aside so she could lay all the dresses in a row. There were seven of them, including the one on the doll, and each one was made very differently with special trimming and darling little buttons that really worked.

"Her brother, Raymond, was a year younger, and he had a different kind of box. It contained the most painted animals in all the world! It had some little boards that fit together to make a barn and a shed, and some painted blocks of hay. The wagons had wheels that really worked, and the horses could really pull the wagons when he pushed with his finger.

"Raymond wanted to take everything out at once, but Mama wouldn't let him. She gave him a board, and she said he could play with only what he could put on that board. She said if they lost those little animals in the quilts, they'd never find them, and maybe they'd get broke.

"She told him that would be terrible because as long as we were going to be living in the wagon, he would need all the toys to play with.

"Raymond got something else that looked fun. Mama wouldn't let him open the can until we stopped for supper. It was full of little sticks that fit together, and there was a sheet that showed how to build cabins and barns and other things. The sticks had a name called Lincoln Logs. Mama said they were named after a president, whatever that was.

"The Logs looked interesting, and Francy asked him if she could play with them with him. He said she could if she'd stay in the back of the wagon the next day, so he would have someone to talk to. She didn't mind that, but he mostly talked to his horses and cows. That was all right because she was busy looking at her doll's dresses.

"It seemed as though she just couldn't get her eyes full enough of the lace and ruffles and the tiny buttons. She looked at the dresses and was happy for each one of them, but she'd really like to have a whole lot more. She didn't say that to her Mama, though, because she knew Mama would say she was being greedy. Mama thought that Grandma Nicolo had been generous enough with the presents so the children would have something to play with while they traveled."

The teacher watched. So different... these four girls. She watched as they bent industriously over their work. She had seen them almost daily for over two years. One learns a lot that way.

There was Carlotta. Sometimes called Lottie. So many of the gifts from heaven were piled on this one little girl. Almost twelve years old, now, and she exhibited every indication that she would be a knock out beauty and that her parents had resisted spoiling her. Good natured, helpful when she assisted the Level Three boys with their math games and sang number songs with the 5 and 6 year olds.

She had a naturally giving spirit and seemed to want only to be part of the group. What would she be when she noticed every head at Carlile Corners turn her way?

She studied as hard as she could, succeeded superbly, and all this with parents who wished only that she be happy. They faithfully saw that she attended every day... though they may wonder why would she need all that learning just to cook, clean, and produce a family? They didn't say that, exactly, but that was the attitude of so many of the adults. The girls studied math "just like a boy" and... why? For what end? But how were the needs of boys so different from girls? Miss Josie could only shake her head and wonder.

At this moment Carlotta tapped the eraser end of the pencil against the frowns on her forehead as she concentrated on a thought. Then suddenly as a spring shower, a small smile appeared and the pencil began scribbling furiously. It was a good thing this essay was to be re-copied. Josie did, however, have a teacher's curiosity to see their rough draft and note the changes they would make on the final copy.

Carlotta, her teacher decided, could go either way. Her parents were not exactly the pioneer type, though they tried hard to be. Their only daughter also tried very hard. She now had three friends who accepted each other for what they all were, girls of a near equal age living in the newness of the Territory. Carlotta might actually have been just as eager for friendship with the girls a year or two younger. It will be interesting to watch her grow up, her teacher decided.

Josie, herself, had her own work to do. Having been reminded by her former tutor that she must concentrate on HAVING A LITTLE FUN, she did not permit her lesson preparation to occupy so much of her time as at the beginning.

She was startlingly surprised when neighbor Brad Cullen had invited her, together with his sister, Janine, and Josie's cousin, Jefferson, (the fellow with the head full of tight red curls), to an outing.

It seemed the small village of Argyle five miles away had managed to acquire a machine that made "store-bought" ice cream. So much better than having to wait until the weather snowed to make that popular confection and then consume the delicacy while hovering over the potbelly stove to keep warm.

The four young people, Josie and her cousin, Jeff, with Brad Cullen, the young blacksmith and his sister Janine, sat around the tiny ice cream table on delicate looking wire chairs, so close that their knees almost touched. How did they ever find so many things to talk about, and why were so many things terribly funny?

They chatted and laughed and spooned the favored dessert. So much was said and laughed about, but later the serious-minded Josie could hardly remember a thing that that had been uttered. Certainly nothing of importance passed any set of lips.

Maybe this was fun…?

Maybe it was just a waste of time, but it didn't seem like it. The foursome went again to the Sweet Shop and on Saturday's every two weeks or so after that.

Brad Cullen was four and five years older than the others and so interestingly persuasive that it was easy to let him direct the festivities.

Brad, himself, had a purpose. Back at the school and with the children around, he had been unable to get any attention from the teacher. She treated him as though he was just one of the community, one who was helpful and solved problems for her, as he had promised to do, so his little brother could attend the classes. Now, however, here at the ice cream table, he could see Josie in a different light. And she, at last, saw him.

Having seated himself across the table rather than beside her, he took full advantage of his position. Josie, he noted, had finally relaxed her squarish shoulders… a little. The chin that was carefully held level was allowed to lower… a bit… and her laughter managed to define her single dimple... right in the middle of her chin. Her well-formed mouth became mobile and even mirthful as she and her cousin teased, and when she batted playful verbal barbs with his sister, Janine.

And his sister, growing up as she did with no mother, was just as verbally proficient especially in the company others.

Back to Josie through Brad's eyes. Tall, for a girl. Shoulders broader, perhaps, than would be considered fashionable. Strongly formed hands and feet that would not be considered dainty... if shoe size was the measure. She wore nice clothes, better than most in the territory, but wore them so naturally and with ease, and not as something to be noticed. Measured steps. Her whole manner exuded confidence, and that was without doubt valuable when teaching children. She knew what she was doing, and intended that her instruction be the final word.

Even with the hyperactive five-year-old brother of Brad's. Josie had somehow intrigued him, giving him no opportunity to argue. Firm, but fair. Stern, but with a smile.

Brad valued this opportunity to evaluate Josie from the social angle. This was because he had already decided, firmly, that she would eventually be his. It might take a while, as she had her own aims, plans and concerns, but he was patient. From the first glimpse, she had attracted him as no other girl had been able, and here she was, living less than a half a mile away.

In the school room, Josie, watching her Level Four girls with their essays, moved a bit to avoid staring and making them nervous. They had all four opted to stay a while to work after the other students had gone. Quieter. Easier to concentrate.

Carlotta was bent over her paper, her hair, fair and honey-streaked, wavy and curled at the end, hung down over her ears and hid her face, but her hand guiding the pencil moved furiously.

"Lottie, almost five years old, rode along the bumpy road, and her thoughts twisted themselves around in her head like tiny ropes. When she asked where they were going, her Mama said 'just down the road a ways.' That was not true, because they had been riding all day. That was longer than 'a ways'. That told her that Mama didn't know the answer, either, so she didn't bother her again. No use to make her feel bad just because she didn't know.

"Papa whistled a tune like he was happy, but then he yelled at the horses. Sometimes he yelled at 'Gee' and sometimes at 'Haw', so that must be the names of the horses, though she noticed he couldn't tell which was which.

"Finally it seemed better to wrap her stuffed bear in his blanket and watch out the back of the tent that was over the wagon. Sometimes both she and the bear leaned over on the pillow and went to sleep. But just about the time she got to sleep, the wagon stopped, and Mama woke her up to go into the bushes and wee wee. Even if she didn't have to.

"When it got dark, Papa tied the horses to a tree. The animals moved around in the dark, and they ate grass all night jingling the straps around their necks.

"Mama made a bed in the tent, and everybody went to sleep right beside the road. The girl heard chirpy sounds all around her, so she whispered to the bear not to be scared. She would take care of him. To prove it, she hugged him tighter.

"Then one day Papa had to keep stopping so Mama could upchuck, and she tried really hard to, but sometimes she couldn't. Then she cried when she got back in the wagon. Papa hugged her and said it would all be worth it, but that didn't help Mama to upchuck when she wanted to. Lottie didn't like to upchuck, but she thought everyone should get to do what they wanted to, if they could. And it surely seemed that Mama really wanted to.

"Just when Lottie began to think she would be riding the rest of her life, Papa told the Gee horse to turn off the road. He was whistling and happy, and he unfolded a tent and helped Mama make a bed in it. He opened the tin box of crackers and slices of cheese, and they all ate.

"There were two big trees over the tent and a lot of little bushes. Mama looked around and told Papa, there's no place to wee wee. Just look around. Papa looked around, and stopped whistling.

"That was when they got back in the wagon and rode back to the town where they had a house with beds. It had a privy house in the back, and Mama was glad. Lottie was glad because there were girls and boys, and they wanted her to play with them.

"Papa came and hugged her and told her to be a good girl for Mama, but he didn't have to say that because Lottie was always good. He waved goodbye and said he would come back for them. The girl waved and then went to hold hands while the boys and girls played 'drop the handkerchief'. They played games until it was too dark to see each other.

"Mama and Lottie got to sleep on a bed in a room with other people, and she was glad she remembered to keep her bear with her. She didn't want him to be scared. Mama liked the room with a bed and they both went right to sleep. There was nothing chirpy in the trees to keep them awake."

When the classroom clock said the girls had been writing for an hour, Josie stopped them. "Enough for today, girls."

They had hardly left when Brad came by with his wagon, dusty and dirty and in his work overalls. He greeted her with a pleased grin. "Janine said I was supposed to pick you up and bring you for supper. I always follow orders. Something about making noodles… or something."

Oh, yes. Concentrating on the girls had taken Janine's offer from her mind. She was going to make chicken noodles, a favorite of her family, and she offered to show Josie how noodles were made. For a cheap, tasty dish, she had said, one couldn't beat noodles, and if there were any left, they were always better the next day.

Not only noodles appeared on the table. Fresh baked blackberry pie, made from the last jar she had brought to the Territory, and there was tender chicken and a salad of new greens. One thing about Janine, she could cook.

Brad appeared at the table clean and shaven and then took her back home in the buggy after they had eaten. He didn't hurry. Brad had noticed that another place where Josie managed to relax was at Janine's table. Smiles. Dimple. Lowered chin. A truly different person from the one in the classroom.

Well, she had that right. The schoolroom was her job, and he was certainly different when he was on his job. Shoeing a horse made it difficult to stay clean and still keep from getting the rough end of an impatient horse hoof in the kneecap. He had bruises to prove it.

It was the next day that Josie's cousin, Carmelita, finished the last page of her essay. It was with a smile and a jab of the pencil on the last period that it was concluded.

Today's contribution went as follows: "It was when she was twelve years old that Lita met her own fairy god mother.

"From six years to through eleven years, she did what the other girls did in the Territory. She ran errands, did small jobs that became harder and harder as she became older and older. Everyone must have thought she did a good job because if they had not they would have told her to do better.

"There were times to play with friends and times that families joined their meals together, but everyone had to work so hard and got so tired the bed was the only place that looked good a lot of the time.

"When Lita turned twelve, she looked in the mirror to see if there were any changes. She really looked, maybe for the first time to see what kind of a person she was. Some days she felt like an empty shell just waiting for the proper filling, like the lemon pies her Ma liked to make. She knew deep down inside that if she told someone how she felt, they would think her crazy... or joking. Other days she felt like she was one great, big question mark.

"Some days were good, though. One job that so many of the girls hated was gathering cowpats, but not Lita. Evenings were best for that, as sometimes they were dampish in the mornings and no one wanted a damp or mushy cowpat. Often her thought went like this... like she was thinking of another person.

"What she likes about that job is that she can be alone when she is actually alone. Much of the time she was alone with other people around, and she thought about the same things every day… mostly about what she had to do next. But while gathering cow pats, she would be out in the fields, and a cottontail rabbit would jump up and hop away, and she would have told him that if he had been really still, she would never have seen him. Maybe he wanted to be seen. How would it be to think like a rabbit and live inside the furry head, behind the big eyes and under the tall ears? Does that sound strange?'

"Poor Lita! Always having weird thoughts that couldn't be talked about. She stared at the row of noisy crows on the barn roof and wondered what they were saying to each other. They turned this way and that, like a bunch of ladies with their cookies and teacups, gossiping on an afternoon.

"Then something happened when Lita became twelve. Somehow it seemed like a 'landing' to her… you know like when you go part way up a staircase, and then there is a little platform and the stairs turn and go the rest of the way up? Well, that's what it seemed like for Lita to become twelve. It was a landing, and now she must turn and go on up to… where? What was up there? How could a girl know where she was going? And whether she should hurry… or slow down. Maybe she should stop entirely. How could she know?

"A look at Mama and it seemed that even she hadn't figured it out, either. Get up. Think of breakfast, think of chores, think about dirty clothes to be washed. These things had to be done, of course, but there should be something else to think on while doing them.

"And then Lita would worry that she was being silly. Or maybe she was like Cinderella and only dreaming that there was something more if she went up the right staircase.

"It was that year that the family had a tragedy. Her mother's sister back in New York had a fire in their house, and she and her husband were killed. They left a girl and a boy with no parents, and the two would be coming on the train to live in the Territory with her family.

"The girl, her cousin, was almost a lady. Seventeen. What would she be like? Would she like Lita, or would she be mad that she had to come there to live? Mama worried about having two more people in a house that was already too small, but she wouldn't have it that they go anywhere else. Family members stayed together, Mama said, and they made room for each other.

"It was pretty much a month before they came. There were things to do there in New York that no one told Lita about, but that is the way grownups are. They tell you if they are of a mind to, and don't if they don't want to. When you're just twelve years old, you're still standing on that landing.

"Then finally they knew when the train would bring them. Lita's brother, Jeff, got to go to meet the cousins. He was the lucky one because he was the only person who could drive the big buggy and that could be spared from the farm for that length of time. Everyone had so much to do, and he would be gone for most of three days.

"Lita wanted to go with him so bad that she could taste it, and it tasted bitter. She knew WHY she shouldn't get to go, but that didn't help. She went to bed and lay awake thinking about how it would be to have a seventeen-year-old girl cousin actually in her house, and then she would be scared that her cousin wouldn't like a twelve year old bothering her. She thought the cousin might not even like her little sister, Esther, hanging onto her like she owned her... as Lita knew she would.

"It was just after noon on the third day, and no one had gotten much done for thinking and watching down the road. Finally, they heard a crunch of the buggy wheels, and the dogs started barking because they knew the sound of the family buggy.

"Jeff pulled into the yard and was hardly stopped when a little boy jumped out and went flying across the yard. Mama caught him, though, because she's had experience with little boys. She looked him over, sniffed a couple of times, and wiped her eyes, and then let him go.

"Jeff was grinning from ear to ear, like he was the one who made the world and hung the sun. He held out his arm like he was someone important, and the lady put her hand on his arm and stepped down to the ground.

"Lita looked at her cousin, and it fair took her breath away. She was tall, almost as tall as Jeff, and she walked even taller, like she knew where she was going and was very brave. Her beautiful cape hung over her shoulders with every pleat in place. Her velvet bonnet was tied neatly, and the brim was straight with a tiny ruffle on the edge. Her carpetbag was looped over her arm, and she looked around and saw Mama.

"She walked toward Mama, and it was a good thing because Lita wanted to move toward her, but she couldn't. Her feet were stuck like she stood in sticky mud. She thought, 'this lady is so beautiful, and she was belongs to us. She is really part of our family.' It was true that her grandparents and Lita's had been the same people.

"It was like the twelve year old suddenly looked up the rest of the staircase and could even see the top! She couldn't see exactly what was there, but she knew there was something up there.

"She watched the beautiful, brave, tired face of her cousin and saw her lips become tight and her eyes become shiny. Mama opened her arms, and the beautiful lady walked into them, and her tears streamed down her face, and so did Mama's. Lita looked and saw the sadness looking out of her cousin's face.

"It was then that Lita felt her stomach and insides seem to shrivel up and dissolve. She felt so sad for her cousin because she had lost her parents, but still she was so brave!

"When Lita could finally move, she hugged her cousin and her Mama together. Papa came and hugged them all, and Jeff stood back and looked at us like he didn't need to see anything else as good as this in the whole rest of his life.

"Somehow… some way… Lita knew a certain thing at that moment. She knew that this beautiful cousin would understand about the staircase and she wouldn't even have to explain it to her in so many words. It seemed very clear to the younger girl that she was just a few more steps down the staircase from this lady, and all she had to do was follow. All she had to do was climb because this lady knew where all the steps were. She knew, because she had climbed them herself, and there were no more surprises.

CHAPTER 2

Lita could almost picture a fairy godmother standing beside the pumpkin that was not yet a golden chariot. She could feel the beautiful gown and the glass slippers almost as though she was wearing them, and they were so much more than she had ever dreamed of. She could almost feel the excitement of what was ahead of her, though she didn't know what it was.

"With her cousin Josie in their house, it seemed everyday that Lita learned something new and had new exciting ideas just pop into her head from nowhere. Josie knew about so many things, and she said it was her job to see that her brother knew what their father had planned for him to know. Her little brother was very lucky, but she, Lita, was just as lucky.

"Lita knew she shouldn't brag about her cousin, but she couldn't keep from telling her friend, Rosalie. Maybe Rosalie was standing on her own landing, too, because she was as excited as Lita was about the cousin, though they still didn't know what of.

"Then when the school happened, Lita thought she would burst. While she listened, she noticed how Josie walked and sat, and how she crossed her ankles. Of course, that's not the way Lita started to act, but she knew that was the RIGHT way for a lady to be, and when she wanted to be a lady, it would be good to know how.

"Then her cousin let the students teach. How did she know they could do such an important job? She would explain something to the older girls and then have them explain it to the younger ones. She let them hold the study cards with numbers on them and let the little kids shout out the answers. The bigger girls felt so important and proud, and they wanted to do a really good job, so the teacher would be proud of them and let them do more. They wanted her to smile at them, but they knew that, at school, they must earn her smiles. Teaching was such fun! And such a challenge!

"Then there was the night that Lita had a dream, and she woke herself up crying. In the dream, she was standing on the landing of that stairway, looking up. While she was looking up, she saw a lady… and she knew the lady was a teacher. She didn't look down at Lita.

"She had a ruler and a pencil, and was talking about measuring… how inches make feet and so on. Lita watched the teacher's hands, and she knew they belonged to cousin Josie. She looked up into the teacher's face and it was… not Josie! The face that looked at her was the same one she saw in the mirror the day she was twelve.

"Then the dream started to fade. Lita reached out with both hands to grab hold onto it, but it was gone like smoke through her fingers.

"She was dreadfully sorry the dream had gone, but she was happy, too. Now she had something to work for. She knew that she had been permitted a glimpse of the face at the top of the ladder so that she would know what she would be when she reached the top. Her hands would be like Josie's… doing what a teacher does, but the face would be hers.

"Whatever it took to be a teacher, that was what she would do. She would work hard and learn everything that was taught to her because there must be so many girls like her in the territory…."

Miss Josie spoke, and the girls looked up at her. "Time to stop, now. I can't let you get too tired, or you can't do your best work."

The flesh and blood Carmelita felt her throat tighten, just like she was being gagged. Looking at her cousin, she pled, "Please let me write just two more sentences! Please!"

Not waiting for permission, she grabbed up the pencil and continued her thought "….girls like her in the territory who stood on their own stairway and looked up at nothing but more steps. Lita knew she wanted to climb up to the top, so she could stand

and look back. That was the way she could show them the way up". Then Lita drew in a deep breath and let it out.

"'That is what I will do,' she promised herself."

Period. Paragraph finished. A smile of relief as she lay down her pencil.

The girls left Josie to her quiet classroom. Of their own accord, she felt her hands lifting up her cousin's essay. She just had to see that was so pressing in the last few sentences that they must be written now. Backing up several pages to get the thought, Josie read of the expectation of her arrival in the territory. She read the descriptive words her cousin wrote about her feelings and the emptiness of her life… nothing but steps going into the great nowhere.

Josie scrubbed away the tear so it would not damage the words on the sheet and continued to read on until she reached the dream. She sniffed, wiped her eyes, and kept reading.

Weary and exhausted at the end of the day, Josie felt the passionate words cause her throat to tighten and her heart to pound. Maybe… just maybe… Josie had actually done something important. Not that she had set out to do it, but accidents do happen.

Her cousin had guessed right. Josie knew the feeling Carmelita had, not from emptiness, but of indecision. Lack of direction. Was this actually the right stairway for her?

Josie felt such a moment of satisfaction. If she had done something, even one little thing, for that beautiful young girl who was part of her own family, then how could she ever again feel that she had done nothing?

Fact remained: Whatever she had done for Carmelita, the girl had done twice that for her. Still she must realize that there was not a teacher at the top of her own staircase, but something more. Perhaps she would also learn in a dream what it was.

Putting the papers back in their folder, she slid them into the desk drawer and called to Flip. "We need a walk. Let's go get the mail." The little dog ran to the door and yipped. He was ready. Always.

It was later, in the middle of the night, that the moon shone like daytime across her bed. But it wasn't the moonlight that had awaken Josie. Far from it. As her consciousness returned, Josie saw in her mind the sheet of paper she had read... the one that Carmelita had written. The page was numbered page 10. That was to have been the last page, and it was not possible that she had completed the entire essay.

Could the girl have misunderstood? Josie could not accept that premise. Her cousin didn't miss much, and certainly not something as important as this assignment. She had seemed so eager. Well, that was tomorrow's concern. Tonight was for sleep.

But it wasn't. Finally, with a resigned sigh, she slid her feet from under the cover down to the cozy fur rug. Flip cocked an ear and leaped up to plant himself beside her. Wherever she went, she would surely need him, and besides... there might be a buttered biscuit that she needed help with.

Josie lit the lamp with a go-fer match and carried it to the table. Removing Carmelita's sheaf of papers from the folder, she flipped through the completed sheets. Pages 5, 6, 7, and 8 were totally blank. Why?

When the question was put to her cousin, she met a wide-eyed look of innocence and a sense that the girl was questioning her as to why there was a question.

"I had to do it that way. The middle couldn't happen until the dream was done. You know...? I know you don't know what the pages say, but I had to do it this way, so it would make sense when I wrote it all down."

Chastened, Josie nodded. She was guilty of prejudging a project unfinished, and she knew it. It was obvious that Carmilita knew what the end result would be, so she had to fit in the middle parts... or something. She put the report into the girl's outstretched hand with a nod and an apologetic smile.

Francine had already found her place and begun. She sat tall and straight as few eleven year olds would attempt. Her long-fingered hand with the blunted fingertips gripped her pencil in the relaxed, slanted position explained in the penmanship book.

Her cursive letters flowed from her pencil in a perfect copperplate script... continuous and oval. It seemed she didn't realize that what she was writing now was just a draft. Her work looked like a finished product. It would be interesting to see what changes she decided to make when she recopied.

She had written, "When the little girl called Francy reached the age of eleven, she could not remember much of the trip in the wagon. After all, she had been barely four years old, but there had been the lovely surprise from Grandma Nicolo. The surprise was even better than going to the Sorbet Shoppe for an ice cream cone... or even an unexpected trip to the playground swings.

"What little Francy saw was a whole armload of tiny dresses that fit a doll. The doll dresses were made out of magic. Miniature over-skirts crocheted from glistening spider webs, trimmed in pearls made from dewdrops. She could only dream of such fascinating beauty. Some dresses were flower gardens enclosed in picket fences made of shiny lace, and whole sleeves were made of the same lace.

"One dress had darling buttons made from flower shapes, and they were so close together down the front of the dress that they almost touched. The little girl showed the dress to her brother who said, 'Uh huh,' and went back to trying to make his toy horses stand up on a board, with the wagon shaking and rattling. She decided then that he didn't get to see any of the other magic things she had been given or he might cry for them. He was only three, and he would mess them up.

"There was a dress made of red velvet, trimmed in pointed lace made from black thread. The dress had a little jacket cut from a thick kind of black cloth and a tiny hat that was just for looks and not to keep warm. The little hat had a ribbon that tied under the chin. Francy had a lot of troubled tying a ribbon, so her Mama tied it, and the little girl slipped the hat off and on carefully so it could stay tied.

"One dress was shiny pink and made out of ruffles, one sewed onto the other, and tiny white buttons from the neck to the waist and on the cuff of each puffy sleeve. The dresses felt so

31

smooth and wonderful, it was fun to move her hand over then, like she was petting a kitty.

"That's when her Mama said they would have to get a wet cloth to wipe her hands if she was going to pat the dresses that way. She said that the old wagon kicked up dust and made hands get dirty, and there wouldn't be a way to wash the dresses for a long time. She knew Francy would want them to stay new just like Grandma Nicolo made them.

"The little girl discovered that when she spread them all out side by side, along with the soft, fuzzy night gown, they made a row as wide as her arms could reach, and she felt like she had the best thing in the whole world. But she didn't because there was more to come.

"The day before the wagon stopped at Carlile Corners, Mama gave her and her sister another present that was soft and wrapped in paper. It was tied with a bowknot in the string, and Francy knew how untie a bow, even if she couldn't tie it, so she jerked on the loose string and the paper package opened.

"What she saw made her gasp so she could hardly breathe. There were more dresses, and they were maybe even prettier than ones she had. Mama showed her how there were four dresses, one for each finger, and one for each year she had birthdays.

"When they stopped for their picnic lunch, Francy and her sister spread out all of their doll dresses, and there was not even two of them just alike. How did Grandma Nicolo know how to make so many different dresses? They looked good enough to eat, and she licked her lips thinking about them. She decided right there that when she was big like Mama, she would find out where to get beautiful dresses like that so she could wear them every day.

"When Papa stopped the wagon for the last time, there was no house to go into, so they lived in the wagon for a long time. Papa didn't care, though, and he whistled and sang all the time he hammered and dug holes. Mama looked tired, but she helped sometimes and was always trying to have something to eat ready because Papa and the helper man were always so hungry.

"Sometimes Francy put her doll and all the dresses in the little box with the handle and played with her brother. He really liked that, and he let her pick which animals she liked to play with. The sheep were nice, but the chickens and ducks were more fun. They stood on little round pieces that looked like a clump of grass.

"Their bigger sister, Rosy, liked to chase butterflies and rabbits, and one time she caught a frog. She could make it squeak, and it surprised Papa, because he didn't think a frog could squeak if it was held. Francy didn't know why her sister...."

Pencils stopped. The time was up. There were other things to do. Josie instructed the Level Two class to play the Domino Game for a while and let Level One watch. It got so exciting sometimes that it took all four girls to keep order. Level Four was always quick to help when things began to get out of hand.

The Domino Game was a middle-of-the-night inspiration of the teacher's. The Caller gave out a number below 25, and the players would race each other to be first to spot the number of dominos with that number of total spots… no more and no less. It was fascinating to watch the speed of their minds as they grabbed out the little wooden squares, their mental activity saying that double blue, blank yellow and yellow/green made 20 (or double yellow and blank green), so then they would need a blank red to make 25 (or a blue/purple).

Once in a while the number was raised to fifty as an extra challenge, and it was a stretch for seven and eight year olds, but even Level One could play if the number was lowered to 10. It was then that a pair was formed with one from each level, so the younger ones could occasionally 'win' and feel successful.

Josie had not intended to peek at the drafts the older girls were writing, but the temptation was just too strong.

Carlotta wrote in good eleven-year-old cursive… letters uniform and spacing correct, just the way anyone who knew Carlotta would expect it to be. "…and the Papa came and got Lottie and her Mama where he had left them. Lottie was glad to see Papa, but it was hard to wave goodbye to the children at the

33

house with the beds. It had been such fun to play with everyone. Sometimes her Mama took her walking in the stores that had clothes and hammers and a lot of things.

"Mama told Papa that their little girl had a lot of fun with the other children, and Papa had put his arm around Mama and told her it would all be worth the trouble, and maybe there would soon be someone for her to play with.

"Lottie heard him say that, and it sounded good. It would be fun to have someone to play with, but she knew the word 'maybe' was scary, because so many times it was a 'no-no.' One couldn't ever count on a 'maybe'.

"When the wagon stopped, there was a house that was so tiny it looked like a dollhouse, and there were a lot of boards laying around everywhere. Mama didn't say much, but she was glad there was a privy house. It wasn't very big, but it would be all right for now.

"Mama tried to cook on the tiny little stove, but a lot of the time she just cried. It wasn't so bad when Papa could shoot rabbits. Mama could make soup and dumplings, and she could eat those without having to upchuck.

"They crowded everything into the tiny house, and then the house grew another room. Papa hung a rope between the two big trees, and Mama fastened the wet clothes there after she washed them in the tiny river.

"Then the Mama got sick again, and Lottie's bed was moved into the room where Mama cooked. The Papa rode away and came back with a woman to help Mama get well. She wasn't very good at it, because Mama cried all night, and sometimes she screamed like something hurt, but Papa stayed by Lottie's bed and wouldn't let her go help Mama get well.

"When it was morning, someone came that they called Mrs. Gray Owl, and she didn't look at all like an owl, but she did have gray hair. Mama still cried, and Papa took Lottie for a walk to count the butterflies.

"When they got back Mama wasn't crying anymore, and it looked like she was asleep. The other woman took Mama's bed sheets and went home. She said she would wash them, so Lottie thought maybe Mama had to upchuck and couldn't get up in time.

"The Owl woman stayed and sat by Mama's bed and kept looking at her. She let the little girl come in and kiss her Mama and said it would make her Mama have good dreams. She put some leaves in a kettle and cooked them until they smelled funny. She said it was medicine for Mama.

"The other woman came back with wet sheets and hung them between the two trees. She had some cookies, and Lottie could have one if Papa said it was all right. She had a big kettle of something that smelled really good, and Papa and Lottie ate and ate.

"When Mama woke up, Lottie got to see her for a minute while she drank her medicine, and then Mama had to go to sleep again. The little girl thought maybe Mama was extra tired, and she would feel good when she woke up.

"Then the Owl woman left, and Papa came and sat on the bed with Mama, and Lottie brought her bear and her doll and got on the bed with them. Mama watched the little girl and then started crying. Papa hugged her and said it wasn't so bad. There was still time. And he said that, anyway, the one they got was just about perfect, wasn't she?

"Lottie thought and thought, and the only thing there was that was new was the black and white spotted cow, and she was a girl, so that must have been what he was talking about. She didn't know what made a cow just about perfect, because she looked just like all other cows, but she really did give good milk. That was a good thing, and Papa and Lottie drank a lot of milk for a while because not much of anything else got cooked. Mama made the Owl medicine out of leaves to drink, and then she slept a lot.

"It was really nice when the tiny house grew still another room, and the perfect cow got her own house that had three sides and a roof. Mama got...."

Carlotta had stopped in the middle of a sentence. Josie had no doubt that her clear thinking would pick up the thread with no difficulty.

It was now easy to see why she had been an only child and how her loving parents had tried to keep that from happening. It just went to show, not everything turned out as one might like it to. She did not try to resist the urge to see Rosalie's latest addition.

"Rosalie got to sit on the seat with Papa most of the time because Francy and Raymond couldn't leave their toys, and Mama had to see that they didn't fall out the back when Papa went over a bump.

"Sometimes the little girl put the doll aside and chose one of the story books. Papa had no trouble reading it while he drove the horses, and sometimes he pointed out a word for his daughter to look at. The story of the three little pigs was a favorite, and 'pig' was a fun word to look at. 'House' was just about as funny.

"One day when he was reading a story about a bean plant that grew all the way into the clouds, Mama put a little package on the bench beside Rosalie but said she mustn't open it until she put the book away.

"Rosalie held the book and turned the pages when Papa said to, and all of a sudden there was a scream from the back of the wagon. The scream was so loud and sudden it made the horses dance on their back legs and make funny noises through their noses. Their harnesses jingled like Christmas bells.

"When Papa yelled "Whoa" and tried to get them to put their feet down, the horses wanted to run, and they went sideways and rolled the wagon down into the ditch. It was lucky the ditch wasn't very deep, because the wagon tried to turn over, but it couldn't.

"Papa finally got the horses to stop and told Mama to come and hold the straps tight because he had to get out and lead them out from the ditch.

"One of the horses was kind of stuck in the dirt, and Papa had to say a lot of cranky words to get it to climb back up on the road. He made them stop then and told them to get their heads together or he would lay his strap against their backsides. He talked just like they could understand him.

"Stuff was tossed all over the wagon, and Raymond and Francy were screaming and crying because their toys were mixed up everywhere, and Francy thought all her doll dresses had fallen out of the wagon. She begged Mama to let her go back and get them, but Mama told her to sit down and shut up because she had done enough already.

"Papa finally took a breath and came and asked Mama what had happened, and Mama said it was just Francy screaming from happiness when she saw the four new doll dresses.

"Papa looked at Mama and said, 'That's all? I thought maybe we had picked up a rattler and it bit someone. How long will it take to straighten all this out?'

"Mama said, 'I don't know, but you can drive on, now. I'll start looking for things. I'm sure all the toys are here… just mixed up in the bedding.'

"Mama made Francy sit in the front of the wagon behind Papa's bench and shut up, but she kept hiccoughing and sniffling. Papa said he didn't feel like finishing the story… he was too hungry and as quick as we found water for the horses, we'd stop.

"Rosie didn't find out until the next day what happened to the bean plant."

Josie chuckled at the widely different versions of the same incident by the sisters. Of course, an almost five year old is much more advanced than a barely four, so it would be normal for the younger one not to remember the trouble she'd caused. At that young age, 10 months could be forever. Another lifetime.

Thinking back, Josie, herself, could scarcely remember distinct events at under six years. Her life must have been smoothed into a regular pattern of days, weeks and years with no total up-turn such as the land run and the cross-country trek. The children of the Territory shared a common experience of having come from somewhere else and were starting from scratch with their lives and friendships.

Giving in to an urge, she turned Carlotta's pages ahead to a further entry. "One day the Papa took Lottie down the road to see another girl, and they had a tea party with her toy dishes. It was cookies and strawberries and something that was pink and sweet to drink in the tiny teacups.

"When they started home, Papa asked Lottie she if liked the tea party dishes, and the little girl thought for a little while and then told Papa, "No." She had decided she didn't want any tea set.

"Papa was surprised and said 'Why not? You had a lot of fun with them, didn't you?'

"Lottie didn't want to tell her Papa the real reason. She was sure he wouldn't like it, but she had to tell the truth. 'I don't want a toy that takes two to have fun. I'm only one.'

"The Papa looked so sad and unhappy, she thought quickly and added, 'There is something I would like. All of the pictures in my color book are colored. When we go to the house with the beds, I could pick out a new book.'

"Papa sniffed and wiped a piece of dust out of his eye, and said, 'Lottie, sweetheart, you shall have a new colorbook.'

"But Lottie didn't get her book right away. When she got home, Mama was out behind the privy house trying to upchuck and couldn't. When she saw her little girl watching her, she started to cry and then she hugged Lottie.

"It was that day that Lottie knew she had done the wrong thing when she had gone with Papa and had fun at the tea party. When Mama got sick and had to have the Owl woman come, Lottie knew she could take care of Mama just as well, and she decided then that she would never go away again and leave her Mama at home to get sick.

"It was already too late, though, because it wasn't very long that the woman came with soup and some cookies for Lottie. The Owl woman came, too. She made Mama sicker because Mama cried and screamed all night, and Papa wouldn't let Francy go help her Mama. He just held her in his lap and hugged her, and he still had that dust or grass seed in his eye.

"It was a few days later that Papa left and brought home a cow that was all yellow, trimmed in brown, and Lottie thought it was prettier than the one with black and white spots. Lottie decided that Papa had been looking for another pretty one, and then he found it.

"After that, when it had snowed a lot, the black and white cow had a little one that looked exactly like a tiny one of herself. That made Papa happy, too, and no one thought about the color book for a long time, but it was fun to go with Papa to milk the new cow. The milk squirted in white streams and made foam just like soap suds.

"A long time after that, the little black and white cow was gone, and Lottie was a big girl before she knew it had been used to make stew and sandwich patties. Eeouuu!"

Now that she had started, Josie was impossibly curious about each new entry. Likely they would be ready for their final sheets within a week as they had been scribbling furiously every day.

Thumbing through the sheets to Carmelita's middle pages she read of the dreary, same thing one day after the other. That was what had made up the daily life of her cousin. At a certain point she had to give up her job of gathering cow pats and collecting the eggs. They became duties for a younger family member, and she graduated to managing the stove for easier cooking, making occasional batches of cottage cheese that took a boring period of stirring, and a lot of the time she was pulling weeds in the kitchen garden.

Little brother Darrell couldn't seem to remember what was pig weed and what was young and tender beets. Both had a reddish stem, and it took someone who could look close. Spring beets were such a delicacy that none must be wasted. Also onions. If one did not put his hands very low, the green top popped off and left the white bulb in the ground.

Once and a while she got to go to the Corner for something, but never alone. She had been nine years old when the Canfields had moved in the house less than a mile down the road. The family who had won that section "froze out" meaning they couldn't stand the hard work and the lonesome days. It seemed that the land the Canfield family had won in the race was not close enough to neighbors, and they had sold and re-bought.

At the first peek at Rosalie, she and Carmelita had been pulled together like iron filings stick to a magnet. Rosalie was almost a year younger, and her sister, Francine, was another ten months below that. The three girls had fun, but often the younger girl was otherwise occupied, and Carmelita and Rosalie were like two peas in the same pod.

Life had been much better after that, but a mile was a mile, and duties on a farmstead were still duties. There were not many occasions when the girls could share duties. Darning sock heels was one of those duties because that job was deemed to be about the ability of a nine or ten year old, and a special afternoon consisted of being together with the basket of socks, poking the wooden "darning egg" into the sock heel and reweaving the hole with yarn. If there happened to be cookies to share, it was an extra special day.

Rosalie had been at Carmelita's house when the news was received that the house in New York had been burned on Christmas Eve. The adults were lost in the fire, but the little seven-year-old boy and his seventeen-year-old sister would be coming to the Territory.

The girls had shared tears over the loss and puzzled with each other over the seventeen-year-old girl. What could she be like? Would she be too important to talk with them? There were not a great number of older girls close by who were not already married. Really... what would the cousin be like?

Rosalie was still eleven, and Carmelita had just turned twelve when cousin Josie had arrived, and later "Miss Josie" had moved into the Sutter place that was built under the edge of the ledge of prehistoric stone.

A school? How could that possibly be, but of course it would be just for the little kids. Still... and anyway, it was something to talk about... and talk about, again. There seemed to be not enough words to describe the wonder of it.

Up until then, Carmelita had not written in so many words about the staircase to nowhere. It had likely seemed something that did not require words because nothing could be done about it anyway. There was no one to tell it to, and she herself knew all about it. But now...?

One page later her pencil had scribbled out the pain and frustration of the stairway, and that her birthday had set her on the landing with no idea what was ahead of her. Then the dream...

Josie sat at her desk within the stone walls of the schoolroom, the early Saturday sunshine making blocks of light on the floor. Coffee steamed in the mug beside her. Toasted biscuits melted their butter on a plate. A relaxing morning.

When she thought of her four girls that she called Level Four, she almost felt her heart would burst with pride. So bright, so quick, so eager... Josie could hardly wait to take them to Oklahoma City for the certification test.

There was no doubt that they would do well, but she sincerely wanted them to have another year. If they already had certification, it might not seem important enough to parents to spare them for another year. There was so much more she wanted for them.

Young Lily Gray Owl had turned six and was doing so well that her grandmother continuously bragged about her, at least as much as her English adjectives allowed. She said so much to her brother, old Gray Eagle, who was a tribal elder, that he browbeat two of his sons into sending their older boys. That was how the school got Johnny Black Bear (who insisted on being Johnny Black) and his cousin, Willie (Running) Elk. The boys were ten years old, but quick and eager.

Old Mrs. Gray Owl had insisted they would be no trouble if they stayed with her and she wanted them to "hear the new words and tell the sound to their tongues." She instinctively knew they would have to deal with the newcomers, and that they were grossly out numbered. She wanted them to be ready to "talk so ears could hear and say book words."

For this, Old Gray Owl would bring more presents to the teacher. One of the gifts was a fur cap, white as snow, tied with a braided leather strap that had been bleached white. Josie stared at it and wondered what Aunt Sharon would say it would be worth in a New York store.

The native boys had now been promised for another year, and Josie was bravely deciding to put them in the new Level Four because of their age and size and the fact that Raymond Canfield had become fast friends with them. Also, there were several girls. It would be a big enough class that the Kiowa boys would not stand out as being a bit behind, and they would learn a lot just by listening.

While Josie was planning her next year, a neighbor was trying to plan the rest of his life.

Brad Cullen had been getting a number of jobs shoeing horses… not his favorite activity, but it was an income. While he pounded the glowing iron, he thought. Tapping the hoof of a bored piebald nag, he thought. Trips to the ice cream store had been a revelation, but Josie was still a puzzle. It was going to take a lot of thought. So he thought.

The school was her first thought, yet she did not give the idea of it being a passion… only a job to be done, and she was going to give it her full attention. She was chatty and teasing with her cousin… he was family. She was chatty and idea-sharing with Brad's sister Janine… she was a co-worker. With him, Brad, she was a polite and reserved neighbor. And that was absolutely not all he would like to be. So he kept thinking.

When the answer came, it was a lightening bolt between one hammer stroke and the next. He and she had nothing in common. There had to be something that was just between her and himself that needed discussion and suggestions. It should be a need that would require a meeting of the mind. But what would that be…?

He was on his way home, the wagon bumping and rolling along the dry ruts of the road, and he was thinking. He spent a lot of time on the road alone, and it provided a lot of thought time. It would really help when he got a shop of his own.

He pulled up to Carlile Corners and went in to check his mail hook. Nothing but a note. Someone needed him down south, and they had sketched a map on how to get there. He sincerely hated these hand-drawn maps. Most of the time the house was not where it had been put on the map, and he could waste a half a day looking for it. Having the name of the farmsteader did not help, either, as the area was too newly settled for knowing who lived where.

Oh, well. He clicked the horse into action, turned the corner, and headed south. Out ahead of him was the pen with Jeff's Conamara horses. The leggy foals had turned into horses, still leggy but filling out fast. The mottled charcoal of their manes showed how they were maturing, and the lower legs were darkening into their signature pattern. Very attractive markings.

Next down the road was the school. Prairie Academy. Josie. Now, if he had the shop right here, everyone who stopped at the Corner would see his sign, and they could bring the animals to him. Also, he would have a place where he could set up the rest of his equipment. His skill was much greater than the shaping of horseshoes.

As he passed the Academy, he admired for the hundredth time the attractive stone work. Old Digby really had a hand with it, and there was still much material available on the back of Josie's land.

Reaching his home, Brad dropped his day's fee into the money jar, and Janine would turn it into food. She did a good job with the grub... did his sister. After eating supper, he seemed drowsy and flaked out early on his bed. Somewhere between the cooing of the doves by the chimney and the morning crowing of the rooster the idea jammed itself into his brain, and he sat up in bed, startled. How could he have missed it? Plain as frost on a pumpkin!

He needed a shop. He, the jack of many trades, could not lay stone with the skill of the old crippled Digby. Josie had stone in abundance and could likely sell it if she had a mind to. There would come a time when the object of his attention would be tired of living in the schoolroom and want a house.

All of these thoughts added up to the perfect answer.

He would say to her: "I would like very much to learn to lay stone like Digby, but he would have to work with me right here. Now, if you would let me put up a house, maybe two rooms to start with, or maybe more, I would see that the stones were brought to wherever you say, and if Digby would agree, I would like his advice so I can learn. I might want to work at that sometime.

"The trouble is," he would continue, "that I would need to do it in spare time, when I have no paying job, and I spend so much time going and coming now, and it is all a waste. If I would put up a little place on your corner, right across from the Corners, customers would bring the work to me and save a lot of time. I could use that time learning about building with stone, and you would eventually have a house. We would both gain."

He could see in his mind that she would treat his statement soberly and thoughtfully, as she did everything. If she hesitated, he would mention that he especially liked the way Digby had finished the classroom floor. She would be doing him a great favor if she accepted his idea. (He knew she enjoyed helping others, and, actually, this plan would cost her absolutely nothing but her permission.)

Then, with a sigh, he told himself that if he could not get her attention in this way, he just as well turn his efforts in another direction. If she agreed, it would likely take a year, at least. If this had been a settled community, there would be activities like hay rides, parties, sing-alongs, and maybe church activities to attend, but there was nothing yet. So he had to get her attention somehow.

There was no more sleep for Brad Cullen that night. He turned over a few time, finally sat up, pulled on his clothes and his boots and slipped out the door. Sitting on the porch step, he worked it out in his mind, right down to the size of shop he would like, and what he would use for a sign.

Next time he went to Argyle, he would pick up a pair of those thick leather gloves like Digby used to lift stone. He was assuming the old crippled man would go along with his suggestion. He would do anything for Josie, and the house would, of course, be hers… whatever way the plan went.

The next day being Saturday, he headed north toward her schoolroom. The fellow down south could just wait until he got there. He could just let that shoeless mare go barefoot for the weekend.

He found Josie at her desk deep in thought. She listened, face as passive as if made of stone. He had reached the place in his persuasion where they would both gain, and she lifted a finger.

"Have you spoken to Digby?"

"No, but I will. I needed your permission first. I really want to learn how he shapes stone like on your floor here. Also, I want to learn how he makes it so smooth."

"Are you thinking you could do this?" Pointing to the floor, smooth and shiny as any tile floor in New York.

Brad felt his heart turn over. Success! "That is what I want to learn. I've learned a lot of things by doing, like putting on your roof, and this looks challenging, but I'm sure I can."

Had he said enough? More words? Too many words? He watched her face. Small smile. Small nod.

"What if you would sketch out what you'd like to do, and we'd go from there. Would you like coffee?"

Just as he would have nodded, there came a light tap came at the door, and it opened. Young girl with dark auburn braids. Sack in her hand and a grin under her scattering of dark freckles.

"Mama took cookies out of the oven. Raisin cookies still hot." A mischievous grin, "Mama made us count out a dozen for you before we could have any, but I put in thirteen." The girl was obviously pleased with herself for the small trick played on Mama!

Quickly as she had come, the girl was gone. Josie offered an explanation. "O'Grady cookies are always good with coffee. I'll get you some. That girl, Bridgit, she's bright as a new penny and fast as a racehorse. I'm counting on big things from her next year. I have plans for this year's older girls that's going to give me more time with the ones Bridgit's age."

Brad was careful not to catch his breath with surprise. This was the first he had heard her discus what she did, at a time that she was not talking with Janine. He had a sudden urge to ask about the progress of Tray, his five year old brother.

Then he thought better of it… there was a chance that he might hear what he didn't want to know! Just now he was not in the mood for bad news. While things were going well, shut up, he advised himself.

A steaming mug appeared, and warm cookies shared the plate with the buttered biscuits.

If he ate slow…? Obviously, he couldn't leave until he had finished the coffee? That would be rude!

She continued in a chatty way. "I have five new beginners for next year, so Tray and Lily and the others their age will sometimes be in the position of helpers. I'll be having this year's older girls doing most of the teaching. They don't know it, yet, but they'll be excited. They all want to take the Certification Test, and they'll do well. Doing actual teaching with Janine and me will give them more confidence."

Brad learned more about the school in the next half-hour than he could have imagined and still left 6 cookies on the plate when he took his leave. He'd stop in Monday with a rough drawing before he talked with Digby. He whistled all the way home.

Josie, with a singleness of purpose, transferred the plate with the remaining cookies to her pie safe, noting the generous slice of crabapple pie left from Aunt Nettie's gift. Smiling to herself, she noted how the pie that was a favorite of hers appeared often when Josie was expected at her aunt's for a meal. The crabapple, a tiny relative of the European variety, grew on large bushes all over the Territory. Spicy and rich flavored, they were most often mixed with honey and turned into apple butter, but Aunt Nettie had a special hand with pies.

Alone, and back at her desk, Josie resumed her thoughts of the next year. What had formed as an abstract cobweb of a thought had turned into a complete and colorful fabric. Josie was certain her interest would wane as soon as Joshua was gone back east, and that was less than five years away. A lot would happen before then.

CHAPTER 3

However, there was the time until then to be filled with plans for the Prairie Academy to be continued when she was gone. At present count, there were two new girls, Eve Adams and America Forrester to be placed in the new level three. In addition, there were five new ones in the lowest level.

The two new Third Level girls had attended school to a minor degree, but reading was still at a substandard level, and math was even lower. They had some catching up to do, but there was the value of competition and being put in with those who were a bit more advanced would undoubtedly spur them on to their best work. At least it was a start. This inequality of age to education was a situation she must deal with for a while.

This year's graduates, the current Level Four girls were her best hope. She had acquired a list called RULES FOR TEACHERS 1872, and even Josie, herself, found it scary to consider. Next week she would share it with the girls, so they would understand why so much was expected of them.

Their penmanship lesson, now that they had practically completed their rough draft autobiographies, would be to create a copy for themselves of the rules for teachers as put forth by the Board of Education for the Territory. It would be added to their folders containing things of importance to remember.

It was Tuesday of the following week that she gathered the girls around the table and read to them:

RULES FOR TEACHERS 1872

Oklahoma Territory
Teachers, each day will fill lamps, clean chimneys.

Each teacher will bring a bucket of water and a scuttle of coal for the day's session.

Make your pens carefully. You may whittle nibs to the individual taste of the pupils.

Men teachers may take one evening each week for courting purposes, or two evenings a week if they go to church regularly.

After ten hours in school, the teachers may spend the remaining time reading the Bible or other good books.

Women teachers who marry or engage in unseeming conduct will be dismissed.

Every teacher should lay aside from each pay a goodly sum of his earnings for his benefit during his declining years so that he will not be a burden on society.

Any teacher who smokes, uses liquor in any form, frequents pool or public halls, or gets shaved in a barber shop will give good reason to suspect his worth, intention, integrity and honesty.

The teacher who performs his labor faithfully and without fault for five years will be given an increase of twenty-five cents per week in his pay, providing the Board of Education approves.

Josie had read slowly and distinctly, glancing occasionally at the wide-eyed looks of horror registered on each young face. She forced herself to restrain the look of satisfaction she felt.

"Now, girls, I want you to relax. This list is for those who expect pay from the Board of Education, and that will not be necessary for you. You will be worth the tuition paid by parents. The lack of schools in the territory gives parents no choice, and even when that time comes, the parents will still wish to pay to get the best teachers. WHICH YOU WILL BE!" This last statement brought a shy smile to their faces.

"There is one small situation I must tell you. Though you could certainly pass the Certification Test at the end of this year, it is now given only to students who have attended the seventh grade.

Due to the scarcity of teachers, I believe there will be an exception made for you if you study one more year, and in addition to that, you are a bit young to work on your own. Especially Francine and Carlotta.

"I will be telling you more later, but I want to assure you that there will be a place for you, even if the test is refused. Parents are desperate to have their children educated, and a certification will mean very little to them, if you can do the job. By this time next year, YOU WILL BE ABLE TO DO THE JOB!" Another smile.

"Next year, you will work in pairs with Levels One to Three for every other week. The week in between, you will attend advanced classes with me. When you begin on your own, you will know more than you will ever need to know to begin to teach, and each year you work, you will gain experience and confidence.

"You will expect the parents of your students to pay you because you are worth it. You have worked hard and earned what you get. They must pay for having their horses shod, for help to stretch fence wire, and expect to pay money for a fancy horse, a good producing cow or a pair of pearl button shoes." This last also brought a smile to the four faces turned to her. Shoes were an important thing to a growing girl.

"One more thing. I have a list of the questions that will be asked you. You will know every one of them at that time. Most of them you could answer now, but I want you to gain speed and confidence on the math equations."

Four faces exchanged looks with each other. It was an eye opener. Exciting, but possible. Scary, but tameable. An exciting future, but one they could earn. Miss Josie had promised!

"Now, girls, we'll get to work. Today, Francine and Carlotta will take over for Miss Janine, on the number cards for Level One. Carmelita will pronounce spelling words for Level Two and Rosalie will listen to Level Three in reading. Rosalie, I want you to take notice of their attention to expression, periods, and question marks. Hesitation before saying a word means that student will write it down for further study. Now go..." They scattered like a flock of doves. They went, their minds seething with the new information that they must put aside for now, but to be thoroughly discussed together later.

When the students were gone, Josie and Janine sat at the small round table on high stools to catch their breath.

Janine, with a smile, "You really stuck it to them, didn't you? They left you with their faces pale with fright."

Josie nodded, also smiling. "The reality of it will be lot worse than that, but this gives them a start on knowing why they have to work so hard. I'll share with you, though, that being scared now is a lot better than not knowing what is expected, or how to get to where they think that they want to go."

Janine gave a knowing nod. "Lucky girls. They will always know that they won't have to depend on a fellow to take care of them. Or worry what would happen if the fellow died, got hurt, or just disappeared."

Then Josie. "Yes, that, and knowing they don't have to abide by the rules of the Board of Education just to have the money. Why they say the teaching day should take ten hours beats me. The brain of a child cannot function if they're tired. Experts are even beginning to decide that children can't work such long hours in factories in the east. Studying is not much different."

Janine had just stood to leave when a sound happened outside the door. She opened it to the sight of her brother removing his shoes before coming in. "Had a smelly job, huh? You think Josie wouldn't want horse poop on her floor? Wonder how you figured that out?"

Turning his face toward her, he demanded, playfully, "Get on home and get busy in the kitchen." Then added, "I'll bring along the Trailer."

Sock footed, he joined Josie at the table. Extracting a crumbled paper from a pocket, he smoothed it out on the table. "I made a few marks. Thought I'd show it to you to see if I was on the right track. Digby said he was ready to start when I had time, so I drew this. See, this room would be 16 by 16 and have an archway door into the next one. It would be 12 by 16 if you think that's a good size. This way there would be something put up for you to see, before additions were made."

Silently, Josie looked at the paper, ignoring the smudges from the work-worn hands. Good size.

"There'd need to be doors on all sides of the big room if the walls were stone. Couldn't hardly cut a needed door through a rock partition after it was put up."

Brad pulled the pencil stub from his pocket and drew a door into the center of each wall. He glanced toward Josie as she studied the result.

She had a suggestion. "Look, try moving the doors off center. Furniture placement would be easier with a wider wall space."

Rubbing out the door marks, he moved them closer to the corner. "That's something that can be worked out exactly on the finished drawing. Otherwise, are the room sizes about right?"

After a moment, she gave a satisfied nod.

"There's a pretty good road worked out back to the rock ledge. Jeff made so many trips with the sled, he just about took care of that." Then an idea struck... maybe an inspiration. "Say, have you ever been back there to see where that rock comes from?"

With a shake her head, she admitted. "No, never thought about it."

"How about some Sunday afternoon that I come cleaned up without horse poop on my clothes and take you out there in the buggy. It's really an interesting sight to see. Rather makes a body wonder how it was formed."

He paused, waiting, and she did not say no. "How about next Sunday?" One must press one's advantage if he had one.

Finally, a nod. "That sounds interesting. If it doesn't rain."

Donning his work boots at the step, he agreed, climbing wearily into his wagon. That shop on the corner would have to come into service quickly so he would have more time.

Then his thought turned to Josie. A girl of few words. When she seemed to be totally disinterest, there she was with ideas for changes. It was going to be fascinating to see how her interest in the project held. He was counting on it being a continuous thing.

When his mind drew up a picture of her, she would be sitting with a pencil and maybe a notebook. Or a reading book. With her head bent in concentration. So, to amuse himself, he tried putting a soup kettle in her hand, or a knife and a kettle of unpeeled potatoes, and the sight was irresistibly amusing. His mind tried standing her beside a cook stove, and that picture didn't work either.

In his mind, he moved her across the table from him in the Sweet Shop with an ice cream dish, and there she appeared, laughing and chatting, the dimple in her chin being more pronounced.

On a whim, he mentally placed her beside him in a single seated buggy behind one of Jeff's attractive charcoal trimmed Irish horses. He put her in her riding coat and pearl button boots. You know, he assured himself, that picture just might work!

A fellow just had to figure out where a girl was, in her mind, if he wanted to be with her... in body! Josie was a challenge. But he'd get there, he promised himself. There hadn't been anything yet that he had really wanted... that he couldn't work out a way to get. And he really couldn't imagine life without Josie.

In Digby, he found a kindred soul. The graying crippled man... the miner from the mountains of Colorado... the man who made the brave decision to amputate half his foot before the rattler poison circulated into his blood...? That man had dealt with his circumstances and found a part of his life that he hadn't known he had missed when he met Josie. Much the way Brad now felt.

"It's actually for Josie," Brad had said, by way of explanation. Yes, he did want the training in placing stone, but he knew he owed Josie a debt for the training of his little brother. Besides, how else could he get her "alone" attention?

He could see that the old man had taken to Josie like a starving deer to a patch of new grass. The old man could see in her the daughter/ granddaughter he had neglected to provide for himself. She had seemed, to him, to have an opening for the father/ grandfather who had been taken from her.

Yes, old Digby understood himself, and also the kindred spirit in the young man from Tennessee. They strengthened each other in their desire to please the girl and care for her.

The old man sighed as he reminded Brad that the stones would have to be furnished by him, due to failing strength and crippled foot, but he would be glad to share his skill in mining the flat flagstones from their earthen bed where they were formed.

Brad nodded, knowing already that the transport of the stones would be his own problem and must be worked out within his own limited work hours. But if that was what was needed to be done to complete his own plans, there would be a way. And time.

The ambitious young man managed to harness the skills of his father in creating a three-sided structure for his new blacksmith workshop. The large sign stated "Cullen Blacksmithing. Shoeing horses a specialty." The sign was cleverly tilted to face Carlile Corners and be easily read from a distance. The old man saw a position for himself in "running" the shop while his ambitious son was elsewhere.

Old Gaither Cullen was naturally outgoing and friendly, readily attracting men of all ages to stop in and have a cup of the thick, acid liquid he called coffee. And later bring their smithing work.

Activity continued in the classroom. Josie was introducing poetry into the class of her pride. Carmelita and Rosalie sat with her at the round table, elbows planted firmly and chins in hand.

The emotional words of the rhyme, "Sail On" were being absorbed. The terror of the sailors, the pleading of the first mate and the dogged determination of the Skipper. The girls knew, for certain, they would be required to explain how the words made them feel... what words they would say if they were on the ship, and what would they have thought might be the force driving Christopher Columbus to continue to sail into what might be certain death.

While discussing the poetry, Josie could hear the clear enunciation of the spelling words and the scrape of chalk and eraser on the slates as sums were being worked out.

A glance toward the window wall revealed Carlotta seated on one of Old Gray Owl's wolf fur mats. Lily sat snuggled close, practically under Carlotta's elbow, with Tray cross-legged beside her. Esther leaned against the wall with her eyes on the cardboard rectangles with words drawn in crayon.

Carlotta spoke with fun on her face like the exercise was just a really exciting game. "We have the 'at' sound that we know. Who wants to put a consonant in front and tell us what it says?"

A frantic mental grab for the single letters produced 'mat', 'cat', 'fat', 'rat', 'sat', and 'hat'. No, Carlotta chided, chuckling, actually 'dat' and 'zat' were not words. A giggle throughout the class.

"Now we have a bigger word. Say 'ame', with a long 'a'." She received total cooperation. "Now, put an 's' in front and what do we have? Sound it out."

In unison the class cooperated. "say..ah..mmee." Then a questioning expression as they did not recognize the word. Carlotta chuckled and explained. "We forgot the rule didn't we? When we have four lettered words with two vowels, and the last one is an 'e', what happens?"

Tray, now six years old, blurted out, "The 'e' keeps quiet so the other vowel can say its name!"

Carlotta again. "Right. Now let's sound the word. Say… ay…mm. The class of five screamed, "SAME!" A nod and a smile, "Right. Now let's change the first consonant."

The result was shouted with excitement. "TAME," "LAME," "GAME," "NAME," and then someone changed the beginning letter to a "C."

"What is that word?" Someone responded, "Same? No, that's not it."

"You're right, Esther. Remember that "C" is a clown and likes to be someone else. Sometimes "C" is an "S" and sometimes a "K." Remember CAT?"

Excited eyes widened in recognition. "It's a 'K'. It says came!"

A pleased smile on Carlotta's beautiful face. "Oh, you are such a smart class. Now let's try 'AKE'." And so it went. Josie nodded with satisfaction… a born teacher of tots, was Carlotta. Such an important job.

Her full attention came back to the round table and the two older girls. "Of course, we know that Columbus did not actually discover America. People had been here a long time, but they were not people could, or even wanted to, put on paper what they had done so others could follow. It took Columbus to document his trip, and Amerigo Vespusious to publish it to paper. We can clearly see why writing down thoughts and actions are so important. Others can build their ideas on those before them, but only if they are written down to be read. By Friday, we will have this memorized and ready to recite with expression."

The class of two was dismissed to return to their story math problems, which they didn't really like, and to the creation of new and difficult problems of their own, which they liked even less. Their teacher, however, was heartless so they bowed their heads to do what they must do.

Brad made the half a mile trek to the back of Josie's quarter section of prairie land to view the rock ledge. The weight of long-ago settling had pressed the organic and inorganic dregs into the marine equivalent of petrified wood. Essentially petrified dirt, and it had settled into layers of inorganic sand and chalky shells, to be separated by layers of organic vegetation, long since decayed and gone.

Left, then, to be pushed up by the heaving of the earth's crust, were the layers of stone, pancaked together and ranging 3 inches thick to a half a foot. By judicious placement of the pry bar, and applying many points of pressure by humans, the layers broke apart. The layers of decayed vegetation provided weaker points for the pry bar. And for the straining humans.

From Digby, Brad learned how to tease and score the stone to release the rock chunks in a size and shape best for building. The skillful use of chisel and iron mallet dressed the stone still further, and the resulting chips were piled aside for eventual uses elsewhere. A young man of a less determined aim in life would have given up as the sweat poured and the muscles ached. Even the blacksmith's hammer seemed light by comparison to this iron pry bar.

The young Tennessee man, however, firmed his chin, tightened his jaw and worked the pry bar under yet another layer of the ancient mineral substance and yet another chunk came loose. If it broke where it was not planned, there was more chipping and shaping to do… therefore, a skill must be learned quickly. The tapping and scoring must be accurate. Digby would accept no less.

A small heap of dressed stone lay on the ledge the following Sunday.

Josie was ready for the sight seeing trip. She was not dressed in riding coat and pearl button shoes, but the young man had no complaints. Hat with wide brim to shield from the sun (woven from cattail reeds by the skillful hand of Mrs. Gray Owl) protected her face. A dress of blue check with ruffles at the wrist (put together by the tiny stitches of Mrs. O'Grady) protected her arms and hands. Her knees were covered by the generous gathers of the skirt of the dress, and her feet were shod in her everyday schoolteacher shoes, worn into comfortable softness.

The slight breeze brought the fresh lilac aroma of New York soap (selected by Aunt Sharon) to his nostrils as he directed the horse down the road created by Jefferson's sled. Early prairie flowers had escaped the soil and anxiously sent up their buds and blossoms to create their desired seed. Colorful carpet of blossoms in the grass.

Brad Cullen sat on the bench beside Josie, his heart pounding in a reassuring rhythm of satisfaction. He would like to consider today as a destination, but he knew it was only the beginning step on a lengthy journey.

Josie sat in relaxed comfort, seeming to need no words. She gazed about with mild interest at the valuable piece of property that she had so hastily purchased almost two years ago. During that time she had not bothered to give thought to anything but her classroom and the training of children, specifically her brother and cousin.

She briefly responded to Brad's comments, which were always framed in business-like words. As if this was just a business trip for her information. As if there were still decisions to be made that required her input.

At the beginning of the stone ledge, Brad pulled the patient beast to a halt and held out an arm to help her step down as she gathered her skirt aside. She stepped onto the stony path, and it was as solid and level beneath her feet as a concrete sidewalk in front of the New York stores. Stopping to examine the heap of dressed stones, she nodded with satisfaction. She could see the touch of Digby as it had been transferred to the man beside her.

The actual person she thought of, however, was her old tutor and his problems. There were several problems that could have been invented here with these uniformly dressed stones and the growing pile of dust, gravel and chips. Interesting. The ledge stretched out before her for at least a quarter of a mile, following the shape of a rounded rise in the land.

Beyond the rise, the small stream of water whispered and gurgled. Sugar soil, it was. So much of it was still made up of the tiny, rounded granules that had rolled and tumbled, always moving down stream. The force of the constantly moving water had cut through the soil down to the ledge in many places, creating a smooth, rock bottom to the stream and keeping the water clear.

Thought problems.

Valuable stone. A problem. Considering the certain value of the stone as a building material, and a knowledge of the desired wall size, (minus the size of the windows and doors when applicable) one could accurately figure the cost of a house consisting of 2 rooms, also 3 rooms or more. One would require a finished drawing such as Brad had presented to her. Then, if a stone floor was desired, it would need to be figured separately as the flat side of the stone would be used rather than the thickness and only one length. Also taken into account would be the irregular shapes.

With a breath and a shake of her head, she pulled herself away from the attractive challenge and looked up at Brad, who asked, "Well, what do you think?"

Josie gazed about her and settled her gray eyes on a massive walnut tree, obviously at least a half a century old. "I see a good place for a picnic someday."

Brad resisted his sudden intake of surprised breath. "Shall we walk over there and see for sure?"

Taking a narrow animal path, they circled among the shrubs and at one point Josie stopped to examine the small nuts on the slender-trunked tree. "Filberts! I think they may have another name here, but they're filberts in New York. They're very expensive, and usually come onto the market only at Christmas. Some people like to put them in a heavy pan in the fireplace till they heat up and crack their shells, but I mostly liked them raw just like they came out of the shell. They're really easy to crack."

Brad nodded with interest. "I've heard them called Chinese chestnuts but I don't know why. These nuts have a relative that grows in Tennessee and Arkansas called chinkey-pins, but they grow on a much bigger tree. When these ripen, we can come and get a lot of them. I always liked them, too, and Janine used to toast and crack them and put them in chocolate fudge."

Making a future plan at this time was a good move so he added, "I'm thinking we may have to be careful to beat the squirrels."

All kinds of plans immediately stretched out before him, spawned by Josie's words. Truth be told, the nuts were getting more interest from her than the ice cream at Argyle, but then the ice cream had been to Janine's liking, and Josie just went along for the ride. Or so it seemed.

The shade beneath the walnut tree was deep and cool and produced an aroma of mint from the depth of leaves. He could picture a quilt spread on the softness of old leaves, a picnic lunch and a lazy day. It could happen. It really could happen!

Josie was chatty on the way back, commenting on this and that, leaving an opening for his responses. As he guided the horse, Brad thought. Yes, this could be the first step of a very satisfying journey, but he was aware there were still a lot of stones to be chipped and hauled along the way before he got there.

It was that night that Josie dreamed again. It was not a dream of the fiery deaths this time, but a peaceful, festive evening with her family in the spacious and expensively furnished New York home. The fruit bowl was heaped with huge gleaming oranges shipped up north from somewhere in Florida.

It was Christmas Eve. Gaily wrapped presents were stacked in the corner. A crackling fire and Joshua's excited chatter livened the spirit. Josie's mother sat in her favorite soft chair, smiling approval over all and her father knelt in front of the fireplace with the popcorn popper in hand. The wire-screened box held, not corn for popping, but the small brown filberts she had seen that day.

Josie nodded as though she was watching the scene play before her. Her father always liked his filberts hot, and the small nuts were beginning to whisper among themselves as their shells weakened.

Beside him on the floor was the crate made with thin strips of wood and half filled with the nuts. Josie, herself, held a wooden bowl in her lap and a nutcracker in her hand. The shells were thin, so it was necessary to crack gently to avoid crushing the kernel. Josh sat at her feet watching his father. He was noisily sucking a red and white stripped peppermint candy cane.

The picture was so clear, and Josie could see herself sitting there and knowing what was going to happen. Still, it was so cozy with the fire and the well-built house. There was no feeling of the freezing wind and the snow that was falling outside.

She waited, waited... something needed to happen. Suddenly the airwaves were split with a series of staccato barks from the small dog on her bed. Startled awake, Josie sat up quickly and heard the yipping of young coyotes working toward acquiring their adult voices.

Occasionally, an adult animal raised his nose to the sky in his musical, conversational howl. The "song dogs" were obviously out to give the pups an educational outing.

When they seemed to get too close, she heard the report from Jefferson's shotgun. Josie smiled. No parent was ever more protective of a child than her cousin Jeff, with his Conamara ponies.

They were pretty well grown by now, having very nearly reached their adult size. He had plans for breeding them in the coming summer as he was so eager to add new ones to his herd.

For the past year he had practically lived with the young animals, sleeping in the barn that was in sight of Josie's house. Only on the coldest nights did he agree to come and bed down in her warm attic, and even then, he was too restless to sleep well.

It would be fun for the school children next year to see the leggy little animals galloping and tossing their heels about as they were being halter trained.

Then Josie's thoughts went back to her dream. She sighed, pleasantly. It was a good dream, and she had not had to experience what would happen later. Too many dreams had seen her fighting through flames and smoke to save her sleeping brother. Too often she had to re-live the frightening jump from her upstairs room to the snow on the yard, rather than to face the flames. And then have to face life without the love and protection of her parents.

But the danger was over, now. Josh was safely asleep with his cousin in Uncle Matt Wilson's house. She was grateful for the remembrance of that last night with her parents. A thread of memory reminded her of the grove of filbert bushes not far from where she lay, and the music of the retreating song dogs sent her back to sleep, to dream no more that night.

Brad, lying in his bed in a house a half a mile south, also heard the coyotes, but having no livestock that could not take care of themselves, he gave them no thought. Rather, he turned his attention to the day with Josie. Things were looking up. Yes, things were looking good. Now, he must plan the next step.

Digby, having been appointed as his teacher, proved to be a cruel perfectionist. Every stone was inspected. Each course, or row, must contain stones of a near equal thickness. If necessary, the rasping file would be used to force the bumps on the stones into compliance.

While the length of the stone could vary, the width and height must be uniform to fit the plan. That requirement involved skillful chipping, and if the chip crack did not happen as planned, that stone must be reworked for another, smaller use. A lot of chips were accidentally made.

Brad had constructed buildings from dimension lumber, and when the initial measurement was made and the frame raised and checked for squareness, the building went fairly rapidly. Not so with stone.

Every new row of stone must be checked with the bubble level and plumb bob, and no deviation was permitted. No stone could argue with Digby's chisel and hammer, and he did not pass on any stone that did not meet with his exacting approval. After all, it was for Josie's house, and she would get the best that Digby could insist that Brad produce.

Slow. Brad had reason to be grateful to his father, without whom his work would go even slower. Old Gaither ruled the kingdom of the blacksmith shop with dignity and assurance. By him, the prices were set. Horses were essential for every occupation, so money would be found for their shoes or harnesses and for the repair of any part of a wagon or buggy that was weak.

The old man set the hours for the work to be brought to the shop. Friendship, gossip and visits were appreciated… for no one liked company better than he. But when it came to money earned, he knew his son's value. Had he not sacrificed to have him apprenticed at the most active and efficient shop in all Nashville?

So Brad spent time thinking. Sometimes things were looking up. Josie had begun taking an interest and often walked down to the worksite. In her quiet way, she toured the work, examining spaces, making plans and decisions. Digby toured with her and apparently could read her thoughts. Anyone could see that these two rooms would not be enough, and the two lean-to wings would eventually be added.

The center two rooms would have the tall attic that was so valuable for many uses when a family was planned. The wing rooms would have a sloped roof that was economical with heat.

Space for an eventual family? Yes! And Brad kept chipping and planning. Time must be pulled aside for picnics, ice cream trips, and get-togethers. Consequently, he almost forgot what a full night's sleep was all about.

The summer passed, and Josie had relented and let Josh and Darrell off easier. Almost. She reduced the required study to one immense problem to be handed to her by each boy each week. Then they would exchange problems and work on the solution.

She would make adjustments to the problems when appropriate and stress that they must work separately as their aim must be to stump the other. They got such a charge when they dreamed up a problem the other couldn't solve without help, their entire summer seemed like vacation, but turned out to be valuable.

Josie smiled to herself with pride at their success, though she knew it would make extra effort for her during the year. The cousins would be considerably ahead of their classmates in some areas and would require more challenging demands in those directions.

That would not be a problem, she had decided, as she had made the decision that she would direct the Academy only as long as it took to find a competent replacement, and for the cousins to reach age twelve. One could do most anything, for a while.

And, oh yes, there were some things she wanted from New York. She needed to ask Aunt Sharon to shop for them. Asking the wife of her New York guardian to shop for her was like giving the lady a present. No one ever loved shopping more than that New York lady, and none were better at it than she. Aunt Sharon had such a lot time and nothing much to do.

Josie wrote, "…Could you look around at all the magazines, especially fashion magazines showing dresses and hats in the latest styles. I have some young ladies here who will wear the pages to shreds, examining them. Also, if there are some paper patterns available for the more simple ones, I could use them, too. But if there are none, the ladies here are exceptionally clever at making their own patterns, adjusting fit, and shrinking or adding sizes. They've been known to ask to borrow a dress belonging to a neighbor, in order to make a pattern. And they don't even have to take the dress apart.

"There's another thing I need. Could you look for books of poetry, both English and American? I have what I think is a budding poet here, and she will devour whatever you can find. I accidentally picked up one of her scribble pages and was amazed at what I saw, and it was certainly not something I taught her. She's only thirteen, and she wrote about a little native girl, six years old, who is in our beginner class. I'll send you a copy of the poem.

THE LILY FLOWER

Lily buds on slender reeds,
Standing high above the weeds.
Sunshine on the grasses fall,
Feeding sunrays... warmth to all.
Plants spring up from winter seed.
Not every plant comes up a weed.
Lily petals spreading wide
Revealing honey wells inside.
Not all lilies grow up wild.
A Lily Flower can be a child.
Brown eyes watching by the hour
Hide deep inside the Lily Flower.
Tiny girl in schoolhouse row
Watching, listening, much to know.
Taller, reaching to the sun.
Girl with smiles for everyone.
Bright eyes watching, growing power
And finally bloom... a Lily Flower!

"Isn't it amazing? The 'Lily Flower' girl was named White Flower but her grandmother wanted it Anglicized, so attention would not be called to any differentness of her race. The girl is doing extremely well and is teaching English to her grandmother as fast as she learns it and also to a couple of ten-year-old male cousins.

As to the poet, I have encouraged her to let me have copies of what she's written. She tries to shrug me away by saying that she didn't write it, she only copied it down out of her head. Imagine that! I did notice, however, that our single grownup book of poetry, the one that the publisher sent us, no doubt, has been checked out by her a number of times. I can imagine that the book may not have sold well for the publisher, as a lot of people don't understand poetry. Well, I understand it, but I certainly can't write it, and I don't seem to find it anywhere in my head that I can just write down!

"So I will appreciate it if you find a book or two, maybe one that is about specific material items rather than philosophy, and contains a variety of rhyme patterns. I think it might help her, though she doesn't seem to need much help.

"I surely do appreciate this. Another thing, I could use several pairs of stockings. Mine created holes in the heels and the lady who does my laundry 'darned' them, but they're getting thin in other places. Thanks…."

Josie smiled to herself over the memory of the sight of the small girl, Lily, when she heard the poem read to the class. Francine had not been especially pleased that Josie asked to read it, but Josie thought it might show the girl its value.

Later in the day it had begun to snow, and Francine stood in the warm room looking out the high window at the younger boys. They were screaming, running, and flinging snow about like a herd of wild things. After a while, she took a seat, picked up a pencil, and scribbled on the back of a scrap page.

LITTLE BOYS AND SNOW

The prairie snow is made for little boys.
They, forsaking all their indoor toys,
Devote themselves to icy, frosty joys.
To wind-swept drifts with joy he goes,
With red and runny nose and frozen toes.
In wooly cap and scarf… and layered clothes.

A pointless laughing battle has begun.
Snowballs fly and small girls, screaming, run.
A prairie snow is made for days of fun.
Climb sloping hill… ride down on sled.
Eats evening food with nodding head.
Exhausted, eyes will close
Before he hits his feather bed."

Josie had watched, amazed, as she had seen the girl scribble fast and make no erasures or changes. It was almost as she had said, it was in her head, complete, and she just wrote it down.

Then it had caused Josie to wonder if that would have happened had she not seen the one poetry book they had, if she had lived somewhere other than Carlile Corner, if she had parents other than those she had, if there had not been a house burned down in New York… and on and on.

Certainly, if she, Josie, had not come to the Territory, some things would have been different. What would the girl have done with what came naturally in her head, and would she just have be forced to deal with frustration because of no creative outlet? One could think and think, and the mind could just not comprehend the consequences of a single event. Even a tragic one that happened a half a continent away.

But Aunt Sharon would take care of it. Added to the letter, "…just one more thing. I remembered a tablet called the Composition Book, I think. If it is still available, would you send me one? At the rate she writes, I'm sure Francine will fill it. On second thought, make it two books! Thanks."

Summer gave her a lot of time not involved with the classroom. It was almost daily, now, that she made the short trip down to the stonework of what would be her new home. Sometimes Brad would be there and sometimes not, but Digby would be around. The walls were now above knee high on all sides.

Her current kitchen inside the cave room had never been a concern, but now that there would be an actual room with walls at eight-foot height, she began to look forward to it. Helping to furnish it would be pleasure for Aunt Sharon. It seemed better to order it shipped out on the train than to get something at Oklahoma City. In her next letter to Aunt Sharon, she'd remember to ask for brochures of what was available.

There'd be the parlor furniture, of course, and a dining table of a more generous size. The bed, she already had, but she could use a number of chairs for the parlor. Also a variety of lamps. Larger rooms with higher walls would require more light sources.

The floor was still a mass of footprints in red-brown dust inside the walls. In her mind, Josie saw the smooth, natural pattern of the future flagstone... the way it would be.

All she had to do was wait. There were times she felt herself being drawn away from the cave schoolroom. A lessening of her interest, if not her zeal. A real teacher would not feel that, would she? It did not matter that she had been lucky in her successes... she would turn the responsibility over to another as soon as that person could be found. That might take a while.

If she should... marry? Well, it could happen. The fact was, she felt a lot different now than she had a year ago when she came on the train. The Territory had become her home and would always be. Who would share her home? Scary thought! Maybe... well, it could be Brad. Certainly that would please Janine. Something to consider... now that she had some time.

She had mentioned to Digby the existence of the grove of filberts, and with a grin he had warned her that squirrels liked them, too. And those tiny rich nuts made good tasting squirrel meat.

Hmmmm, and she had eaten a lot of squirrel stew during last winter. It had seemed that on her most weary days, there he was with food and quiet. How would she have felt about the Territory if Digby had not been here? Or the rattlesnake bite? Or the stream that flowed through the property that had attracted Digby to camp there? So much to think on, if one just let oneself.

It had been late in that summer that a sad incident happened to the Canfield family. Grandma Nicolo, the great giver of gifts, had passed on to her reward. She had long been put away by the time Julia Canfield had been notified of her mother's death. Such was the mail service.

CHAPTER 4

In their childish minds, the children did not so much miss the association with her, as they had been so young when they had come to the Territory. Rather, they saw the endless parade of wonderful and thoughtful gifts they had received over the years. The parade had now ended, and they sighed over the loss.

They were, however, very wrong. Grandma Nicolo had seen beyond her death and bequeathed to all of her grandchildren ten golden coins. A veritable fortune! Of far more value than childish minds could conceive, but they were not to receive the sum until age 21 or until their parents requested. The indulgent parents did, however, offer the children one special expenditure… if they could choose one thing they really, really wanted, they could have it now.

Rosalie, the oldest, had not hesitated one minute. "I know what I want, and I'll always want it. That fancy bed that the Sutter family had to leave and Miss Josie has now. That's what I want, with all the fancy vines and flowers made out of iron, and I'll paint it in colors I like. I want the cover for it, too. And the top ruffle and a beautiful spread."

Her eyes shone as she smiled and sighed a contented breath. Well, that was easy. Josie would be a good help in locating the bed, and it was a good choice, her practical parents knew. A good iron bedstead lasted past the life of one's grandchildren, and their Rosalie was not one to change her likes and dislikes with a change in the weather. Like some teenage girls.

"And you, Francine? Do you want a bed like that?"

With a shake of her head that made her dark hair sway, "I want dress material for at least ten new dresses, and I want to make them myself with Mrs. O'Grady helping me. I want patterns or pictures from New York, because I want them to be comfortable and very, very pretty. I don't know how much that will cost, but that's exactly what I want. And another thing, I want a pair of white, pearl button shoes."

Her parents stared amazed. Where had this child come from? Certainly she couldn't be theirs. Her mother found her voice, "Francy, honey, why would you want ten new dresses all at once? You have plenty of nice things to wear…?"

Francine was ready with her answer. "I want them because what I have now is not what a school teacher would wear. I have 'little girl' dresses. I want to be ready to teach when I need to be, and I know it'll take a year, at least, for me to sew them. Will they cost too much?"

With a shrug in agreement, they turned to Raymond, their youngest. "And what would you really, really like to have?"

The eleven year old boy thought hard for a short moment. "Do we still have any of those molasses cookies? I'd like to have a handful of them, and then go see if Luke and David want to go check the river for catfish."

"Nothin' else?"

"Hmmm. I don't think so. Do we have any cookies left?"

"Take 'em and go, son. You've made your parents happy." They could have added, it's nice that you plan to be a little boy for a while yet, and nothing could please us more. There followed a glassy rattle of the cookie jar lid and a slam of the door. Raymond was busy being eleven.

The news of the legacy passed quickly over the Corners territory. Carmelita's eyes shone with pleasure at Rosalie's gift. To be truthful, she had felt humble that she had the gift of Josie and a view of the top of her stairway, and Rosalie had not been able to share it with her. She sensed that only she could see the real value of it. Now that Rosalie would have her own wish, Carmelita felt they two could be more even. It was best when friendships could be even, and she had long known that her friend had adored that bed, even before it became Josie's.

It was Francine's choice, however, that had the community agog. Dresses? She had nice clothes already, and she had another year of school? And why did the fabric and patterns have to come from New York?

Mrs. O'Grady, however, smiled with satisfaction. She knew the pride of having just the thing you knew you wanted, and the older lady was pleased to be was chosen to be part of the acquisition of the items. She also felt an anticipation to see the actual fabric to work with actual store-bought patterns instead of creating them herself, and she might even get the opportunity to advise the girl on the trimming.

Also, the sewing lessons would work out well. She was currently instructing her Bridgit in stitching buttonholes and pleats. Also tucks and flounces. Bridget, however, was a small girl with rounded shoulders, and there was not much height to work with. Francine Canfield, on the other hand, was tall for her age and had excellent shoulders. She could imagine Francine at fifteen or sixteen. She would be a dream to fit with expensive fabric!

And Josie was facing another year and another set of students. It was pencil and notebook time. Now that she had made a decision about last year's Level Four, she went about dealing with the new one. The one arriving next September.

There would be four boys. Raymond Canfield, barely eleven; Jacob, ten; and the two grandsons of Mrs. Gray Owl's brother, Gray Eagle, Johnny Black Bear and William Running Elk. Both were Raymond's age, and Johnny had decided that he was Johnny Black, and he didn't need the 'Bear' part. William also decided to dispense with the 'Running'. Elks always ran, so there was no need to mention it.

Both boys were very clever, but had had no access to the book based education. It was Gray Eagle who got his wish. He wanted them to learn counting because the best jobs they could get would be with the newcomers and he intended that they 'not be cheated in their wages'.

That seemed a reasonable level to reach in a year, and could surely be learned somehow. The matter was partially solved by the effort of small Lily Gray Owl during the summer. Under her grandmother's orders, she had attempted to pass on what she had learned of reading and numbers, and had been surprisingly successful.

Old Gray Eagle, native tribal elder, was proud of his bargain with his sons for the future of his grandsons. The fathers would have had the boys hauling coal from the next county to satisfy the demand of homes and business in every direction. The old man bravely insisted that he could do as well as the both of them because he would haul coal, nonstop, using two teams of mules. So far, he had done well.

So, with the four boys, Josie added the girls. There was Kristy and Gwinnie McLaughlin and also Patricia O'Day and Bridgit O'Grady.

There was a new girl with some schooling who had moved into the area. Eva Adams was the age of Patricia, and it was hoped she would learn fast and be able to keep up.

So, four boys and five girls. That clearly meant that she would take over their training herself, which was what she had felt would be necessary.

The next was Level Three, with six students. There was Josh, her brother, and Darrell, her cousin. Isaac and Luke were next, and there were two girls, Bettina Stewart and America Forrester.

Josie was not sure of America's background, but she could hardly put her in with Level Two, which was Tray Cullen, Lily Gray Owl, Esther Wilson, and David Stewart and America's own brother, Homer.

There was a new crop of beginners. Marshall Adams, brother to Eve, and Benjamin Worth. Three girls, Addie, Evelyn, and Annabelle.

She nodded with satisfaction. Twenty one students were just about capacity for the classroom, leaving room for an addition or two as time went on. If the parents were required to pay $1.50 per student per month, that would add up to at least $30.00.

Then, $30.00 divided among 4 girls would be $7.50 for each.

She had not told Carmelita, Rosalie, Francine, and Carlotta that they would be the 4 girls receiving the $7.50 for themselves.

It was, however, Josie's intention that it be part of their education. They were worth something, and it was good for them to be able to convert their worth into dollars and cents. Josie felt that it would be more business like and create a knowledge of their own importance. And earned skill.

Josie had selfishly determined to herself that her first graduating class would have certification and practical experience. For her, it was an exercise in determination. After that, what they did with what they knew would be up to them. Josie continued to feel her interest pulling away from the school and moving in another direction. Strange thing, the way a consuming desire could fade away like fog in the valley when the sun came up.

First to come from New York was the soft-sided package containing the requested stockings, along with lace camisoles and ruffled petti-slips. Sharon Blaine had not been able to resist tucking into the package a beautiful silk scarf. As she admired it, Josie could not help but smile. It was lovely but not nearly so creative as the one knitted for her by Mrs. McLaughlin, or the bonnet/scarf combination made of rabbit fur created by Mrs. Gray Owl.

She folded the silk scarf and set it aside. It would make a gift, sometime. Perhaps to Janine who would love it, and the pale blue of it would set off her white skin and dark hair.

School would begin in one more week. And it would be an interesting one. Such a help was Janine, that Josie wondered what she would have done....

Next in the mail came the hard box with the magazines and poetry books. That was when she called in her four helpers.

The wrapping was peeled away before the four sets of eager eyes. They knew this must be extra special... for them to be in attendance. The first sight of the shiny covers to the fashion magazines opened their mouths in anticipation, and the interest grew as book after book was set aside to see what else was in the box.

Then the patterns! Sharon had actually managed to get a book of patterns by a company called Butterick. It was dated two years ago, but that was no matter. Leaning their heads together, the girls examined a few pages, then closed it to be enjoyed later.

Then there were the composition books. A bundle of 8 of them were still in their factory wrapping. Wealth! She opened the bundle and displayed a lined, stapled book with hardboard cover. "Girls, these are books for something special that you want to keep and they can fit in your folders. When you want one, they will be here in my desk."

Francine stepped forward and carefully removed one from the stack, a small smile on her lips and a knowing glance at her teacher. She tucked it protectively into her spread fingers.

"Now, girls," Josie began, "find a place to sit because I have a plan. Next fall I will be teaching only Level Four. I will begin searching for some one to take over the school as teacher, and they will begin by teaching only the lower levels, while I take the large class of Level Four."

Wide and concerned eyes as the girls looked from one to the other. What was going on?

"So here is what I planned. While I'm looking, I need for the four of you to help. You will work in teams of two, and the partners will be changed about to give you experience in working with another person. Rosalie and Francine will not be paired together... As sisters, I think they've already had experience in working together." A giggle passed around."

Josie continued, "While two of you are practice-teaching, the other two will do a bit of advanced reading and work on a few other subjects to have you totally prepared for your Certification Test. While Carmelita and Francine are doing the teaching, Rosalie and Carlotta will work with me. Next will be Francine and Carlotta working together, and it will be their responsibility to put together a lesson plan outlining a weekly goal and how they plan to reach it. I will approve the plan, but it will be the responsibility of the teachers to make it work.

"Now the other thing I want to say is this. The parents of the community know the school is valuable, and things of value cost something. You are aware of the way your parents and others gave me presents, food, and help with transportation. Now it will be different.

"A tuition of $1.50 will be required for each student for each month, in addition to the basket of cowpats for the stove. The amount of the tuition will total maybe $30.00 a month and that amount will divided among the four of you." More wide-eyed glances at each other!

"I'm telling you this now, at the beginning of the summer, so you can think about it, individually and together and you will be a help to each other making your plans. Any questions?

Silence! Stunned, wide-eyed and closed mouth silence!

Josie nodded, knowingly. "There will be a lot of time. Questions can come later." Dismissing them with a smile, she watched them revert from amazed teachers-in-training to giggly girls gathered around the magazines. Francine turned the pages slowly, examining every dress, shirtwaist, and even the pages of ruffled, plain and sophisticated bonnets.

It was during that summer that Brad proposed to Josie the first time. It was a casual, off-handed proposal, meant to test the waters.

The stone house had finally reached the roof, but only after each and every stone had been inspected and approved by Digby in his roll as trainer. The dimension lumber used for the roof was something Brad was acquainted with. He would not need Digby until he began the side additions.

Finding time for work on the house, and also to sleep, along with creating his blacksmith business was about all the young man could manage. "Looks like I'm going to have to move in, up here, to get something done." Josie had already moved everything but her bed, and the stove like Aunt Nettie's that had been ordered.

With a knowing look at Brad, Josie responded, "I'm moving that bed in here soon as I get cousin help."

Brad grinned, companionably. "That's all right. There's plenty of room for the two of us."

At this point, Josie found duties to attend to, and Brad was satisfied. She didn't yell or throw anything at him. Things were looking up.

It was late in the summer that he had suggested making the deal with her cousin next door. "You ever think about it, Josie, you could do a good turn for Jeff, and he'd be able to help you."

Now that he had her attention, he continued, seriously. "This big old quarter section you have, you know you'll never need to use it all. Here's what you could do. So he explained it.

Jeff needed to set himself up permanently, with something he could count on, as now Doug and Junior had taken over the Hastings place. The older brothers had left fencing and cross-fencing, and Jeff had dreamed of being able to use it with more animals. His adoration of the Irish Conamara horses had only increased, but the money to purchase more breeding mares had not.

"What you could do would be cut this tract in half right down the middle. The school would be on one side and all of the fencing and sheds on the other. Now if you were to deal with him to give you a pair of his fancy carriage horses, ones of your choosing, and if you kept the first hundred feet of the corner for the blacksmith shop. He could sled the stones for your room additions in partial payment.

"It'd be a pretty good trade, and he might even toss in a good saddle horse to balance off the stones from his part of the ledge. It could be a lease until all accounts were settled to your satisfaction."

Josie paused, then, "Do I need horses?"

"Certainly you need horses. You'll need them to pull the closed-in carriage you'll get for a wedding present. Then, who knows, but that there'll be a handyman around here that needs a fast saddle animal."

"Digby couldn't ride a saddle horse."

"Wouldn't be Digby. I'm fairly handy, wouldn't you say, and for a fact, I'm a man. That'd add up to a handyman, wouldn't it?"

Josie ignored him and went about her business, but his sharp vision of her reaction produced a tiny smile. Enough said for now.

But then the trade began to sound good. She and Jeff got along famously as friends. This way, he would have the freedom to build himself a permanent house, and maybe he'd live here when he married. Maybe it would be Janine?

And there was the stone ledge that others seemed to consider so valuable. There was no way that she would do anything with the stones, and if she did, the ones on her half would be more than plenty.

Another thing entered her practical mind. If those stones were so valuable, why couldn't Jeff sell some, and that would give him money for horses? That could work, couldn't it? They were good looking animals, and the more she saw them, the more she appreciated them. Big... strong... and trainable.

This way they would always be next door, and with this trade she would still have the corner. Actually, Brad had a good idea. And, of a truth, he was exceptionally handy. And a man. A good looking man, at that!

The decent stove arrived and was installed with a proper chimney. As she stood before it, Brad could not hold back an amused grin. A totally unnaturally picture and absolutely out of character. Like an armadillo riding on a race horse! Would she ever use it? Anyway.... it was there.

The suggestion of a land trade also made Jeff Wilson breathless and heart-stopped with excitement. Stepping off his half of the stone ledge, he had the impression that he was walking on gold coins. Dreams could come true.

A sign in the blacksmith shop and another over the mail hooks in the Corners stating 'BUILDING STONE FOR SALE' brought an immediate response. In this building-material scarce land, the activity was hardly a surprise.

A letter to Green's Farm where he had purchased the young horses, assured him they had a pair of mares who were well-patterned with gray and charcoal and bred to studs of the same pattern. They'd hold them for him.

"I'm thinkin' you'd not have a particular use for the foals from the carriage horses…? These here I raised are first rate. Brad should check 'em out."

It was Josie's turn to have the small amused grin. How did it become Brad's duty to check out the horses she would be trading for? Anyway….

More words later. Brad, the negotiator, was not through. To Jeff, privately, "You'll be bringing a couple'a mares home from Green's Farm, won't you?"

At Jeff's nod, he suggested, "You'll be goin' through Oklahoma City, and if the new carriage was ready, your team could just hitch on and bring it home, couldn't you?"

It took every cent Brad could scrape together to arrange purchase of the closed-in carriage, but he thought the gamble was worth it. Surely it would cement his chances. And face it… if she turned him down, what good would money be, anyway?

It made conversation for a week when Jefferson Wilson came into the Corners holding the reins behind a matched pair of Conamara mares, heads high, gait steady, and rounded rumps swaying, swinging their charcoal trimmed tails back and forth over their flared fetlocks.

Behind them was the carriage.

The carriage had the appearance of a storybook picture, or a vehicle that had just come from the streets of New York City, or maybe Chicago. Painted pearl-gray with trim of black and silver. Someone must be out of his mind to order something like that out on the rugged plains of Territory. Wherever would a fellow drive something like that? Whose was it, anyway?

Josie happened to be at the Corner checking the mail hook when the crowd from nowhere seemed to gather. Staring up the road, she gasped with astonishment as she saw a piece of New York City coming toward her.

Tears formed and ran down her cheeks. A moment of homesickness? A sight from the past… the place of her birth, from which she had been so abruptly yanked?

She saw not the crowd gathered around her. She only saw the smiling face of her cousin and the lift of the mare's heads. She saw the swing of their trimmed charcoal manes and the shine of the silver on the harnesses.

Jeff stopped, leaped lightly to the ground, and held out his arm to his cousin. Josie stood tall, chin lifted. She gathered her skirt in one hand and extended her arm toward the smiling, curly haired redhead. Then she stepped into the carriage. With a word neither to the right or left, Jeff stepped aboard once more and clicked the animals into action. Josie leaned forward and waved with both hands while riding 'in state' to the schoolyard.

Stepping down, assisted by her cousin, she tossed her head and smiled. "I see the horses I want. You're welcome to every baby that comes, I just want these."

And with that, the deal was sealed.

It was in December that the marriage happened. The carriage made a return trip to Oklahoma City, and the couple spent a week enjoying holiday activity.

They came back to a community party held in the stone ledge schoolroom. It was practically a day-long celebration in which many excited children were treated to a ride in the carriage behind the fancy animals. No current resident of the Territory would ever forget the marriage celebration of Josie Wheeler and Bradley Cullen.

Neither could any of those who observed the courtship have ever thought it would be any other way. It was obvious that some things were meant to be.

It was in September that the foals began to drop. The boys in the classes could hardly concentrate. Janine often took the five year olds on the eighth of a mile walk to watch the action of the fascinating, long-legged little animals as they attempted to stand on their wobbley stilt-legs. Heel-kicking and head-tossing. Tail-switching and tumbles as they sought to gain the proficiency on their miniature hooves.

Jeff managed to find time to lean his elbow on his side of the fence and entertain the keeper of the children, and Janine seemed adequately entertained.

And he had been lucky. From Josie's carriage mares, he got a colt and a filly, both of the color he wanted. In an amazing streak of luck, his four mares produced three gray fillies, but lo and behold! What now....?

What should happen next but the dropping of a chocolate brown colt with the scruffyness of his ancient, equine, Viking forbears. No less a thoroughbred Conamara, the Viking strain had remembered the time a darker color was desirable in the northlands and had thrived on the windswept Islands north of Ireland. Orkneys. Hebrides. And other smaller islands where the fierce blow off the sea could cut through a person like a knife. Darker color and scruffy coat were a survival adaptation, but it clearly had no place in Jefferson Wilson's corral.

Francine and Carlotta took their turn to come to the paddock to gaze at the newest members of the community. The tall, black-haired girl immediately fastened her dark eyes onto the 'ugly ducking' of a colt.

"Chocolate!" she announced. "How much do you want for him, Jeff? I'll buy him right now if you'll keep him for me for a year and train him. He's exactly what I want."

No one was surprised. No one could ever remember seeing Francine Canfield being hesitant in a time of decision. What she wanted and felt, she knew instantly, and did not change. The money she paid for the animal, together with some from the sale of building stone, purchased another two mares. Jeff's herd was off and running.

Chocolate was kept and fed with Jeff's herd, and duly broke to a saddle, but more importantly, he was taught to accept the discipline of the double tree of a buggy tongue. The little fellow was taught to back his quarters between the buggy shafts when ordered to, in order to be more easily harnessed. He learned to march along like the best of them, obeying a light touch of the reins. Intelligent Conamara, he was… just a horse of a different color.

Francine's father made the trip to Oklahoma City and returned with the best-made 'lady's buggy' he could find. He brought chocolate colored paint for the buggy so the animal, and the conveyance would match. Somehow he knew it would have been Francine's wish.

He was happy to do it, as this buggy was the instrument that would bring his daughter home on weekends and during summers, and it would last her for decades.

It was during late November that the students of Level Two were working on their penmanship. Actual lead pencils and lined paper. A luxury. The assignment was this.

Miss Carmelita had explained it carefully. They must think of what they wanted to say before they wrote it down. In fact, they must first write it in chalk on the slates. It must be a sentence about what they would like to receive as a present for Christmas.

She was specific as she said it must start, "I would like to have" and contain the word, "because." If they had trouble with spelling or letter formation, she would be glad to help.

Silence and a lot of concerned lip-licking. Tray's hand shot up, as it usually did. "Miss Carmelita, can we make more than one wish?"

After a minor hesitation, the teacher nodded, "You may write more than one sentence, but every one must start with "I would like to have', and contain the word "because."

"Thanks," Tray responded, and the next sound was the hurried scratching of the chalk on his slate. The others followed his example, as they usually did.

Carmelita chuckled and smiled at their requests. Every child had at least two requests. Tray requested another sheet of paper.

When she collected the papers she had acquired, she counted a total of seventeen requests. Penmanship could be better, but it was early in the year, and their hands were still small and unaccustomed to a pencil. Chalk was the most often used piece of writing equipment. The content, however, was most impressive.

Forming itself in her mind was an amusing scenario. What if someone decided to take over the job of Santa Claus and make Christmas come early? He would tell everyone that he was now Santa Claus. He would say he needed help in deciding what gifts to bring. These are the letters he got, and he couldn't fill a single one of them. In the end he was forced to hand the letters over to the real Santa.

With a few twists and turns, she incorporated the letters into a story to use as part of the entertainment for the Christmas program. Due to the smallness of the room, only the immediate parents were invited to the party. A few examples of class achievement were shown and refreshments were served. Excited children and proud parents made the whole exhausting program worthwhile, according to the four teachers. As a finale, the false Santa Story was read.

Giggles happened as Level Two class recognized their own offerings, and parents were soon laughing with their children.

Josie had no part of the program and sat as one of the guests. When the False Santa story was read by her cousin Carmelita, she saw what she thought was an important potential. With a shrug and a smile, Carmelita handed the story to Josie when requested.

The next mail that went to New York City contained the story. Aunt Sharon might enjoy it, and it was truly an example of what could be done....

Sharon Blaine read the story and placed it aside, slipping into her winter fur coat. Putting it into the hand of the editor of the local paper, she felt satisfied and ready to let fate take its course.

She was notified that the piece was "charming," and they would like to byline it as "A Note from the Western Prairie." They thought it would be well received as so many of the residents of the City had friends and relatives who had gone west.

They would title it, "Why Christmas was Late That Year." Would Mrs. Blaine give them a release from the author?

Sharon spent only two sleep-disturbed nights over the illegality of what she intended to do (and her husband an attorney, for goodness sake!) but proceeded as she had always known she would. Knowing time was the element if the paper was to use it this year and knowing there was not enough time to ask the girl, she penned a release and signed (horrors!) the name of Miss Carmelita Wilson of Prairie Academy School.

Excitedly buying a dozen of the papers and clipping out the story, she enclosed it with the money order the paper had offered her, made out for $10.00. A letter from the editor complemented her (without knowing she was barely fifteen) and advised that they could use others under the same byline if she would honor them with the submission.

Protected between covers of stiff cardboard, Sharon mailed the copies to Carlile Corners, in care of Argyle, Oklahoma Territory. Josie found herself swallowing with difficulty because of the emotion and pride, but Carmelita burst into a flood of tears, hiding her face in her hands. Somehow, actual money seemed to be the marker of success. The validation of true talent. Someone must be willing to pay for the product for it to become real and have actual, measurable value.

Rosalie grinned with shared pride but did not understand the tears of her friend. Or the validation of coins earned. "Carmelita said a long time ago she was going to be a writer. Why is she crying?"

Other offerings were mailed to New York City.

THE WRONG COLOR PONY (who was picked by a beautiful lady as her own because he was the color of the chocolate she loved.)

THE LAST PUPPY (the runt of a wolf litter who found himself alone when his parents thought he could care for himself. He saw a reflection of himself in the water and knew he was an adult.)

THE CHRISTMAS HAT (a man got a hat for Christmas so he cut ear holes in his old one for his mule to wear in the sun. The hat blew away, landed in a tree, and a bird made a nest in it. A mouse climbed the tree and nipped off the tie strings to line his nest. The hat fell out of the tree, and a chipmunk hid from a coyote in it. The wind blew it against a weed, and a prairie dog pulled it into his hole as nest material.)

SONG DOG (the coyotes who lifted noses in a howl to compete with the buzz of the bee, croak of the frog, chirp of the bird, and whistle of the wind.)

WHERE DID THEY HIDE MY LEGS? (a young tadpole that had only a tail and worried about his legs, but finally they did appear, and he still didn't know where they had been hidden.)

There were many more, and each one brought a letter of thanks and a money order payment. Carmelita carefully put the printed stories in a protective folder and cashed her money orders in Argyle. She knew the stories were not nearly as good as she wanted them to be, but they would be saved to look back on and smile. Someday she would write really good stories.

To the neighborhood, however, second looks were cast toward her with wonder. She was their own Carmelita! She was the one to whom was paid 'enormous sums' for words she just pulled out of her head. Now think about it, how magic was that, I tell you! After numerous requests, she pinned a copy of each story above her mail hook for a few days to give those who wished a chance to read it.

Carlotta, with her soft fine voice, taught songs to the children. When she ran out of the ones she knew, Sharon Blaine searched out a book of children's songs and sent it, hoping the girl could work out the tunes. Or maybe invent new ones.

Francine was a teacher. She was able to stare soberly and firmly at any small boy and influence him to produce his best work. The smiles and hugs were afterward, when he had done well, and that made it worth while. Hugs were brief, but given in the classroom so others would see.

Janine read stories to the younger grades and took little ones out for exercise. She was extremely conscientious in whatever she could do, in return for the education of little brother, Tray. The well-stocked library with books for "older girls and ladies" made the duty a pleasure most of the time.

Josie managed her class of nine. As helps, she had a full folder of things she had used last year, and there were new ideas that came along. The assignment of creating their own problems was still valuable to encourage thinking from more than one direction. Last years problems could be used, as well.

Her four boys were interesting. There was Raymond Canfield, brother of Rosalie and Francine. Raymond was able to nudge a seat partner with his elbow, whistle between his teeth and roll a pencil noisily across his desk and answer every question quickly and thoroughly. Giving it a lot of thought, Josie decided to let it go. Raymond was a born leader, and a leader acquired followers. His classmates could do far worse than follow him.

Jacob, over a year younger and also in the class, had a distinct hero worship of Raymond and his quick intelligence and could only be helped by example. Then there were the two grandsons of Gray Eagle, Kiowa tribal elder. The two boys, Johnny and Willie, also strove to follow the example of Raymond. There was no way to totally "catch them up" with Raymond, but they gave excellent attention and were bound to pick up a lot, just by listening.

Josie could smile a bit over the thought that Lily Gray Owl was the younger cousin of the boys and was in Level Two. She was intensely attentive to everything that went on. If the boys misbehaved, she was sure to pass the information along to her grandmother, and the boys were staying with her grandmother for the year. It was Josie's decision that the best plan was to let Raymond lead, as that was certainly what he would eventually do.

As the school year progressed, it came time for the 2000 word essay which would constitute the final grade for grammar and punctuation. It was not unexpected and was looked forward with a variety of stages of enthusiasm.

The girls had been preparing themselves, so to speak, by dredging up their favorite memories. Girls just naturally seemed to have more details that were important enough to remember.

Some of the boys, however, found themselves dreading the ordeal and scrounging for enough words to fill out the requirement. The cousins, Johnny and Willie, had spent a lot of their life together as best friends, and their combined, shared memories added up rather well.

Then, there was Raymond Canfield. He treated this assignment as he treated all assignments. It was not a surprise, so therefore he was prepared. His effort went as follows:

"If small Ray had been asked for his first memory, he would have told about the magic box. He must have been about three and a half and had found himself in a wagon with a tent covering, moving behind a pair of horses and going somewhere. It didn't matter where. Just doing something different was interesting to him at that age.

"Then they handed him the BOX. It was a big box, but Ray was a strong little fellow and had no trouble lifting it. Holding it tightly, he crawled on his knees to the back of the wagon, over the boxes and sacks, the messed up quilts and a lot of pillows. There, he opened the magic box.

"His first glance showed a lot of small things with bright colors. He learned later that they were made of wood by a neighbor of his Grandma Nicolo and painted by her with a tiny brush and a lot of kinds of paint.

"There were cows and horses, sheep and goats, chickens and ducks and also dogs and cats. Some of them would stand up by themselves, and others, like the chickens, had small round pedestals to stand on, and their feet were surrounded by green spikes that looked like grass.

"Farther down in the box were the wagons and carts with wheels that really turned. They were painted in wonderful colors… even the spokes on the wheels. There were little leather harnesses that hooked over the horses' heads and attached to the wagons. There were things to haul in the wagons like sticks of wood, 'rocks' made from wood and painted, bales of hay made from blocks of wood. Everything was painted to look exactly real.

"The rest of the trip after that, little Ray didn't remember much except the magic box and its contents. There was Mama and Pa to take care of eating, sleeping and keeping clean, so the little boy had nothing to do but play.

"Eventually the long trip was over, and the magic box was placed in the room where he would sleep for the next lot of years, but it didn't get as much attention as it had on the trip.

"After the trip was over, there were real things to do with real dogs and cats, baby calves and chickens. There were times of following the horses and the plow as Pa made trip after trip across the ground so he could plant seeds.

"All of the days seemed a lot alike and interesting. There were other boys to play with and a nice creek with fish. There were rabbits to chase and birds to feed. Then came the day of the giant horses.

"When Ray first saw the giant horses, he thought they should be in a storybook like the bean stalk that Jack climbed up into the sky. The animals, four of them, actually, were eating grass in the yard of the people who lived across the road. Ray just couldn't keep his eyes off those horses, and the man who owned them let the boy see the foals the mares had produced.

"By now, Ray was a bigger boy and had a lot of chores to do. There was hay to rake and gather and pull up into the barn loft with the platform and pulley-rope. There were beans and peas to pick in the blazing sun, and there were times that he walked behind the plow to plant the gardens. He also pulled a lot of weeds in the garden to feed to the hogs.

"There were many things to think of while doing these chores, but the thing he thought of most were the huge black horses with the fringe of lighter color around their feet. If he had those horses, he could likely pull the whole world. Or, at least, a big chunk of it.

"If someone had a pair of those, he would have no trouble having a good job. Ray had a couple of friends who liked to go with him to watch the horses. The three of them would lean against the fence and talk about the things those horses could do.

"Ray wanted some horses like that with every bit of longing there was within him. Sometimes he talked with Pa, and Pa would listen, and stroke his chin. He would look like he wanted to say something, but he didn't. He just listened.

"Then there was the day, and it was not long ago, that Ray was talking with his Pa, and said, "Do you think I could ever have a horse like that? For my very own?"

"That's when Pa nodded and smiled, like he was finally going to get to say what he had been wanting to say. He said, "Son, I believe you could. There's the gift your grandmother left you, and if the owner wants to sell a pair, you could probably have enough money to buy them."

"When Ray heard his Pa say 'pair', he breathed in a deep breath because his head was a little bit dizzy. He had been thinking of only one. Then Pa had more to say.

"'Now, son, if it was me, I would prefer a pair of the foals as soon as they were weaned from their mother. You are too young to do much with the grown up horses right now, but you are the perfect age to train the young ones as they grow up. I think we might look into it. I'm certain you will take good care of them, because you and Johnny and Willie have the print of the fence wire on your faces from looking over the fence.' Then he grinned, and his eyes twinkled.

"After that, the boy didn't think about whether he would get the horses, but he thought about what all they would do. One thing they could do would be to pull the big coal wagons that are so heavy. The coal is dug out of the ground a few miles over past the ridge, and a lot of horses get so tired they have to rest a lot. Sometimes the wagons are not filled full because they are so heavy.

There was so much to think about if one had animals like those.

"After that, Ray began to ask the grownups and Pa about how much money was paid to those who hauled coal. He was rather good at making up problems over at the Academy, so he began to figure on how much money could be made that way.

"Ray is certain this is the way he will go, just as soon as he graduates. He would really like to remember more about this but he can't. It hasn't happened yet, but it will! Ray will not stop until it does.

CHAPTER 5

Miss Josie smiled a small smile and nodded her head. She would have expected no less from Raymond Canfield and was certain she would eventually see a lot of the Clydesdale horses performing a variety of duties, likely some of which had not yet been tried.

Watching the boy, and the others, was like seeing a flower bud in spring, not knowing exactly how it would bloom out. Or perhaps a pupae-case swinging from a limb. What brightly colored butterfly would eventually emerge?

Raymond's sister, Rosalie, when asked what she wanted from her inheritance, she knew. She had never mentioned it to her parents, but she knew, and it was something that was beautiful, useful, and would never become outdated.

When Francine was asked, she knew... and had never mentioned it to her parents, but she knew. Her ten plus dresses would be beautiful, useful, and totally appropriate for her dream job.

Young Raymond had no idea of what he wanted until he saw the Clydesdale horses. Then he knew, and was never distracted. Beautiful, useful, and would make a lot of money for him.

The Canfield family was continuously interesting to Josie. There was the oldest girl, Rosalie, who was the perfect 'second in charge'. She chose a position of assisting a leader, and she had forged a bond with Carmelita, less than a year older.

Instinctively, she chose a 'leader' and followed, knowing followers were just as important. She was a team player and had very good ideas. She happily carried out the plans of another and was the perfect "lieutenant" supporting the "general" in charge.

Francine was not a leader or a follower, but an "independent". She created her own plans and required no help in perfecting them and carrying them out. Neither did she dispute another's right to do the same. She expected to work alone. She chose the wardrobe she would eventually wear to teach. She decided on the books and training material, and her fortunate gift of money would enable her to furnish them.

She was a born teacher, stern, fair and encouraging, as well as generous with praise for a job well done. She set her own goals and proceeded to meet them.

Raymond was the complete package of male ability and would not necessarily follow the path, but rather, would create the path, and bring others along with him.

The Canfield sisters' younger brother Raymond was strictly his own person. He was the leader who would attract followers without trying. Handsome, tan skinned with black eyes and a heavy brush of black hair. He automatically treated the two native boys as though they had been as fortunate as he and therefore knew all that he knew. That attitude went a long way toward encouraging them. He treated Jacob as a kid brother whom he liked. Jacob thrived on attention from his idol.

Josie imagined Raymond in a few years... Solidly in his own business with Johnny and Willie nearby. It would be like the planet called Raymond circling the earth on a set course, bringing along the satellites of the two native boys. Old Gray Eagle would have been proud. He had clearly seen the way the 'old life' would go, and he had been successful in rescuing two of his grandsons. They would be an example to the rest.

All in all, the four boys of that class had created their own welded group. The girls were not so. Eva Adams had fortunately been able to occasionally attend school and was not far behind the Irish girls, Patricia O'Day and Bridgit O'Grady and the McLaughlin sisters. They had fun. It was their intention to enjoy life, born of family background and genetic inheritance. They possessed the firm feeling that fun was what life was for. They totally lacked the seriousness of last year's Level Four, but they were very interesting.

It sometimes took more effort to influence them to work, but somehow the work got done, and test papers proved it.

Unlike the individuality of the Canfield sisters, the McLaughlin girls, Gwendollyn and Kristollyn, were identical halves of the same apple. Less than a year apart, they had depended on each other for approval and assistance from the time they learned to walk and would likely continue to do so. Last year they were round faced and dimpled, their light brown hair shaggy about their gaily laughing faces. Dresses with flouncy skirts bounced around their knobby eight and nine year old legs, and their elbows were still awkward and sharp boned.

This year, after only a year, they acquired angular faces with cheek bones lightly outlined, hair trimmed into a face-framing fringe with a braid starting at the crown of their heads and plaited within itself all the way to the nape and held by a colorful ribbon. Below the ribbon, hair extended below their shoulder blades in a thick switch that would have been the pride of any show pony. It was impossible to picture one of the girls alone, so closely they stuck to each other. No set of twins could be closer.

The other two from last year's Level Three, Pattie O'Day and Bridie O'Grady, were taller and noisier this year. They possessed a great sense of humor, and they built on each other's words. Red hair and milk white skin of southern Ireland, they also acquired the violet eyes common to the region. The girls were not related that they knew of, but they were sure to have had common ancestry not many generations back.

Laughing and lighthearted, they treated the school assignments as they would a job of gathering cowpats. It was a thing to do because it must be done. No second thoughts. None of the four girls lacked ability, but there was not the fierce determination of last years Level Four, or the eyes on the goal to make the best of the gift of school that they had not expected to get.

There was one other important difference. These girls had three years of school, where the first class had only two to achieve the same result. It was now their second year, but they did well, just as they had intended to do.

Eva Adams, new to the territory was a social accumulator, gathering everyone around her and seeing the best in everyone. First to pick up a fallen toddler or to reach out to a friendly dog, nothing passed her attention, and she obviously enjoyed the noisy group at the school. Her former schooling had been in St. Louis and rather strict and formalized. Eva treated her homework assignments as gifts and presented them in complete fashion.

As Josie considered the girls, Eva was the only one she would guess would choose to teach, but the others must qualify. Later it would be different on the Territory, but at this point, the options were few. In addition, the parents were firm. It was a sacrifice to let children of eleven and twelve spend the time in school, and their folks intended that they make it worthwhile. Little girls must grow up fast. So must little boys.

It was around the middle of November that Josie began to suspect her family would increase. By the New Year, she was sure. As it turned out, she was one of the lucky ones who was not flattened by morning sickness, and she sailed on through with her plans. The first to know of her pregnancy was Mrs. Gray Own, though no one had yet been told except Aunt Nettie and Sharon Blaine.

The old Kiowa woman smiled widely, her many wrinkles arranging themselves across her face. With an approving nod, she held up her hand with two fingers extended. Meeting Brad outside the Corners, she stopped him, scooped her hand out over her own stomach and pointed to him, then raised the two fingers, smiling happily.

With a grin he responded, "Josie is expecting twins? Tell me, are they boys or girls?"

A sly smile and a shake of the head. "Surprise," she told him and headed on with her own business.

Josie's obliging sons made their arrival in the heat of early August, and Josie was her old self by the opening of the school year. There might have been a childcare problem if it had not been for Digby. The crippled miner from Colorado added that particular skill to his many others.

The boys were named Aaron and Adam and spent many hours in the room beside the school and were fed by their nearby mother when necessary. Also on rare cases of fussy-ness Janine could handle most situations. And there was Aunt Nettie always ready and eager to take over for her dead sister's grandsons.

It was fifteen months later that the twins were joined with two more, born on the same day. James and John made their appearance in late November, with Janine filling in with the current Level Four. Under Josie's guidance, she assigned the math equations, the outside reading, and on one occasion, held their class in the new rock house down the road. The Oklahoma weather being on one of its contrary notions, it seemed better that the class come to Josie than have her come to them.

This class contained her brother and cousin, and she was serious about having them ready for their further education in New York. There would be a year between, the year they would both be turning twelve, the one where they would study alone on material sent by their guardian, Attorney Elias Blaine. After that, well, it seemed the two families would be saying goodbye for a while to Joshua Wheeler and Darrell Wilson.

But now there was a current matter. Thinking back, Josie wondered how different would be the life of sweet natured Carlotta Owens if fate had not presented itself in an unthinkable situation and drawn her into it through no fault of her own. It had been the girl's decision to take off a year after receiving her Teaching Certification, but that year was cruelly taken from her.

There was the training year while Miss Josie continued with Level Four and set the girls about acquiring practical experience in teaching. This worked out well, as they were essentially too young to be on their own, and the extra year was a benefit.

They had worked hard. Rosalie Canfield had dimpled and grinned charmingly as she confided to her teacher. "Miss Josie, I was thinking it'd be different after I got to teaching. There was Francine and me all huddled around the lamp in the kitchen finishing our homework, but now Francine is there working her thimble and needle, and it's Raymond and me still on lessons.

Sometimes it's Carmelita crowding in with us while she and I work on lesson plans."

That had happened after the training year. It was now, at the close of the term, that with nervous trembling, her cousin, Carmelita and her close friend and helper, Rosalie, presented themselves before the teacher.

Carmelita began, "We've been thinking, Rosie and me, I mean Rosie and I. We been talking about the teaching we did… And we were thinking, if you were to think we aren't too young, even though the beginning age for teacher is 14… Uh, well we wanted to ask you…."

Josie, having realized this was likely coming, had wondered how it would come about. "Yes?" she encouraged.

"Well, for next year," she paused and looked at Rosalie who smiled and nodded encouragingly. "We thought we could try, maybe for a year, to take over by ourselves. Carlotta isn't ready. She thinks she should spend a year with her parents, and Francine can't tear herself from those dress patterns. It's just the two of us, but we think we could do it, and we're going to have our Certificates by then. I mean just to take the lower Levels…?"

Two pairs of anxious eyes fastened on her and waited expectantly. Josie hesitated, enjoying their eagerness. What better crowning of her efforts could happen than her own cousin following after her? Carmelita was a person of direction, and Josie could see a part of herself in this almost fifteen year old.

Finally, she could hold them in suspense no longer. "I think it would be a very good idea. You know what you're getting into and you would have each other for support. Let's try it for a year and see."

Josie found herself smiling back as two pairs of excited arms hugged her in their relieved joy. The next item on their agenda was the Certificates themselves.

How could any of them have known that Carlotta's life would take such a turn as it was about to?

It was now the last of April in 1897, and the school year had come to a close. Carlotta Owens held her earned coins warmly in her hand as she entered her own room. Such a lovely weight. Seven silver dollars and two quarters. The two quarters would be added to the two she already had and changed into another dollar.

That would make exactly 60 of them that she had earned by teaching at the Prairie Academy. She had worked with the Canfield sisters, Rosalie and Francine, and with Miss Josie's cousin, Carmelita Wilson. She had learned small bits from each of them and was sure she had furnished a few bits of her own.

This was the VERY FIRST thing that she could remember that she had done by herself that was totally successful. The coins were proof that she could accomplish something.

Her father had always furnished necessities and even luxuries, so there was nothing she needed to spend the coins for. But she had sighed with satisfaction every time she had thought of those silver rounds.

As an only child, a favored daughter, she had very little family responsibility, and a considerable amount of guilt. Her mother's health was, as referred to by others, "delicate." It was only recently that Carlotta had tried to convince herself that she had nothing to do with that. She had often felt that this was somehow her fault, but now she knew differently.

She had learned that her mother's three different "sick spells" were her attempts at producing another child, and each had been met with loss and disappointment.

She also finally understood that it was NOT small Carlotta's fault, even though she had been sent away for a while each time. Until recently, it had SEEMED to be her fault, or why could she not stay and take care of her mother, instead of neighbors coming in? Did that mean she could not do a good job? But even the neighbors had not been able to keep her mother from getting sick again.

Carlotta had reached the point of dreading to be gone from her home unless her mother seemed in very good spirits. She attended to her job at the Academy with enjoyment because her progress and activities seemed to be of great importance to both parents. They always wanted to hear every small detail of her day.

Many times she wondered what it would be like to have a sibling to share the attention of parents.

And now she was going to Oklahoma City to take the test for Certification to teach. Not that she would take a job anywhere. She was the youngest of the four girls, but not by much, and they all had ideas of what they wanted to do. Carlotta didn't.

Carmelita and Rosalie had their thoughts on replacing Miss Josie at the Academy. They always were best friends. What was a BEST friend? Carlotta had friends… and there were always things to talk about and girls to laugh with, but one special one? Well, perhaps it would happen later.

And Francine, less than a year older than Carlotta, would not be included in the indecision. She already had definite plans. She was always quick to prepare for what she thought would happen. It had been fun to be paired with her to teach.

Just now Francine was busily creating a wardrobe that she would need when she got a job. She had not even taken the test, yet, and was already getting ready for… something? What would it be like to be certain that you were on the right path to where you wanted to go? Well, it could happen later… couldn't it?

Anyway, her parents seemed excited that she was going to take her test. She would be gone for three days and two nights, and that seemed like a very long time to be away from home.

Now, Carlotta, she chided herself. Even if you stayed home, you couldn't keep things from happening. Maybe bad things. They happen anyway, and besides her mother had seemed so well lately. Papa had insisted that she rest every afternoon, and when he came in after his work day, he would sit on their bed and talk. If Carlotta was at home, and she usually was, she could sit with them, and they asked her plans and discussed what was happening in the community.

So what was the problem? The trip sounded like fun, and since Miss Josie married Miss Janine's brother, there would be six of them going, and that sounded like a party, all by itself. Besides, she tried to convince herself, if she got the Certificate as Miss Josie said she would, that would be another thing that she had accomplished, all by herself. Something that proved that she was worthwhile.

That, and those 60 silver dollars she had in her room. They were so shiny and beautiful, she couldn't bear the thought of spending them for something. Maybe she would keep them forever, like the Certificate. Anyway… that was something to think about.

She smiled to herself with satisfaction. Surely everything would be all right, and she was doing the right thing. She had looked at Francine's new dresses, the ones that she had made all by herself with instructions from Bridgit O'Grady's mother. Such tiny stitches… That seemed just like Francine. She would do what she was told and do a very good job. She would decide what she wanted, and she would get it.

"Maybe I should learn to sew," Carlotta told herself. "I might think it was fun, and it would be something else that I did for myself and by myself."

With a nod of satisfaction with the idea, Carlotta folded her clean, embroidered items of underwear and tucked them into the suitcase with the leather strap that kept it closed. The girls were instructed to pack as small as possible as there would be six of them, and space was limited. A dress could be hung up and worn again, but underwear? No. Face cream and hairbrush. Yes.

Clasps to hold back her hair would be worn, not packed.

As they placed themselves in the double-seated buggy, and suitcases were stored in the boot, there was not yet a speck of daylight. It was a very long trip, and an early start was needed. Even then it would again be dark when they got there. Her parents had been assured that a room was arranged for the girls for both nights.

It was a day for excitement. Everyone was giggly, including Miss Josie, which seemed really strange. It was just like she took off her teacher clothes and put on girl dresses. After all, she was only five years older than Carmelita.

Even Brad, the fellow she married, seemed excited. He almost seemed like a little boy who finally got what he wanted for Christmas, and maybe that was actually what had happened.

Before they got there, the horses were dragging their tired feet, and all the girls were asleep, leaning against each other and thoroughly crushing their carefully ironed dresses. They were met by a man with a lantern and taken to their room.

There were two big beds, and the girls hardly woke up as they removed their dresses and hung them on hangers, then tumbled in the beds. Francine was only moments behind Carlotta as she tried to fluff her sagging pillow and crawl under the sheet. If there were any sounds that night, none of the girls heard them.

The sun was high before anyone's eyes were opened. Finally hunger got the best of them, and they yawned, stretched themselves awake, and took turns washing their faces at the washstand.

Such fun to seat themselves at the diner and decide what they would eat. Miss Josie told them to eat a lot because they couldn't have anything else until after the test. It started at 8 o'clock and lasted six hours. There would be a break after one hour, and she had promised to have a sweet drink for them to pep them up. It was all planned and all Carlotta had to do was do what she was told. Miss Josie had told them.

Miss Josie would have sandwiches for them at 12:00, and that would carry them through until the test was over.

Carlotta didn't feel at all nervous, as Miss Josie had promised that they were all prepared, and all they had to do was to read the questions carefully and answer them fully. Every section of the test was time limited, and if they finished before the bell, they must look over their answers, but be careful about changing them. Most of the time their first answer would be the best. That's what Miss Josie had promised.

Breakfast. Eggs, maybe? Skillet browned potatoes for certain. Sausages that perfumed the diner, crusty brown fried pies that were piping hot from the oven. Apple, cherry, peach, and berry. Steaming peppermint tea with cream. Miss Josie had ordered pies to take with them.

There would be almost hour to look around on the streets of the Territory's biggest city. There were stores with glass-fronted windows. Clothes… shoes… jewelry. Such fun to look at with the other girls. Like yesterday, everything was giggly.

Then they were seated in rows, and Miss Josie left them. Suddenly, it became real that they were about to earn recognition for the last three years, during which they had done almost nothing but study, recite, and assist the younger grades.

Carlotta glanced around her in the large room. There were girls like herself, several older ladies, and even some young men. It was so quiet, they could have heard a pin drop on the wooden floor.

Test before her and a pencil in her hand. It seemed somewhat like a dream from there on. She did not have to know how the dream would turn out, or that she was actually awake. She met each question thoughtfully while knowing it was something she had been taught, so she must only decide the correct way to state it.

Holding her pencil as she was taught, with the proper slant, she formed her letters exactly. Her numbers were carefully readable, like those she had put on the cardboard squares for the Level One numbers class. It seemed hardly any time that the first hour of the test was over.

Already? Time for break?

A thermal jug held the steaming tea that she hadn't realized she needed. The sweet and comforting warmth seemed to fill her with satisfaction as she looked around at the faces of the other girls. Small smiles of pride and confidence were exchanged. Just as Miss Josie had said, they were well able to pass this.

Teacups drained, and the break bell rang. And the time passed.

At last, there were only sixty more minutes, and Carlotta would have the Certificate that she earned by her own efforts, just like the 60 silver dollars in her room.

Test at last completed… and there were two whole hours to walk around on the streets and look at new things. Such fun to hear the comments of the other girls, sometimes funny. She felt herself full of contentment, like this day was a gift that maybe she deserved, not like a birthday present that she got just because she had lived another year.

Gathered again, the formerly quiet group was restless, and it was easy to hear tense breathing. Names were called.

Then she held the sheet of stiff paper and read, "This to certify that Miss Carlotta Owens has been tested and proved herself...." It was over. A shiver of relieved excitement.

Was it a moment of sadness that passed over her? Project completed. Nothing now to pull her forward like the preparation of a phonics games for Level Two. Nothing... not even the Certification Test still hanging out in the future. Everything done. Completed.

With a deep breath, she squared her shoulders and firmed her chin to meet the rest of her life. She was confident that she would know what to do when she got there.

Before they went back to their rooms, the girls were taken to the Ice Cream Dish. Vanilla, chocolate, and strawberry ice cream. Sweet and comforting. Conversation was pleasant but no longer giggly. Bread and meat sandwiches were bought for breakfast as they would be starting home long before daylight. A long day of travel. Maybe they'd even stop at Argyle, if they got too tired and the horses gave out.

Miss Josie and Brad had gone to their room, and the four girls were alone. Sitting on their beds, crosslegged in their nighties, they found things to talk about. What they had seen... what they might like to have... but not one word about the black and gold-lettered Certificates being kept by Miss Josie in the stiff sided box.

Strangely, the certificates seemed like old news that needed no more thought. Just something they had expected and gotten, much like supper at the end of a day.

It was past midnight before they folded over with weariness and slept, but it didn't matter, because they could sleep all the way home, which was almost what they did. They actually did spend the night on the canvass soldier beds in Argyle because the horses were refusing to take another step.

Steaming oatmeal with brown sugar for breakfast and then on their way again. Home. Everything would be just they left it, and only the girls themselves would have changed.

But that was not to be the case, at least for Carlotta.

A horseback rider had met the buggy just outside of Carlile Corner and had talked privately with Brad. Then Miss Josie talked. The girls did not ask the subject, it was none of their business.

Instead of letting the girls out at the school, Brad took the Canfield girls by their house, swung around to the Wilsons for Carmelita, and proceeded on to the Owens farm.

Before they reached the house, they could see the wagons, buggies, and saddle horses around the house. What was going on? Carl Owens stood by the gate like a statue, stone faced, waiting for his daughter. Carlotta's heart began to pound like a blacksmith's hammer as her premonition of disaster began taking shape.

She stepped down into the arms of her father, and she saw his eyes, shiny with moisture. She whispered tentatively, "Is it Mama?" He could only nod.

"But is she all right?" That was when a sob broke in his chest, and he shook his head. "No, my darling, and I'm so, so sorry."

"But, Papa…?" Carlotta felt herself being moved into a circle of arms and soft voices. "Carlotta, honey, your Mama, she's gone. It was so sudden, and there weren't no way to get word to you."

"Gone…?"

"Yes, Sweetheart. It was a snake bite out in the fields. She was bitten on the leg and gone before…."

What followed was not a dream, but a nightmare. Piece by piece the story came out, and words began to be connected. It had all happened during the time Carlotta was bent over her paper, applying her careful script to her answers. Once more, Carlotta had not been there when her mother had been in trouble, and this time it had been fatal.

A matter had been discussed, and Carlotta had been aware that her father had long been interested in having his own captive catfish pond, water fed from the little river, and kept just for his own enjoyment. Or possibly that of a neighbor. He had even picked out a place, and it was one of the subjects discussed during the afternoon visits with her mother while she was resting.

Carlotta had not known when it would be started, just that it was something in her father's long range plans, along with several other things like the wind operated propeller that would draw household water from their well.

It had seemed that, the day being so warm and sunshiny, it was an ideal time for him to take her mother out to see where the pond was planned. He had hitched up the small "ladies buggy" and packed a picnic lunch. He had put a quilt and pillow, as well as a light, covering sheet into the buggy, and they were looking forward to an escape from regular duties and a way to take their minds off their only daughter who was undergoing such an important test.

They were determined not to talk of her but turn their attention to other things, as she would soon be home, and they could enjoy her report together. As they always did.

After driving past the little river and showing her where the canal would be that would fill the pond, Carl Owens had spread the quilt and unpacked the lunch. It had been a special time.

The Territory weather, so often too hot, cold or windy, was ideal. There were birds, butterflies, and grasshoppers alive in the fields, and there was a feeling of wealth and comfort all around.

They had enjoyed the picnic, and Carl had put the remains back in the basket, fluffed up the pillow and spread the sheet lightly over his smiling, relaxed wife. Then, knowing she would doze in the warmth, he waited until her eyes were firmly closed, then strolled back to the place of his new pond.

He was just stepping off the dimensions, though he knew this was rather premature, when he heard his wife's scream. He turned on his heel and ran his fastest as the screams continued.

She had never been given to hysterics, but the anguished tone of the screams fairly tore out his heart, and his feet seemed to be made of lead for all the speed he made.

For days and years afterward, he berated himself for leaving her, though if he had stayed, he might also have been napping. Neither of them would have seen the prairie rattler as it moved onto the spread quilt, its forked tongue waving in inquiry. The sensation of warmth of the human pulled the reptile forward, and it slipped, unnoticed into the warm folds of her petticoat ruffles.

The smooth warm flesh had the aroma of food, so the small reptile sank his bare fangs into the soft warmth, just to check it out. The venom-coated fangs cut into a network of capillaries, sending their poisoned blood back to the beating heart. Such was the consistency of the venom that it had mixed instantly with the blood.

Unbearable, scalding pain was instantaneous. Screams gave vent to the horror and tensing of muscles, but the fate was sealed. Moments before the horrified man grabbed the reptile by the tail and crashed its head against the hard ground, the damage had been done. Still, he slung the body of the rattler against the ground again and again, giving vent to his rage.

Grabbing his precious wife into his arms and sprinting to the still hitched buggy, he lashed the unfortunate pony unmercifully as it galloped toward his house. The speed was useless.

By now, the venom had filled her body, and the pain had thrown her into unconsciousness. Blessed relief from the pain came at a price, and her voice quieted, only moments before her breath ceased.

Carl could only scream for help from neighbors who were too far away to hear and could not have helped if they had.

And now, Carlotta had returned to a crowded house of mourning, and the mother she loved covered by a snow-white sheet. She had turned from this one to that one for some iota of comfort, but faces were only sympathetic. There was no sense of it all, except the clear and present fact that she had left a mother, relaxed and happy, and had returned to find her gone. Forever.

It was only at the threat of an attack of evil spirits from Mrs. Gray Owl, that the girl was not told that her mother had, once more, attempted to produce a sibling for her only child. The old Kiowa doctor demanded silence. "That girl got more in her backpack than she got strength to hoist," the bent old woman declared, her usage of English improving immeasurably. "Ain't no cause to add to it." They didn't, and certainly her Papa said nothing.

Her mother was committed to the ground in the marked off space in the rear corner of Miss Josie's quarter section, the place set aside for the purpose. It was with fierce argument that Carl was kept from laying her to rest on his own property. The other men knew he would never let her rest in peace, but continue to devote his life to her if the grave was close, and there would be no way that the pond would ever happen. He would need the pond now, and anything else he could try, as he had been totally wrapped up in her frail life and in his inability to make it continue.

And then the neighbors were gone. As it always must be in a place of so many pressing duties for every person, work was the master. They had helped with food, which was not eaten. The old woman doctor come and talked, but left, knowing she had accomplished nothing. She was also fiercely convinced that the thirteen year old girl not only had more than she could carry, she was now heaping even more pain upon herself.

Father and daughter, who had always been close now became strangers. When they were in a room together, they avoided a glance that would add to their combined pain. Guilt. As though by their own individual effort they should have kept her alive. Even if God didn't, they should have, and they would not let themselves be comforted.

Miss Josie came, but she herself was so young and so recently bereaved, she felt she was doing more harm than good. The girls of the class avoided Carlotta, as though her pain might be contagious, and they sensed, as well, that they could not help.

Father and daughter wandered through the house, sketchily attending to what must be done, eating because they each expected that of the other one. There was love between them, but no connection of sorrow, being unable to lean together for comfort.

Guilt. The man… for not staying with her and the girl… for going away on a selfish errand.

Carlotta lost interest in herself. Her shiny curled hair hung in tangles, and she did not leave the interior of the house for days at a time. Only vaguely aware of her father's self-destruction, she pulled herself through the next three months.

Fall weather approached and the season changed. Carlotta chanced to stare at herself in the tall mirror of her mother's old room, and could hardly recognize the pathetic ghost that stared back.

Something within her finally blossomed into the knowledge that something had to happen, or she and her father would physically join the woman they both loved. Something… but what? She only knew that it must be done by herself and not her shell of a father.

She pulled her mother's writing drawer from her desk and took it to her own room. There, on her unmade bed, she began to sort through letters received, especially those from Annette Carpenter, her mother's closest friend still in St. Louis. Annette had never married, and had often mentioned a visit, but it had not happened. It was a long ways from St. Louis to the Territory.

A journey of that distance was not to be taken without due consideration.

Carlotta put her letters in a pile and returned the drawer to the room she still considered her mother's. She had tried not to notice that her Papa slept in the overstuffed rocker in the parlor. She had told herself that her mother was not going to return to the room, but had yet to convince herself not to treat it like a shrine.

But now, her good sense said something must happen. The last three of Annette's letters had not been answered or even opened. Her Papa must have picked them up at the Corners and put them in the drawer.

With a sheet of her mother's precious linen stationery, she began, "Dear Annette." Now what?

In her beautiful script, as perfect as that in the teacher's copybook, she pretended this was an essay for her class, centering her mind sternly on the task she had assigned to herself.

She related the activities of the summer, beginning with the trip to take her test, and ending with her fear that her father was trying to kill himself so he could be with her mother. She added that just yesterday, he had neglected to come into the house when dark came, and when she had found him sitting in the buggy in the yard, she had tried to get him to come in. He hadn't seemed to understand what she was saying.

She placed the necessary postage on the letter and sent it off from the Corners. In the last few years, the mail service had improved so much that a letter could leave Argyle and reach St. Louis as soon as ten days.

Annette had read the letter three times before she had exclaimed, "Oh, that poor child! If that father of hers is determined to starve himself to death, I'm going to go get that girl. After all, I have the right. Her mother was my very best friend."

As it happened, Annette's 'baby brother', fifteen years her junior, had been at home at the time. Ralph was a route man with his own stocked trailer, and he made a good wage from supplying outlying homes with life's necessities, as well as a few pleasantries and an update on the local news.

He countered, "Now, Sis, not so fast! That girl is actually not your sole responsibility, and there must be neighbors and such." But when he saw his words falling on deaf ears, he commanded, "All right, get yourself ready, and I'll take you there. Upset as you are, no knowin' what could happen to you on the way out there into no man's land."

It had taken two difficult weeks of travel on the road, but Ralph was hardened to the reins and made time where he could. He had arranged a fast trade of his matched carriage horses, the pair that attracted attention and admiration for his business, and had acquired two teams of shiny black Clydesdale horses. These heavy bodied animals were built for work and not for speed and were able to plod steadily for hours, leaning their muscled bodies into the traces and pulling heavy loads with the weight of their own bodies.

Ralph, with wisdom ahead of his nineteen years, knew the journey would be hard, and he'd need extra strength for the load and on the long days of travel time. His double buggy was heavily built, and the trailer behind it was loaded with merchandise.

Paring the weight down where he could, he managed to be ready in two days. It was either that, or his sister would step aboard the Santa Fe and go on her own, and from what he heard of the Territory it might well not be safe for a woman traveling alone.

The hard two weeks of travel had been divided between the two teams, one pulling during the morning and the other in the afternoon, traveling far into the night. The team not pulling was hitched behind the trailer, resting while walking.

He reached Argyle and over-nighted in their dormitories, the canvas soldier cot feeling like a king's feather mattress to the exhausted young man.

Gathering his sister aboard immediately after the oatmeal breakfast, he headed south as he had been directed, looking for a business establishment called Carlile Corners located across from Cullen Blacksmith. How could he miss it, and he didn't.

Further requests for information took him to the front gate of the house belonging to Carl Owens.

Annette, now rested and in her full quota of indignation, accepted help down from the buggy, only because of her tangle of petticoats. Many a lady has fallen into the arms of someone because she did not wait for her undergarments to straighten themselves out.

A knock at the door, summoned a fair-faced young lady, skinny to the point of protruded bones showing and hair a frightful mess. Eyes narrowing and squinting for a closer look at the daughter that her friend, Maudie, had described as beautiful. Well, maybe.

"Would you be Carlotta Owens? I'm Annette Carpenter. I was your mother's best friend...."

The waif standing before her gasp, "Oh, you're Annette! I need you! Thank you for coming so fast!"

Annette wrapped comforting arms around the thirteen year old as a mother would wrap her new-born. "Darling girl, I came. I'm so glad you wrote. I was worried about your mother's health, the way she was. And I got no letter…."

"Way she was?"

Doing a quick double take, Annette explained, "Oh, she always was so delicate, and I worried about her out here." That much was true. Apparently Carlotta had not been told of the attempt to once more… to… well, perhaps it had been for the best.

Carlotta's father was met in a totally different manner. "Carl Owens, aren't you knowin' this here child is starvin' herself to death, a'worrin' about you? Just look at her! What're you two eatin' that's got you into this shape?" The question did not expect or receive an answer from the surprised man.

Annette had cast her eyes quickly around the house in an efficient appraisal and found it abysmally wanting. Such a nice place it was, but what hard treatment it had. That nice carpet… it ought to be a crime to be allowed to endure anything like this.

Father and daughter stared at this hurricane that had descended upon them, until a young man stepped into the room. "I'm Ralph Carpenter and that windstorm over there is my sister. She's had months of worry and grief over her friend and then two weeks on the road to get thoroughly worked up. She isn't dangerous, really." He smiled his easygoing salesman smile and extended a hand toward the man.

Annette had disappeared into the kitchen. Carlotta followed, apprehensively. Annette poked the stove lid lifter into the stove lid and peered into the cold ashes. "I need some wood for this thing, honey. Where would I find it?"

Carlotta shuddered into life and led the way to the woodshed. Two loads were carried into the woodbox, along with a few dry cowpats, and the ashes were shook down. Viciously and noisily. Firewood was expertly placed and lit and was soon crackling its warmth. "Now, these here dishes. They're gonna get a cold bath 'cause we need the time. I'll need more soap than this here…."

CHAPTER 6

The girl opened a drawer and took out a fresh bar of lye soap. A swipe of the dishcloth against the soap and a mound of bubbles appeared. Dishes were slipped into the water and wiped, then doused into the rinse water. Carlotta found her senses and grabbed up a wiping towel.

Potatoes. The starter of any meal. Bacon. Onions. Eggs? Yes, lots of eggs. Flour.

Meanwhile Carl Owens was recipient of a detailed explanation of the way to sell household products to wives to whom a store was not handy. Next, the distraught man heard about the way the wonderful Clydesdale horses had pulled the load through two states. They were expensive, but worth every penny. Obviously, it was necessary to get his sister here where there was a need for her.

Carl Owens, having no knowledge that Annette had been notified, was still amazed at the activity around him. One thought had stuck in his mind, though, and he wondered, was he actually starving his daughter? He hadn't noticed.

Fragrant aromas came from the kitchen. The crackling sound of the fire warmed the house even before the heat had reached them. Carlotta watched the activity around her being stirred to an intensity that her mother had never inspired. Though she had never seen this kitchen before, this friend of her mother's seemed to know where everything was kept.

At this moment, she watched Annette grab up a potholder and open the oven door. In slid a pan of perfectly formed biscuits, and moments later, a pan of fruit followed, sweetened with sugar and cinnamon and topped with strips of rich dough.

She lifted the lid to the stove reservoir and tested the water. "Honey, I think this here's warm enough. Get me a bucket, will you, and dip in some water. I'm gonna help you wash that beautiful hair that your mama told me about. Move now...."

Carlotta moved. What a feeling to have this woman's capable hands reaching above her and massaging her scalp, rinsing and re-sudsing. Her mother had never done that. At least, no time that she could remember.

The barely warm water soaked strength into her as the comforting words wound around in her mind. She's doing this for me because she was my mama's friend! I did right to send the letter... Guilt momentarily fled.

Annette took a moment to bang open the oven again, whirling the biscuits and cobbler around to brown on the other side. She drove the spatula fiercely under the potatoes, efficiently turning them over to cover the onions and eggs in the heavy iron skillet. "I make this stuff a lot for my brother. He could eat a horse sometimes. He's gotta be wastin' away from hunger."

The brother had enticed Carl out to examine his horses and also his salesman wagon. "See how this shelf makes a good bed? Many's the night I spent sleepin' in here. Works good. Got a Colt 45 if someone gets it in his head to cause me trouble."

Opening a wooden chest he explained, "Crackers and cheese. Got a place for other things if I'd find 'em along the roads. Not a bad life, really. I don't stay in no place long enough to let folks get mad at me." This was said with a knowing smile.

The men were called in to eat just after Annette had managed to pull a brush through Carlotta's squeaky-clean hair. "You know, honey, this here's gonna make you feel a lot better. Nothin' much gets a girl down like tangly hair."

She leaned away to look at the girl, face on. "Your Ma was right, sweetie. You are a pure looker. Gonna leave 'em dead in a year or two. The last letter from your mom said you were takin' a test to let you teach school. Was that true? I couldn't hardly believe it, but she don't lie. Just look at the way that hair works itself into curls. Such a fortunate young lady. It'll be a shame to have to pin that up some day."

Annette had poked her head out and called the men in to eat. The table had not been set, but Carlotta put herself toward getting it done. The smells were so tempting, she thought that she, herself, also might be able to eat that horse. Or at least help that fellow... Ralph, was it?

The meal finished and put away, the cyclone of a woman set herself against the next item of the day. She let herself into the room that had obviously been Carl and Maudie's. With a yank and a fling, she had the rumpled sheets on the floor and was searching the closet for clean ones. Carlotta helped.

Carl gasped. "Annette! That's where she...."

But Annette cut in. "Carl Owens, don't you shout at me! I'd do anything in the world to get that girl back here, but it can't be done. That don't mean we gotta go with 'er. I gotta have a place to sleep tonight, and I got it from a good source you ain't usin' this good bed."

During this tirade, she had shaken out the bottom sheet, then the upper one. She whipped the wrinkles from the fancy spread and smoothed it down the edges of the bed.

Then continued, "I'd be glad to tell you, I didn't make this long trip out here to help you. I come on account'a this child that Maudie told me so much about. This poor girl lost her mother, and then she lost her pa who wanted to leave her and go to her mother. She lost everything dear to her, but I ain't standin' by to let it continue. Now, this here girl needs me 'cause she sure as shootin' don't have you. Quick as I can get it done, I'm aimin' to take her back with me to St. Louis. That's where a girl like Carlotta belongs. So if you don't want me to do that, you're gonna have to shape up to be a man and stop me." With a snap of the wrist, she slid the pillows from the rumpled cases and popped them into clean ones.

"Now, Carlotta, honey, let's go see what we can do to your bed. Help me gather up these here dirty sheets, and we'll have time to suds 'em out and dry 'em this afternoon."

Carlotta was still trying to gather the ends of her thoughts together. She had never seen a force like this, much less been the object of it. Gathering the bedding in her arms, she followed to her own room, and watched the performance repeated.

Later, after wringing the clean sheets into the laundry basket and locating the broom for Annette, she took the sheets to the clothesline. With a deep breath, she drew the spicy fall air into her lungs. Pegging the bedding onto the line, she remembered an old duty of getting eggs. It had been a week at least since she had gone to the henhouse. Would the eggs still be good? Well, the weather had been cool…. She'd ask Annette.

She returned from the henhouse to meet the household dirt being gathered into the dustpan. Somehow, a kettle of beans with ham chunks had appeared on the cookstove. Ham slices filled a bowl on the table.

"Figure on potatoes with ham gravy for supper. Them bean'll never be done in time. They'll be good for tomorrow. Would ya happen to have green beans canned?"

Carlotta shook her head. Nothing much had been done with the kitchen garden all summer. She and her father had spent their time in private mourning and in avoiding the sight of each other. Sometimes pain in the face of one you loved just made your own pain worse.

"That's all right. Let's go look at that garden. I'd reckon we'll find somethin' we can use."

Carlotta followed with a basket. "Look at them beans! Full pods dried on the vines. We'll get them tomorrow. Now, I see turnip greens, and we can get the turnips, too. Onions… good. No time to cook with them but we can have 'em raw. They need to be pulled and dried. We'll do that tomorrow, too."

The meal appeared just about the time the early fall darkness had happened. Lamps were lit and plates set around. Steaming platter of browned ham slices in the center, dishes with brown gravy, mashed potatoes, steamed greens, and fresh slices of onion were set round about.

Annette commanded heads to be bowed for a full thirty seconds of thankfulness, and then she opened the oven door releasing a gust of pleasant warmth and aroma into the kitchen, along with a pan of perfectly browned corn bread.

A pleasant stream of her chatter pulled the meal along. "Some of that milk that's feedin' them hogs needs to come in the house tomorrow, Carl. Till we get things goin', some cottage cheese'll help fill out the meals. You need to get out there and pick them beans that're just a hanging on the vines. Then them vines need to be yanked up. Ralph'll help you for one day, but after that he needs to be on the road to set up some customers. I'd reckon you got neighbors a'plenty that'll like a peek in his sales trailer."

She dished up the cold fruit cobbler left over from lunch. "Carl, a bit of top cream'd be good on this desert. I'll take some off that milk tomorrow that's goin' into the cheese."

"Little brother" Ralph buried his attention into his food, forcing his mouth to keep from a grin. These two unsuspecting people had just witnessed his sister in a bout of nervous energy, and it could last a few days. He hoped they could survive. During those days, things would get done that they had never heard of. Good mind reader, too. He had planned to give one day of help for this poor lost man, but first he would set up a route so he could make a bit of money.

Between bites of cobbler, and from the corner of his eye, he studied the girl. If he hadn't known his sister, he would not have realized this was the girl who met them at the door. Still skinny, but such a beauty!

What an invitation to disaster she was! Trouble could happen anywhere around her in this wild new country. He nodded in agreement with himself as he realized she needed a guardian just to stay safe. A face of absolute perfection, she had, and it should not be created in this girl-hungry land of ambitious men. And its share of evil men.

The moon rose over the Owens homestead, lighting the yard of the house. The walls of the house contained four opinions. The girl in her cozy fall nightie sat on the edge of her spacious bed, her

111

mind a turmoil of thoughts. She, the one who was so careful not to disturb the powers of humanity, had actually written the letter that had called down this person who changed lives in one single day.

It was not that she disagreed. Suddenly, there was decent food. Instead of ducking into himself, her father seemed to lift his head and face outward. And she herself? It seemed in spite of her part in the change, she felt contented.

What was it like? There had to be comparisons… as she had learned to make in school.

…As a boat hooked on shoreline snags, can be loosed and allowed to flow itself into the current.

…A buggy that was stuck in deep mud, finally yielding to the efforts of the animals in the traces, could now roll along the road, shedding chunks of its former bondage from the wheels as it rolled.

…A twisted rope finally released of its coils and flowing out strong and straight.

…A house turned upside down… now…? Well, time would prove something, wouldn't it? It needed some thought.

Stretching her feet under the fresh clean sheets, she remembered again the smell of the bedding items as she had removed the pegs and taken them from the line. Sharpness in the fall air and the vague hint of lye soap's cleanliness. A remembrance of another life? A return to… what…? Then with a sigh, her eyes closed and did not open until morning.

In the double marriage bed of her best friend, the woman from St. Louis sought to sort out her feelings. That girl! She was worn to a sliver by some burden she was carrying. There was hope, though, because she knew to send out a cry for help, though she didn't know that was what she did. She was in a bad way, but there was still hope for her.

The man, though, may be totally hopeless. Sure, he lost the woman he loved, and he must grieve, but then he must let it be. That should have been over months ago, and now he should be thinking of the good she had brought to his life and the daughter she so greatly loved and had now left to him.

Annette had roared into his house, shouted orders, and demanded certain activities that should have brought up the anger and indignation of any man alive. But he had registered nothing.

If Ralph had not come with her, she would be tempted grab up the girl in the dark of night and catch the first toot of the Santa Fe going east. With that teaching Certificate, she would be lapped up like a bowl of cream before a hungry cat. But of course she couldn't possible do that. Maybe there was hope. Ralph would be doing to that man what he did best, and he had produced sparks of... well, maybe something. Perhaps she could find out what was still inside this man. He could not have been this way while Maudie was sending all those letters of happiness.

Turning over, flipping her pillow to a cool side, she forced her eyes to close and her thoughts to subside. Tomorrow would be another day.

In the parlor, the man settled into his overstuffed rocker, intending to relapse into his zombie consciousness, hoping for a spell of relief from his devastation. Relief did not come. He saw, instead, the freshened face of his daughter. He had become accustomed to her pale, wan appearance. Had he actually committed a grave error and turned selfishly into himself?

And this Annette. He hadn't known her very well, and he certainly did not remember this side of her. A female whirlwind who, herself, had suffered the loss of a close friend. One would never know it, though, and she had shown zero sympathy to him. And the young man... Ralph. He had some good ideas.

The young fellow, managing as he had without ever having a mother, or a father, and now not yet twenty, he had done marvelously well. His own efficiently-operated business, obviously successful enough to buy those frightfully expensive horses. A pair of those horses alone would buy a Territory homestead.

Crawling out from under the quilts, he had piled onto the rocker, he stood, squared his shoulders and walked out into the moonlit yard. A fresh, chilling breeze came from the south.

It seemed to blow directly through him cleansing his body and clearing debris from his head. Such a different feeling.

Why had he just stood by and let that woman tear into the fabric of his despondency? Why had he not sent her from his house and his life? The reason? He had certainly deserved every disdainful word she had flung at him. What now?

He had no answer. Tomorrow, however, would be a new day, and then he would see how he felt. This moment, however, he felt an exhaustion that went through him with more chill than the south wind. Stepping back inside the door, he tossed the quilts down to the floor, smoothing them out. Flung the pillow after and settled himself into their warmth. The next day, he could not have said when he fell asleep if his life had depended on it.

At the crow of the rooster, Carl opened his eyes to sunshine through the window, the parlor door discretely closed, and his body rested as it had not been for months. Sitting up on the floor, he rubbed his eyes and the stubble of his beard. Shave. That was the next thing, and then he'll see.

In the double buggy, twenty-year-old Ralph was stretching awake. Through the night he had been comforted by the contented huffs and snivels of his four horses that he had turned loose in the fenced yard. Thoughts came flooding in, picking up where they had left off last night.

Nice place this man has here. He must have given a lot of thought to making it this way. That was certainly not the way he had seemed, last evening, but then... (and he had grinned with pleasure at the memory of his sister's blustering attack), yes, last night he had seemed... well, what could one say? Best to just hide... and watch!

As Ralph had been growing up, his sister had often lit into him in the same blistering manner, and he usually needed it. He remembered that it always helped him to, as she always said, get his "head on his shoulders."

Today was another day, and the aroma of frying bacon was flowing across the yard. Time to get up and get things started. It should be an interesting day.

A platter of eggs. A pyramid of biscuits. Bacon piled like cordwood onto the platter with the eggs. Her search for jelly or preserves was fruitless, but Annette had found the honey.

When she had the four of them settled at the table, she announced, "Heads down, everyone. We got things to be thankful for, and we need strength to get through this day." After a short moment, she announced, "Thank you, God. Now everyone, eat everything you can because what's left will face you at the next meal. Carlotta brought us such a pile of eggs, we'll be forced to have bread pudding for lunch. If I can find the cinnamon. Bacon into the beans with the ham if you don't eat it. Dig in, folks."

Biscuits were buttered. Food was passed. "Carl, couldn't help but see a foundation made for another room. What happened to get it stopped?"

Without waiting for an answer, she continued. "Gonna need that room. Either you or me, one of us, needs to have a place to sleep. If you need someone to hand you nails, or somethin', you got this girl, here. She'd be good help. Course, I could use her, too. We need to catch up on a few things that seem to'a gone to pot."

Carl nodded. It was starting already, but the woman was right. He could have that done in a couple weeks, or less if the young fellow was around to help. Seems he wouldn't be, though.

The fellow was currently opening biscuits and stuffing them with bacon. "Carl, which direction would be best for the first start? Maybe a place that'd have the most cabins with families and women who needed kitchen stuff? 'Course, I'll get around to every direction sooner or later. Be all right with you if I leave one team of horses in the yard? I noticed a fair amount'a grass they could mow down."

Without waiting for an answer, he produced a metal bucket and carefully set his biscuits inside. "Sis, you got a hunk'a that cobbler left over?" Cobbler set into the bucket and lid closed, he stood. "I'll be off. Think I'll go south first off. Be back by night. I'll stick around tomorrow to help." And he was gone.

Things in the house progressed rapidly to the sound of saw and hammer and no request for his daughter's help. The beans bubbled their way to tenderness, the fresh milk was set on the back of the stove to clabber. More cornbread graced the table for the midday meal.

Ralph returned encouraged. It was, as he knew it would be, a mission of mercy to homestead cooks who always ran out of this and that.

It had been late in the afternoon that Carlotta had hesitated, towel in hand. "Uh, er...."

"Honey, you just call me what ever you want to. Ann, or Annette or even 'hey, you'. What did you want to say?"

"I was, uh, it was what I thought of. I have that big bed in my room all by myself. I don't mind if there was someone else in the bed. In Oklahoma City I slept with one of the girls, named Francine. We weren't crowded at all. I thought if Papa.... Well if you...?" Her glance begged for help.

"Honey, that's a sweet offer, and I might take you up on it, but not just yet. Sometimes a fellow just has to have something behind 'em to keep 'im movin' forward, like sleepin' on that hard floor to punish hisself. Seems he sort'a got stopped. Fellows just got'a have a thing to do or they get droopy... and don't never get started."

Carlotta nodded. She'd noticed that. Annette had more to say.

"Tell me, dear, what is it that your Papa likes to do? Besides look at his hayfields, that is."

The girl thought. "He use to like to talk with Mama and do things for her."

Annette nodded. "And what about for him? What did he talk about that he'd like to do for himself? Like maybe fishing, or something?"

"Well, there was the catfish pond."

"Where was that? Here on your land?"

"No, well yes... it was something he was going to dig. We got a little river that runs back in the pasture. He was going to make a pond and fill it from the river and put catfish in it. It was a place back... where... I mean, it was...."

The woman stopped her, saying gently, "Not now. Sometime you'll tell me, but not today. This pond, now, was he going to dig it himself?"

She thought. "No, I think there was someone who helps to move dirt, or something. But I don't think he wants to, now, because it was back where...."

"I know, honey. But that's where it needs to be, and tomorrow I'd like you to show me where it is. Can you do it?"

Could she? Well, she'd have to sometime, so it might as well be tomorrow.

Annette tossed crumbled biscuits into the milk, egg and spice mixture, and shoved it in the oven. Crumbled cornbread with eggs and a lot of onions, stirred in with left over bits of meat made a stuffing, and served with turnips diced, steamed and browned in bacon bits.

It was the next afternoon that the woman and the girl stood by the stream of the little river and looked out toward the flat, marshy place. "It was there where all the sumac bushes are. It was gonna be dug and a canal made to the river that could be closed up when he wanted it to be. Then he'd put big fish in it and cattails and things so the baby fish could grow up without being eaten."

Annette nodded, smiled, and nodded again. "Perfect."

"But Papa may not want it now on account of...."

"Honey, he's got no choice. Somehow he's gotta come out of the way he feels. He needs to begin to feel lucky that he had his Maudie for a while, and that he still has you. He could'a married someone who didn't make him happy. He could'a lost your mama when you were born, and maybe lost you, too..."

She hesitated, then continued, "...the way I lost my mother when Ralph was born. I was a big girl, a little older than you when it happened, and my Pa, he couldn't stand the sight of it and walked away, leavin' us both. Ralph never saw his pa, or his ma either.

"A fellow just can't let stuff get in his way. It piles itself up. He needs to move on, and your Papa needs to move on. We're gonna be kind and help 'im to do it. Just leave it to me, honey."

All the way home, Carlotta wondered if she had done something wrong to be so informative, but it was too late now.

It was a week later, on a day that Carl had to make a trip to Argyle, that Ralph did not go on the road, but disappeared on one of the horses. He came back with a smile and no explanation, and the next day there came to the house a man pulling an apparatus called a dirt slip.

Hitched to a pair of the Clydesdales, the dirt slip began to remove layer after layer of soil from the marshy sumac grove. Ralph and the man adjusted the big iron blade at an angle and the massive horses pushed their weight onto the traces, inching the machine along. A squash and a slurp and another pile of the black sludge moved toward the bank of what would be the catfish pond.

By noon, the pond was so deep that Ralph could stand in the basin and never be seen from 100 feet away. That meant about 10 feet deep counting the piled up sludge. The thing was, all ponds tended to fill in a bit at first, so he kept scooping until it was 2 feet deeper.

The two men were slogging back to the house in their knee high boots when Carl returned on horseback. He gasped, open mouthed, at the men and the horses pulling the metal apparatus. Ralph called out cheerfully.

"Carl, good to see you. Somethin' come up, and I made a decision. Hope it was all right. This here fellow, he heard I had Clydesdales, and he has a job comin' up where he was gonna need a little extra horse flesh. Hoped I could trade out service, so we looked around. Your daughter had told Annette that you had thought'a makin' a catfish pond, so we looked around and found what we thought'd be the best place." He paused to let Carl close his gapping mouth, then continued.

"The thing was, we didn't know where'd be the best place for the canal to fill it, so we let it be. 'Course, winter rain's gonna fill in the basin anyway, and that canal could happen anytime after that. I'm thinkin' by spring that basin'll be settled good enough to put in the breedin' stock. Right now I gotta help this fellow git this rig to his house and leave the team with 'im, so maybe I could use that animal you got saddled…?"

What could poor Carl do but vacate the saddle and watch him move off, following behind the huge metal blade of the dirt slip. He gave a glance toward the unfinished room, then turned and walked away toward the bank of the little river.

Standing on the slosh of mud, he stared into the hole in his back pasture. It was at least half again the size he had envisioned and certainly as deep. Absolutely perfect. He had thought of the canal so often that he had a picture of it in his mind. It would have a shut off screen so that a full river would not bleed away his fish, but it could be used to let in fresh water for filling it when necessary.

His pond. He really wanted to be angry at the audacity of this young man to presume on his land, but the gift was so perfect, he couldn't maintain any irritation, let alone anger.

It was, indeed, a new day, and he might just as well learn to live in it. It was evident that his daughter was happier, and he certainly owed her something after the summer they'd both had.

Supper was a silent affair until it was rescued by Annette. "Carl, you wouldn't'a known the onions we pulled up on them two rows. Never saw the like, some of 'em wouldn't fit in a tea mug. Maybe not even in a soup bowl. We got three bushel baskets full and dumped 'em in the shed. Likely there's at least one more basket full. We'll braid 'em up for hangin' when we get 'em all pulled." A short silence and she continued.

"Sure liked the look of them. Sometimes I used to bake 'em stuffed with sausage like we got here. Ralph liked 'em when he was a little feller."

And Ralph put in, "Liked 'em even better when I got big and ugly." The chuckle that followed loosened the tension permitting this and that to be discussed.

It was a couple of weeks later that a beautiful November day happened, as it often did in the Territory. Carlotta mentioned, "I'm thinking I should go down to the school and get my Certificate.

I'd like it if you'd go with me, Annette, and you could meet Miss Josie. Late afternoon would be good, closer to time class lets out."

They walked the distance in friendly companionship. Josie was glad to meet Annette, and her first assessment was that she was fit for anything. Her thick hair of deep brown, just a touch of red, was tendrilling out from the edge of her bonnet. Rounded face, broad cheek bones, firm quick steps, and hands that looked as though they had accomplished something… all these things she took in with the first sweeping glance.

Josie also liked her look of affection with just a touch of possessiveness when Annette glanced at Carlotta. A sigh of tentative relaxation came next and settled over Josie. She had known her first impression was usually her best, and she was certain that this woman who appeared from nowhere was the best gift Carlotta could have at this time. It would be interesting to see how it went.

After a short conversation and a promise of more later, Josie returned to her class, and the two ladies headed toward their home with the Certificate.

The new Carl gazed over the pen at his overly fat… should have already been butchered… male hog. This was an exhausting fall duty, but winter meat depended on it. Every year he put it off… it had been such a trial of strength to Maudie.

Annette, however, had met the whole idea with wide eyes and a smile of anticipation. Ralph postponed his selling trip, and the two men slaughtered the beast, hoisting it with strong chains and pulleys into the butchering tree.

Future tenderness of the meat demanded the carcass hang out in the cold air for at least one night. Annette and Carlotta took a cart and gleaned a load of mesquite brush for the smokehouse. "Puts that extra flavor in the meat, I think."

Carlotta wasn't sure, except that it had not been done before. Bundles of the brushy sticks were tied together and stacked into the smokehouse to be handy.

Knives were sharpened with the whetstone and Mason jars were gathered, washed, and set in a shining row, ready to be filled.

Annette was a bundle of energy and could hardly settle herself to sleep.

Carl, dreading the next day, also had trouble getting to sleep. The floor was hard, the weather was becoming chilly, and as he turned over for the dozenth time, he decided this was just not working. But the meat came first.

Together Ralph and Carl carved on the hanging carcass with the sharpened knives. The younger man was a fast learner, and by mid-morning chunks were sliced away from the bones and taken to the kitchen. Like a savage warrior, Annette attacked the gifts, hacking the slabs into pieces of a size that would fit into a teacup.

Carlotta stoked the fire under the wash kettle, drawing from the nearby pile of dry cowpats. When a pan was full of meat chunks, she brought them from the kitchen to the boiling water over the fire. It had to be watched continually because no scorching was to be permitted.

When the meat had become tender, it was returned to the kitchen and packed into the sterilized jars. The lid was firmed and, in groups, the jars of meat were again brought to a boil.

Later, set in rows, the filled and processed jars marched down the side of the kitchen floor. A quilt was spread over to keep drafts from cracking the precious containers.

"How did you learn to do all this?"

"Child, this here come second nature. There ain't much to do with food I've not done. Back where I worked, we bought filled jars like this from farm women, and they were glad to tell how they did it. Proud of how hard they worked. We used this kind of canned meat for all sorts of meat dishes."

Carlotta was fascinated but decided this might not be the time to ask questions. Annette was rubbing the salt mixture into the slabs of white fat streaked with pink lean. The separate slabs were wrapped in old cloths and packed into the wooden chest to cure. Bacon. Breakfast gold. Fragrant aromas at sunrise.

Hams and shoulders were rubbed, wiped clean, and hung from the hooks in the smoke house ceiling. Fresh bundles of dampened mesquite sticks were applied to the smoking pile, causing wisps of aroma to filter out from between the loosely fitted logs. At no time had Carl been obliged to touch the meat after it had been delivered to the kitchen. He could only stare at the speed and skill of the woman behind the sharpened knives and was glad to be rid of the job.

By mid-afternoon of the second day the project was completely done, and the two from the kitchen sat down for a cup of tea. "Annette," the girl began, tentatively. "I'm wantin' to ask a question, but I don't know if it would be polite."

"Child, you ask away. Anything you want to know."

"I mostly want to know about before you came here. You said your mother died birthing Ralph, and your pa walked away. I'm thinkin' you weren't much older than I am now. How did you get along? Did your family live close?"

"Shucks, child. Your mama didn't say much to you, did she?"

Whereupon, in true Annette manner, she corrected the situation. Yes, that had been true. She had tried to find a job, but it was impossible with a newborn baby. Her mother's parents had given up life in St. Louis and had headed back east. Even though they had crossed the mile-wide Mississippi safely, the family had camped in a valley unaware of a rainstorm up river.

Scraps of their wagon were found first, then the human and animal remains. One horse had managed to work himself to shallower water, even though still in tandem and harness. If her mother had lived, they would have gone east, too, but it did not happen. The two children remained.

Her Pa walked off, unable to function under the pressure, and within days young Annette had realized there was nothing to do but check herself into the orphanage. With the other girls of her age, she had worked hard for her keep and kept up with Ralph.

Being his only relative, she was repeatedly encouraged to let him be adopted. Healthy male babies were in great demand, but she refused. It was amazing to her, looking back, that they allowed her that decision. Someone must have been looking out for her… and him.

At her eighteenth birthday, she had been 'aged out' of the orphanage and had insisted she be permitted to take Ralph, then almost three, with her. She had to pretend she had found help for the both of them and that they would be fine.

Had the orphanage not had its own problems with funds and overcrowding, she may not have been permitted to take him, but she did. Now she really MUST find a way to take care of them both.

In the institution she had learned much about food and its preparation and had seemed to have a natural talent in that area, so she sought work as a cook in eating establishments nearby, but there was the problem of keep for the small boy.

Being resourceful, she noticed certain other girls who were left with their own small child by a fellow. So many of the fellows seemed anxious to get themselves killed or jailed... or they just walked away as her father had. Single men could make it alone.

In these cases, the smaller cafés often arranged a room for the kitchen help in return for paying them less. Room and food was often easier to furnish than money, and she fortunately found a place where she was treated well. Also, food was available for Ralph.

It was hard to leave a child alone all day, with only a peek in on him during quieter moments. It flashed through her mind that she could yet let him be adopted, but the idea only made her more fiercely determined to keep him with her. He was HERS! She had earned him, and she demanded her rights.

It was at that establishment that she learned cooking methods, ways to deal with people, and how to manage her tiny salary. It was at this time that she had met Maudie. She confided to the girl, "Likely your mama told you we knew each other since we were toddlers at our mama's knee, but that was not the case. It only SEEMED like a long, long time. We hit it off from the start, and she moved in with us. She was a big help with Ralph at that time, because he was so quick and active, he was everywhere." Annette had smiled fondly at the memory.

"Where was mama's people?"

"Gone, honey. That old sickness they called the ague hit 'em, and they were gone in days. So was their son. Your mama had to sell the house for money to live and then had to make her own way. Same as Ralph and me."

Annette went on to say that when he was six, Ralph was given a paper route in the area. Older boys were in demand for harder work, so as soon as a child could read numbers, he was allowed a chance with that morning and evening chore. Ralph was quick and friendly and was often given gifts of clothing, maybe lightly worn shoes and sometimes actual coins.

"Now, Carlotta, honey, you should'a seen your mama at that time. When she was fixed up, waitin' on those tables, she was so beautiful to make a grown woman cry and a man fall at her feet. She used her smiles to get tips that made life easier for the three of us. Don't know what would'a finally happened if your papa hadn't come along. They took a look at each other and were both goners."

So Maudie had married Carl, but the girls remained close until Carl got the 'go west' fever. Soon after that, the old couple had to give up the café, and Annette went on to a better paying job and by then Ralph was in school. He still delivered the papers before and after school and did whatever errands he could. Finally, he got a job in a stable caring for horses and was given time to go to school. He learned a lot there among the stables and the rough men.

A part of his job was to transport businessmen in buggies to their place of employment. He was a great one to talk with his passengers, and he picked up a lot of knowledge that way. He also listened well.

At thirteen he was out of school and working full time. He met a route salesman and knew immediately that he would be good at that job. He was at least two years working on getting a horse and a suitable rig, but after that, the brother and sister finally had enough money to dress well and 'circulate in polite society'.

With a small, conspiratorial smile, Annette confided, "I wasn't ever able to get tips on account of the way I looked, but there was them that really liked good food better'n the appearance of the waitress. I attracted customers because they liked the way I cooked, so I was paid more than most cooks." Carlotta could readily believe that.

Then Maudie and Annette kept in touch by letter, unsatisfactory as it was, for the next years. Maudie had repeatedly insisted that Annette must make the trip to the Territory, but after the hard life she and Ralph had experienced, now that things were easier, the brother and sister were reluctant to change. Should have been braver, no doubt. But, of course, what had happened to Maudie would still have happened.

Annette suddenly jumped to the present. "You know, child, I'm thinkin' there's somethin' else out in that garden we haven't got out yet. I'm going out there with a shovel, and if you'll grab that basket…."

Annette examined the dried vines in the garden rows. She wasn't sure, but there seemed to be… Yes! Look at that! Sweet potatoes. Just what we needed to work up with last year's ham's now that we got more." A few turns of the shovel, "Pick up a basket of 'em, honey, and we'll see what else there is."

The "what else" was the white potatoes. Good. The supply was getting a bit low. The stalks of okra were stripped of leaves and bare, but the long, pointed pods were still green.

"Just look at that! I see the makin' of Creole gumbo that was so popular down by the river. The farmers brought 'em to the kitchen all dried out like this, and we ground 'em up. Do we have a grinder?"

Carlotta thought, then she shrugged with doubt. "I'll ask Papa. I think we have. I've never heard of eating something called gumbo."

It was Annette's turn to shrug. "You may not like it. Maybe you have to be born to it, but Ralph sure likes it. We've got rice, peppers, and tomatoes. We'll try it out. We can use cottage cheese instead of rat cheese. What did your mama do with the okra?"

"She fried it in a skillet with tomatoes. Sometimes put it in the soup. We liked it."

Within days the rowdy bull calf followed the hog into the butcher tree. Sharp knives and Mason jars again took care of a lot of the meat, and the smoke house did the rest. Beef jerky could be used so many ways.

Between other duties, Carl and Ralph worked on the new room, it finally being ready for the shingles. It was nearing to Christmas, now, and the prairie winter had set in with a vengeance. The shingles were tacked down with red and frostbitten fingers, but it was finally done.

Neither Annette nor Carl moved into the new room. On the twentieth of December, the four residents of the Owens household took a meaningful trip over to Argyle and came back a family. Almost. The new relationship between Annette and Carl took on a different path, and they became as near a family as any of them had expected to be.

The parlor floor was vacated and Carlotta again had her bed to herself. Ralph gratefully moved from his chilly van into the new room, and the marriage bed was once again in double occupancy.

Many eyebrows were lifted and re-lifted, but few whispers actually became accusations. It was for certain that Maud Owens was not going to return, she had been properly and extensively mourned. Annette had brought her brother to a place where his services were badly needed and gratefully used. Carlotta acquired, while not a mother, something possibly better for her at this time. She now had a helpful friend who loved her and gave her the confidence to be a girl again.

Most of the Territory residents decided, after consideration, that the four individuals had done what was the best thing under the circumstances. Another thing was that concern and neighborly guilt were now absolved. The girl and her father had returned to their former state, if not possibly better. Certainly, Carl, relieved of his concern for his wife, was freed to better his accomplishments.

He leaned over the rail fence of the pigsty, eying the half grown animals. There were two young females with qualities he liked and should make good brood sows. Pork was always in demand, even young started pigs sold well. It was not for no reason that the squealers were often referred to as 'mortgage lifters'.

CHAPTER 7

Now that the land run was long passed, all the residents had sometime ago proved up their land. Some had sold and gone, hence the need for mortgage lifters to help the newcomers to pay off their new estates. A trip into Argyle, or even Oklahoma City, took care of any extra porkers.

Carl found energy. A day of work did not leave him 'wiped out' as it had, and he often tramped to the back of his land to the river to check on his fish pond. Catfish coming along! Sheets of ice were forming over the water now, but it didn't bother the native grown fish. It was just part of their life, and their bodies knew to shut down to minimum until spring. Carl looked forward to catching a mess of fish in an hour's time. That Annette! What a surprise!

The army outpost just over the ridge had also shut down to a minimum as the weather turned bad. Crimes just seemed to happen more often when the weather was pleasant, but now there were a number of restless and bored young men.

Young men from the outpost looked for entertainment other than gambling their meager wages back and forth from one pocket to the other. Swapping nickels, so to speak. Some liked to hunt, and the issuance of a rifle and shells could often mean a few meals of venison for the whole camp, or at least a good rabbit stew. Squirrels a'plenty, and their current cook could even make possum into a palatable meal.

The soldiers wandered as far as the settlement of Carlile Corners in search of different scenery and were pleasantly faced with a number of very attractive girls in their teen age or about to enter it.

Occasionally the young men were invited into homes in groups of two or three for food and fun, songs and stories. A pan of popped corn, flavored with cinnamon and honey, was a treat for the young men lonely and away from home.

The two young people in the Owens house were tossed together in a pseudo-sibling relationship not of their making. Carlotta was still trying to pull herself together and be a normal, going-on-fourteen, girl, and she viewed Ralph more in the visiting relative category. Pleasant to have around, at least for now.

A brother-sister relationship was totally foreign to her, and she could not place him there. One did not miss, on the most basic level, a relationship that one had never experienced.

As for Ralph, never having had a sibling near his age, felt much the same way, with a small difference. He had an inborn instinct to protect a thing that was his, and this beautiful creature was a part of his present family, for good or bad. Not being blind but having perfect eyesight, also being of the same age as the young soldiers, he could not help seeing that Carlotta was extraordinarily beautiful.

He naturally tended to feel possessive toward her as one might view a shining gold coin that he must not let go to a thief… one that was up to him to protect. Or perhaps an exotic bird that must be guarded from predators while not disturbing its habitat or lifestyle. This creature was not to be captured as his own, but to prevent it being taken by another.

It was for this reason that Ralph and Carlotta found themselves often at the same place at the same time, unplanned. Entertainments found in large cities did not exist on the prairie so the young people must make their own.

It is possible that the old-fashioned hayride as an entertainment had originated in circumstances such as these. Wagons were easily available, hay was abundant and places for a group to gather were rare. Ralph was pleased to draft his Clydesdales to the harness. He always had a rested pair, and the exercise was a benefit to them.

A large wagon could carry a sizeable group, and being from a wide geographical area, an extensive variety of songs were learned. A ride around a mile-square section was a four mile circuit…

around two sections was six. Songs, shouts, and laughter made up the evening.

When the group returned, cheeks rosy and voices hoarse, there would be a bonfire. Adults would join in, bringing candied corn and marshmallows brought out from Argyle. There would be steaming milk flavored with vanilla, eggs, honey, and cinnamon… spiced eggnog.

The young men would eventually be sent back to their barracks, tired and fed. The locals would be dismissed to their homes, and Ralph would gather Carlotta, as though it was a natural act for him, which it had become. On reaching home, she would slide from the haypile and disappear to her room while he would put away his animals, as he would any possession of value.

Ralph also, with astute vision, noticed that the blue-eyed beauty with the golden curls and the perfect features tended to pull attention from most eyes. Young men stared as they would at a painting that they did not expect to be real. Actually, the fact that Ralph was always on hand may have created the general feeling of her unattainability.

During the next months, he tried to be available at night, so sometimes he was found starting his route long before dawn. Responsibility was a thing he had naturally felt, likely from the age of three when he sensed he must entertain himself for long periods and postpone his fun and happiness until his sister returned. Delivering papers and handling the coins had cemented the tendency.

It was near the following summer that Jake Fuller appeared on the scene. First he came with the other soldiers though he was maybe two or three years older than most. He seemed to keep himself apart and he came without his uniform dress as some of the others did, and he lost no time fastening his eyes onto the picture perfect girl. At the same moment, Ralph realized the glance, and Jake caught Ralph's reaction.

Jake had intentions. He was nobody's fool, and he would be patient to get what he wanted. He hadn't minded taking his fellow soldiers' meager wages in a gamble, but that was hardly worth the effort. He wanted more.

Jake had another talent. Like Ralph, he could talk. He managed to avoid attention to his attraction to the girl and center it onto the fellow. Aligning himself with Ralph, he managed to build a welcome at the Owens house and enjoy a number of Annette's home cooked meals.

Jake had learned an educated vocabulary and found reason to hint that he was an officer and that the other soldiers were in his 'outfit'. He also magnanimously shared that he felt 'on the level' with them and wanted them to feel that way with him. Nothing wrong with that.

Carlotta, in her inexperience, listened, laughed, and talked with him. Shared the porch swing. Took short walks about the farm, enjoying this young man who was so obviously impressed with her family. Ralph felt uneasy but tried to drown the feeling as being jealous over something that was not actually his. Carlotta had a right to her own life, and so on.

Besides, he had work to do. After some months when Jake seemed to manage the loan of a buggy and asked to take her for a ride around the section because 'it was such a spell of good weather', Ralph could not actually invite himself along.

This was the situation for a couple of months as the year ran into summer and Carlotta neared age fifteen. Ralph heard the picnic being planned by Jake, but Carlotta's father seemed to consider it a normal thing… of beginning courtship, though Jake was years older.

The thing was, Jake acted so gentlemanly! Maybe he was. He had let it slip that his family had a business in Oklahoma City and sold building material for the many new houses going up in that town. Also, he said when he fulfilled his duty to his country, he would be settling there to help his father and brothers.

Even Annette seemed blind to any problem, so Ralph decided he was acting out of place and turned his attention away. He combed his red-brown wavy hair, scraped away his red-tinged beard, and put on a clean shirt. The blacksmith shop was always interesting, and a fellow learned so much about the neighborhood in a place like that. He didn't learn anything about Jake, though, as the locals considered the fellow was just one of the bunch of soldiers who came, served their country, and went home. The local men didn't actually remember which one he was.

Then came the certain Saturday. Ralph Carpenter found things to do at the picnic that Saturday until almost dark. He was relieved to meet Jake on the road, returning to his outpost. The fellows lifted a hand to each other as they continued in opposite directions.

When he reached home, Carlotta was telling the older couple what fun she had and how they had stopped at the Shady Ridge Academy and peeked in through the windows at the place where Francine had classes. They'd had ice cream at Argyle, and he had brought her home. Perfectly normal.

Ralph, he sternly admonished himself, get on with your life. The girl has a right to go where she wants and the fellow is, after all, an officer, and they had to be a cut above the soldier riff-raff. Didn't they?

Of course, Carlotta would attract that kind of a fellow, and she had a right to decide for herself what she wanted. She had a right to say no if she didn't like it.

It was two weeks after that when another date was planned. The pair had fun in Argyle, window-shopping and eating ice cream. He had a vacuum bottle filled with a hot liquid as they prepared to leave, because he explained with a wink that he planned to go the 'long way', and they were sure to get thirsty before he got her home.

The 'long way' was unfamiliar to the girl, but attending to the road was not a thing she normally did. She commented that she did not remember where they were, but he reassured her he did. He explained that the soldiers knew the whole area, and it was now time for a tea and cookie break before they headed back.

He stepped out of the buggy and drew out the two mugs, also a package of cookies. Pouring her a cup of steaming liquid, he handed it to her and poured one for himself. Leaning back comfortably, he let the horses rest while he chatted about this and that and what a nice place Oklahoma City was.

The drink was soothing to her, and the cookies were tasty, then he took the rein and turned the horses, pulling the buggy back onto the road. Carlotta leaned back and shut her eyes, lulled into relaxation by the jiggle of the buggy and crunch of the gravel under the buggy wheels and the horses' feet. She was unaware of his hands as she was eased over and let down onto the seat of the buggy. She did not note that the buggy was no longer moving.

The world was pitch black all around when the unusual pain struck her very being, taking away her breath with its force. She screamed in fright and horror, her voice exciting the horses who reared, squealing.

A force struck the side of her head on one side, then the other and her left ear burned as though it had been sliced with a knife. A hard hand caught her next scream with a slap across the mouth, and a voice ordered her to shut up or she'd get more of what she got. It told her she had to be 'broke in', and it just as well be here and now, as later. A third force against her head shut away the pain and all other feeling… as she felt herself sinking into unconsciousness.

Her next feeling was that of being scrunched up in a… what…? Where in the world was she in the middle of the night and how did she manage to hurt herself so badly? Especially in the place where the pain was centered? Did someone find her after she had been hurt and was now taking her home? She tried to lift her shoulders, and a firm hand pushed her back down.

A voice faintly familiar demanded. "Just stay down there where you are if you know what's good for you. This is the beginning of your new life, Miss Beautiful. You're gonna have a new job and make a lot of money."

Carlotta forced her voice, 'But I have a Certificate to…."

The voice began to laugh loudly. "Teaching!" he sneered. "That ain't no kind of a job for a beauty like you. You just lay there and get better, and we'll be in Oklahoma City by morning."

WHAT… was going ON! As her head began to clear, she started to remember. Jake. Picnic. Saturday. Home. Papa and Annette. WHERE was she? She closed her eyes tight to shut out the pain, and the crunch and jiggle of the buggy eased her gradually out of any conscious memory… at least for the moment.

She opened her eyes again to daylight and the insistent voice of Jake stopping the horses. "Listen, Miss Beautiful. You're getting a name change. From here on, you're Sophie. That's a name that'll fit your new job. Now I'm goin' into this diner for food. You sit right where you are, because your dress is a mess. I'll bring your food out. Don't you DARE try to run away."

With that, he stepped down and disappeared into the diner, carrying the vacuum bottle. Moments later he reappeared. He had biscuit and bacon sandwiches and a hot drink. Something within her caused Carlotta to shudder at the sight of the bottle.

"Go ahead and drink, Sophie. It's just tea. When I want you asleep, I'll put you to sleep so you don't need to be frettin'."

She obeyed. She realized she was hungry, and the hot tea was soothing to her aching head, if not her body. It seemed, from the road signs, that they were now in Oklahoma City, but he kept driving all the way through town.

On a road heading straight north he stopped. "Now listen at this. You got to take yourself a good sleep last night, but I drove all night long. I'm tired, and I'm gonna take a nap. You're gonna drive this team, and go slow. They're really tired. If someone stops us, you're Sophie, and I'm Hiram. We're married and on our way home, just up the road. Got it?"

She nodded. She got it. Taking the reins, she spoke to the team. Five minutes later the exhausted horses stopped dead in their tracks, and the sleeping man beside her did not notice.

Carlotta rested the reins resolutely in her lap, sighed deeply, and set her mind to thinking. Fact one. (Miss Josie had spent a good bit of time teaching her class the methods of analysis and how to set their facts in order.)

Fact One: She, herself, had done nothing to put herself into this situation. Perhaps she had been too trusting of Jake and had not been thinking... but that was the way she was.

Fact Two: Something terrible had happened, and the man who had pretended to be her friend was actually a savage who could possibly be a murderer.

Fact Three: She must exercise total control over her emotions until an answer came. There would be an answer... wouldn't there?

Fact Four: She had no idea where she was, but she was beginning to realize what he had in mind for her. It would be stupid and possibly fatal to strike out walking... wouldn't it...?

Fact Five: ...Surely there was a fact five.... But her mind drew a blank.

She had no idea how long she sat there, thinking, before he startled awake and sat up. Forcing herself to think as one with steel nerves, she bravely offered, "The horses... They're done in, and they wouldn't walk." Now it was time for him to hit her, but he didn't.

Nodding, he said, "Give me the reins. The horses are right, and we'll go back and find a place for the night." With shouts, curses, and a whip on their backs, he got the horses to move, and fortunately, they had not gone far from the last town.

With the animals in a stable, he arranged a room for the night. "Now, don't you think on slippin' out and me not lookin'. Not if you want to live. I got friends here, and I paid one of 'em to sit back'a the door all night. Any move outta you, and he'll yell."

Then, with a chuckle at his own cleverness, he added, "Told 'im you was my wife, and I wanted privacy, and after that, I said to 'em you'd been known to walk in your sleep." Somehow that idea was something he found terribly funny.

Once more he forced her into submission, threatening a beating if she resisted or screamed. "What you got ahead'a you, Miss Sophia, you gonna be glad you already got broke in when some 300 pound fellow comes at ya. But think on this, you're gonna earn a mint'a money. For me."

Later, when he had turned over and stretched out, he advised, "Now while you're thinkin', and I know you're gonna, see you remember this. Beautiful girls are everywhere. I been through all this before, and you ain't all that special. Just remember that… if you want'a keep on breathin'." Then he went to sleep.

Carlotta thought, as he had said she would.

Fact Five: It now appeared to her. She believed him when he said she might not be breathing. Dead, she would be out of options. Submit until the moment came, perhaps she would live. Be brave no matter what happened.

She was awake the whole night, but no better Fact Five presented itself.

Back in Carlile Corners there had been no sleep in the Owens household. A lighted lamp was set in the window. Tense adults stared at each other's faces hoping for an answer. Where could she be? Of course, all kinds of things could happen along the way in this vast and open Territory, but this young man, a military officer… shouldn't he be able to handle problems? Shouldn't he? Surely they'd be here soon and be able to tell what happened. Wouldn't they…? Of course they would!

With the wisdom of his almost twenty-three years, Ralph's thoughts were along a totally different line. Over the past weeks he had tried to develop a relationship with this man. The fellow was slippery as a snake about his past, what his family business in Oklahoma City was, and about his life at the outpost. Certain things just didn't add up.

Ralph had made allowances because it seemed the fellow might become part of the family. There'd need to be a place for him, but try as he might, Ralph could not place this man anywhere in relationship to Carl and his sister. Or, for another fact, himself.

Saddling a horse, he rode down the section lines. In the dark of the night not much could be learned, but it would give him thinking time. And the relief of actually doing SOMETHING.

As the moments passed, his whole being became heavier and more depressed. Something was terribly, terribly wrong, and he hardly let himself dare to think what it was. One thing he knew, he must prepare himself to find out. Immediately.

Galloping back to the house, he released the saddle pony and harnessed a pair of the tried and true Clydesdales. They were slower, but his premonition told him speed was not the answer now. It would be patience. This situation would seriously require his ability to talk with anyone and get answers. It would need his ability to assess personalities that would furnish the best answers.

His buggy was harnessed and ready when he told the anxious parents his plan. With pleading eyes, they hoped for his success. Annette, with sisterly concern, refused to allow him to leave the house hungry. Eggs. The universal healing food. Sandwiches made with leftover biscuits and meat.

When he hugged her goodbye, she left a teary, moist patch on his shoulder. A handshake with Carl showed shiny moisture in his eyes as well. With a deep breath of resolution, he promised, "I WILL find her, and I WILL bring her back. Trust me. If I don't come back tomorrow, I will drop you a note in the mail whenever I can. I WILL be back with her."

Quietly closing the door behind him, he could only guess what the next days would be for them. Also for himself. He remembered with clarity that he had not inadvertently said he would bring her back alive.

The first stop would be the military outpost, and the rising sun caught him in sight of the establishment, its stockade of cottonwood poles weathered to a silvery gray. A bugler alerted the soldiers of his approach, and he was met by a decorated officer, face weather-lined and beard grizzled. His gun was at the ready.

To the commandant, who appeared to be not much older than himself, Ralph explained his mission. With a sympathetic shake of the head, he was told that there had never been a Jacob Fuller, officer or not, posted at the base. Neither was an incoming officer expected.

Ralph knew the man was telling the truth, but he was prepared. "Sir, would I be permitted to talk with your men?"

"Friend, I can't see how they would know this person if I didn't."

Ralph leaned forward and looked into the face before him. "Sir, I beg you. This young lady was a beautiful girl, and she's missing. She left with a man of that name who said he was stationed here. She is a member of my family, and I will find her. Your men are sometimes entertained in my community, and I'm acquainted with some of them. They may have something to say that will get me started on my search."

He hesitated, then remembered the value of the personal touch. "The young lady's name is Carlotta."

The youthful commandant relented. The group of young men instantly recognized Ralph and his question was like a kick at a beehive, as information came at him. Bussing and insistant.

"Jake Fuller? That's what he's callin' hisself now? He's Hiram Scruggs, and there ain't no time he was ever a officer."

"Drummed out, he was, and I was the drummer. Two weeks ago, weren't it?" He looked at his fellows for confirmation.

"Two weeks if it was a day. Should'a been shot, instead. Army didn't want'a mess with 'im."

"Didn't want to waste the bullets, neither."

"Weren't nothin' too lowdown fer the scoundrel to do."

"Said to us he was after another pretty girl to make 'im some money. Said the money the army paid was a joke."

"Pal, I hate to say this about your sister, but I'm thinkin' he may'a took a girl before... Maybe some other time. Didn't say what happened to 'er...."

"Reckon I could guess...."

"Family business in Oklahoma City? That'd be a laugh. I'd say his business'd be farther north. Likely Guthrie."

"We been wondering if that girl, your sister, knew what she was doin'. Didn't seem like she did."

"Didn't know at the time you was her brother, or we'd'a said somethin'."

The five young men stared at Ralph, their eyes naked with sympathy. "We don't like sayin' what we just said to 'er brother, but you needed to know. We're hopin' you got a gun and ammo with ya."

There were nods of agreement. "If'n you don't, the commandant, he's a good fellow, and he'd furnish ya. That feller gave him enough trouble whilst he was here, that if'n we'd'a took a gun to 'is head, ain't nobody here'd testify agin 'im."

With eyes narrowed and mean, the young drummer added, "Hated it he only got bein' drummed out. I even thought'a hittin' 'im with one'a my drumsticks, only it'd'a just only made 'im laugh."

As Ralph thanked them, and prepared to take his leave, the commandant was waiting. "Friend, I apologize for not knowing more. I keep forgetting how clever these men are, and how well they can size up a situation. This has been a lesson for me. Now, if we can furnish anything...? No? Well, we wish you luck. That man is a...."

Ralph couldn't resist giving help. "A devil?"

"Yes, sir." With that, the young officer saluted Ralph and turned back.

Armed now with this information, he considered it much better than ammo, and Ralph clicked the Clydesdales onto the road.

As he passed through Argyle, he posted a note. "...Carl and sis, she's been abducted, but I have learned a lot I can use. Be brave, and I'll tell you more when I can..."

With each mile, Ralph settled himself farther into the knowledge that this would not be easy. North through Oklahoma City... maybe a check in with the law, just in case. But the part about Guthrie had a ring of soundness. A scoundrel of Jake/Hiram's ilk would not leave a true tail. He'd lay down false markers. The 'Oklahoma City family business' was obviously a detraction tossed his way. It was certain, now, that the deed had been well planned.

It was at about five miles that his mind presented him with the remembered fact that a homesteader to the south had lost a buggy in the night a week or so back. Three guesses as to where it was now. Also, there was certainly one or two farmers who had lost a horse in the well-known midnight raid.

So now the man had a buggy and team, also Carlotta, with his ideas of how she would make money for him. Sickening thought.

At Oklahoma City, the law listened with sympathetic ears and took notes for their own further possible use, but they could not help with information about either of the abductor's names. Who knew what name he was using now? And they had plenty of stories of their own, as frontier towns attracted its share of seedy characters.

As he had expected, Ralph would need to head north in the morning. Checking into a room, he spent a restless night and had a good breakfast remembering his sister's admonition. (Nothing important could be accomplished on an empty stomach.)

Carlotta was shoved up a narrow outside staircase and into a large room, bare of furniture except for two beds and a room divider.

Seated on one of the beds was a girl of about her age. Curly red hair, now in a mess but still attractive. Small face, pointed chin and huge eyes. The eyes cut into Carlotta's direction, but her body made no perceptible movement. Seated in the middle of the bed, she had her knees drawn up to her chest and firmly hugged by thin arms. Pointed chin was bent forward.

Carlotta was shoved down on the other bed and told to stay there. He would bring her food. She nodded, silently, and he left.

The girl in the room whispered, "Isabelle."

Carlotta quickly sorted within her mind, and decided on her true name. "Carlotta" she whispered back.

Food was brought. Not bad, actually. Large biscuit split in half and liberally topped with sausage-flecked gravy. Extra biscuit with jelly. Hot tea. The girls ate in silence.

The door opened, and a strange man stepped into the room. Looking from one to the other, he chose Isabelle. The divider was stretched between the beds. Carlotta got her turn before noon. Pain. Screaming pain, but she made no sound.

Food arrived again, but pain had removed all hunger. Be brave, she told herself. Eat it all. Be ready. Stay strong.

Days followed. It was on the morning of the fourth day… or was it the fifth? Isabelle was silent. Sleeping, Carlotta hoped. Pain subsided when sleep came. For some reason, Isabelle had been brutally struck by the man who seemed to act as though he owned her. Who knows what Isabelle did after that, but if she could sleep… well….

When hours passed, Carlotta decided to check on her. Creeping around the room divider, she gasped in horror. The girl's right arm lay over her chest with her supper knife loosely clasped. Her left arm was by her side in a pool of dried blood. There were bloodstains on the sheet, cover, and pillow.

Her hand caught her scream of terror before it left her mouth, and Carlotta tiptoed back to her bed. With the hairbrush she was provided, she nervously untangled her hair, put down the brush and lay back, her face toward the far wall.

In mid-afternoon Isabelle was removed. Bedding and all rolled together, Jake/Hiram helped the other man to remove her from the room, and in an hour or so they were back.

A blindfold was applied over Carlotta's eyes and a gag stuffed in her mouth. Rolled together in her bedding, she was carried down the narrow stairs. Placed on a platform (wagon bed?) and moved over rough and pebbly ground. She heard conversation, but could not make out the words.

In due time she was taken from the vehicle and moved into another room. Blindfold removed, she saw the room was similar to the one she had left. The air was damp, and she thought she heard the sound of running water. River? Had that been what they did with Isabelle? No! She would not think about that.

Somehow, the customers that she had been brought here to entertain knew where to find her. Including the 300 pound one. About noon another girl was brought in and put on the other bed.

At the small opportunity she had to peek, she saw her roommate. Very young. Twelve? Freckles and a long braid. Maybe waist length hair. Someone would have had to take care of it for her. Someone looking for her? Would they know where to look? How would someone know where she was? Or where either of them was?

She had entertained ideas of escape at first, but since the move, it was hard to be hopeful.

Ralph had never been in Guthrie, but he knew it was a fast growing town, filled up in a day at the time of the land run in '89. Well, now to get down to business.

Experience had told him that there were places to go for information. The blacksmith's shed or livery stations were good. So was a train depot if a train came through that town.

So, Santa Fe depot it was. There, directly behind the depot was a café with a sizably hungry clientele. That was also a good sign, so he went in. He had noticed a row of neat rooms beside the café, and there were likely to be vacancies now, being the middle of the day. Someone in the café would know.

Good food. He remembered Annette's advice once more. Eat when you can. The manager was a talkative fellow named Samuel Littletree.

Yes, there was a vacancy. How long would he need it? Not sure? Well no problem. Here on business? The law? Sure thing, mister. His own brother was the deputy sheriff here. We can settle you in and take care of your animals. Point you to the law when you're ready.

The sheriff was a hard faced, stocky fellow with a ring of red-tinged gray hair growing into his collar. He listened. His expression appeared that he seemed to think nothing that could happen in this wild town was amazing. It also seemed that he could handle whatever it was.

"Kidnappin', you say? That happens here, and we got the expert in that field. That feller even had ta rescue his own little niece. Name'a Jacob Littletree. He's on his way in right now. Give you some coffee?"

Ralph had just enjoyed good coffee at the café. Surprisingly good, actually. The last thing he wanted was the re-boiled, acidy brew made in places where men accumulated, but it would be ill-mannered to refuse.

Jacob Littletree arrived. Tall, hair as black as midnight, eyes like lumps of coal. Expression serious and hard to read. Listened as though he was copying each word into a memo in his mind.

Girl almost fifteen. Fellow that pretended to be an army officer. Courted the family before abducting the girl. It all sounded just too familiar.

Name could be Jake Fuller or Hiram Scruggs or any other that came to mind. For certain he'd been in trouble before and might be known locally.

Deputy Littletree nodded. "Now that name 'Scruggs' rings a bell. Had trouble some months back, maybe a year, but it seemed to be connected with gambling."

Nodding knowingly, Ralph continued, "There's one thing that might help. One of the fellows that knew him said he was looking for a girl to make him a lot of money."

Jake's lips clamped sternly and his eyes narrowed. "Helps a lot, mister... uh?"

"Ralph Carpenter", he supplied. "The girl is my... stepsister...."

The deputy paused a respectful moment, then requested, "Give me an hour or so. Where'll I find you?"

"Oh, down at your brother's place."

The deputy nodded. "Look for me soon. You used to a saddle? Could be you could help."

So Ralph went reluctantly back to his rented room. This deputy impressed him totally. Back to the Santa Fee station. Checked on his Clydesdales. Both of the huge beasts were licking up the last of the grain in their troughs and eying the filled hay nets attached to the wall. Good folks here. He'd like to take a nap to be refreshed, but he knew it was useless, tensed up as he was.

Good as his word, Jacob Littletree appeared in the doorway. "The fellow's back and he's one we've had in our sights. Usin' the name'a Hiram Scruggs and workin' with another fellow that's been duckin' us. Trash collectors found a body back'a one'a the boardin' houses earlier this week."

Ralph felt his heart skip and his chest constrict. He held his face expressionless. He would take her back as he had promised, but this was not the way he had hoped.

The deputy continued. "Girl about thirteen, curly red hair…."

Ralph felt himself relax and hated himself for it. Whoever she was, she belonged to someone who was no doubt now searching frantically.

Jacob again. "Got a line on someone… might be him. Moved out leavin' paid rent on the books. Tells me somethin'. He went in a hurry. Had another girl with 'im but don't know nothin' about 'er. Got myself onto checkin' likely places and wouldn't mind a ride-along. You got a piece?"

"Colt 45 all right?"

"Get your gear and we're gone. We'll get you deputized as posse, and that'll give you authority, happen we have to split up."

Business taken care of, the men rode away on well-kept, well-trained animals. The town of Guthrie seemed to have no end. Well built houses were constructed beside shacks hastily thrown together. Business was being conducted out of wagons and tents. "Ain't near as bad as it use to be. Years ago it was mostly all tents. Some was livin' in cardboard boxes. If they was lucky."

Ralph purely hated the words they had to use hunting for this fellow. It was bad to tip their hand that they were the law, but it seemed the only way information could be gleaned. And it was slow.

Much too slow.

Carlotta's new roommate was Mary Lou. Imagine! Mary Lou… and if she didn't manage to stop screaming, she was going to be… no, don't think of it. She hasn't been hurt enough yet to make her use the knife to her wrist… not yet but….

Business seemed to be terribly good for the next two days. Carlotta was relieved there was no mirror because she must look a sight. She had, however, learned to send her mind on a 'journey', as she told herself. This would not last. Papa? What was he doing now? Somehow she couldn't quite bring up a picture... Now, Ralph, hmmm.... But how could he ever find her? He couldn't even know which town she was in. Certainly, she didn't know.

The two fellows... could be they were getting careless. She could hear a few words sometimes. Not enough, though, to be helpful.

Moved again. Despondency settled around her. Thoughts of what was going on, and what all could happen to her. If she was rescued, how could she face anyone after all that had gone on with her? How could she face Papa? She also knew what could be going on inside her.

At the next meal she let the knife slip down into the sheets, but Hiram noticed, and found it. It caused her a whack in the head that left her mind circling.

Could she manage to choke herself? Hold her breath? No, she had tried. It just made her pass out, and then breathing started again.

Mary Lou was taken away and replaced. Carlotta was too busy thinking to be curious as to why she was gone or to see the new roommate. Concern with herself.

There had to be a way to die, because she surely did not want to live. That was a certainty. Even if she was rescued, an impossibility, of course, she still wanted to die.

Starving would take too long, and besides, there was no place to hide the food she didn't eat. There was a gas light fixture overhead but it was high, and would torn sheets strips even reach that far? Hanging would be risky, and she might be caught trying. She needed to think of something that would be a certain success.

Ralph posted his third note. "...no real news, but it's possible that Guthrie is the right town. Getting good help from the law...."

It was discouraging and depressing. The element of the city that engaged in prostitution was clever and crafty. Somehow they managed to move around, making no effort to hide where they no longer were. Numerous hints came to nothing... only empty buildings. Officer Littletree had to leave him for a while to tend to some emergency, but Ralph slugged on alone.

Finally, on an inspiration, he left his horse and neat clothes and wore ill-kempt work clothes retrieved from a dump barrel. He pretended to be a potential customer. Picky customer. Lookin' for "real beauty with yeller hair." Pay extra if he could find one. Young. Then success... finally...

"Yeah, mister. They got a looker, and I know where. I been there. How much'd it be worth to ya to know?"

Ralph resisted the impulse to wring his stupid neck. Told the fellow he'd think on it and be back. Where would he be found?"

Ralph knew that if this snitch was on the level, the man would need help to stay alive. The snitch sounded good to his word but was obviously an amateur. Didn't seem to know how much his information was worth. The thing was, he got greedy and went to the pimps for a cut on the fee for sending a customer.

The pimps laughed, put a bullet in his throat, then bound and gagged the two girls. Dumped them in a wagon and headed out.

The officer and Ralph had found the empty room, no surprise, but also found the remains of the greedy snitch. Stretched out by the doorway. Room smelled of perfume and hair on the pillows. The men could almost imagine the beds were still warm.

What now. Look for a wagon (?) and two men (?) leaving town (?) or just relocating (?). Which? Make the best guess. That's all you have.

Officer Littletree knew his way around, but Ralph, knowing how clever these men were, convinced the lawman to let him split up and take the main drag. Experienced lawbreakers sometimes realized it was often safer to hide in plain sight, and it was a good plan.

Two old men with hair grown over collars, slumped on the buckboard of a wagon. One bony horse tugged between the shafts of the doubletree that attached him to the rickety wagon. Ralph, badge inside his shirt, with Colt 45 on his hip, purposely cut off passage as the old horse ambled around a corner.

Jake/Hiram peered from beneath his ragged straw hat and around his greasy beard and instantly recognized a face he had known down at a place called Carlile Corners. Gouging his elbow into the ribs of his companion. "Law man! Run!"

With not a hesitation, the two men on the buckboard seat leaped off either side of the wagon and dashed toward the first cover. Ralph lifted the gun and aimed at the foot of the despised Hiram and fired. Foot and shoe disintegrated into a dusty, bloody cloud.

The startled nag hitched to the wagon started backward, sending the wagon rolling down the way they had come. Unable to stop the backward roll, the horse reared and neighed, and two strong young bystanders dashed out and held to the tongues of the doubletree.

Officer Jacob Littletree, on horseback, galloped after the fleeing man, and it was no contest. Hands cuffed behind him and a rope lassoed around his neck, he was returned, stumbling after the horse and the lawman with the gun.

Ralph ignored the result of his gunshot and leaped into the bed of the wagon. Bound and gagged, and rolled into bedding were two frightened girls. Heart beating as though it would break through his chest, he pulled back the bedding and looked into the face of Carlotta.

Jacob had freed the other girl and removed the gag. Gladys, or whatever her name used to be, shrieked for joy at the sight of a deputy uniform on the man who had freed her. In a rapturous instant, she threw her arms around him and kissed his cheek.

Carlotta, on the other hand, bowed her head and began to cry.

So much had happened in Ralph's mind, and none of it was good. He found that he wanted desperately to free her, take her in his arms and kiss away her tears, but he remembered she was the stepdaughter of his sister, and she must be taken home. He did, however, help her from the tangle of the bedding, so she could stand on her feet.

"Ralph! How did you…?" Her sobs robbed her of words.

CHAPTER 8

I t's all right. I found you." He looked at the lawman's smiling face and heard him say, "She must be the one!"

Ralph took her to his room at Littletree Inn and ordered warm water, towels, and a hairbrush. Leaving her in the care of the Littletree's he went shopping. Never in his short life had he bought a garment of clothing for a female of any age. But then, he had done a lot of things in his short life for the first time and would undoubtedly do a few more.

He found the store offering ladies wear, spotted a sales person of Carlotta's approximate size, and ordered a change of clothing "from the skin out." To answer her questioned look, he continued, humorously, "Fell in the creek?" It seemed to work.

The dress, white with sprigged blue flowers, was his own choice, and included a classy looking cape of matching blue knit. Also a lace trimmed bonnet. He decided she'd have to pick out the shoes herself, to get a fit.

Returning to Littletree's, he found the matronly cook had taken over and was trying to comfort the sobbing girl. He passed the clothes through the door and went to the café for coffee and courage. Why would she be crying… still…? But then, he had never assumed that he understood girls. Actually, he had never tried or really cared until now. He had actually heard that not even women understood women.

Finally he remembered his sister's remedy. Carlotta had to be hungry. She would eat, and then things would be better. Meanwhile it was note-sending time.

"…Sis and Carl. Found her. Quite shaken up but all in one piece. An older woman here is helping her. She needed a bath and clothes. I got her outfitted, and I hope she's able to take a nap. She looked very tired. I haven't been able to talk with her yet. More tomorrow if I can. Ralph…"

The woman reported, "Took 'er peppermint tea and got 'er calmed down some. Wouldn't say to me what all happened but she said there was something she wanted her brother to do, and she'd tell him tomorrow. She wants you to stay with her tonight, so we're movin' in a soldier bed for you."

Well, good! He'd be her brother if that was what she wanted. And tomorrow she'd talk. But, yes, Annette, she needs food now. Quick as she wakes up I'll see to it.

He checked on his animals. Contentedly munching hay from the net. He decided to appease his restlessness by checking in on the lawman.

"Yeah, that other girl, she could talk and said she lived in a settlement other side'a Cottonwood Creek. One of the men drove 'er home in a buggy. That fellow you aimed at, he ain't gonna get too much use outta that foot. Doc had to take it off and part'a his leg. Gunpowder. Gonna need a statement outta you before you cut out for home."

Ralph nodded. "Sure. Want to thank you for your help. Good thing to get rid of those characters."

"Yeah, but they're like mushrooms. Pick one off and two pop up in the place. 'Course, that just makes me glad to do the job I always wanted to do. I told you, didn't I, that another body showed up? That's two killins' and a suicide in the last week. Girls. Just little girls."

Ralph was silent, just shaking his head in dismay. It could so easily have been Carlotta and likely would have been if he had been a couple of weeks later. Fellow like that Hiram, he'd just use 'em up and destroy the evidence. Then he'd just move on to someone else.

The deputy sheriff stroked his chin, thoughtfully. "You ain't thinkin' on a job change, are you? The force could use a fellow like you, fast thinkin' and sharp shootin'?"

Another head shake. "Nice offer and I'll remember it. Fact is, I promised to get this lady home so folks can stop worryin' about her. Plan to check us out tomorrow and head south."

"Well, luck go with ya if I don't see ya again."

Ralph headed back to Littletree's. Carlotta had done a lot of sleeping, but some of it might be the result of the medicinal tea that was given her. Anyway, that gave him time for planning. It was note time, and then they'd head on home leisurely and let her rest on the way.

"…Dear Sis and Carl She's all in one piece, but she's been badly treated. I'll tell you more later. We'll be a week or so on the road for reasons I'll explain when I get there. Believe me, and stop worrying. There's wrong been done but nothing that can't be fixed. Ralph…"

Annette nodded at the good news. "Badly treated. That could mean a lot of things."

Carl agreed. "You knowin' your brother's way of sayin' things, how bad is it?"

After a telling hesitation, she responded. "Not good, I'll say. But he don't lie when he asks for time, and he's got a story. We gotta count on that and just wait."

Ralph really wanted to take her to the café for breakfast before they left Guthrie, but the seriousness of her face when she said there was something he needed to do for her made him hesitate. Likely better to bring food to her and not take a risk.

Carlotta ate the food with the determination expected of one who would use the strength to accomplish a disagreeable job. Eggs, gone. Fried potatoes, following closely. Tea, gone. The last biscuit? Going, but she was chewing with concentrated determination.

"Now I'm ready. I gotta have you do something that needs to be done. I was making plans when you found me, but now you can help."

"I'll do what I can."

"Good. Promise me you'll do this. I want you to kill me. I heard water behind that last place I was, and I was figuring how to get to it and drown myself, but your gun can do it quicker."

Wide-eyed concern! "You want me to… kill… you…?"

Firm, and with determination. "Yes. Quickly. I can't be let to live anymore."

Now Ralph was presented with a problem. He had studied the words folks used, even back as a paper carrier. The way folks said something could mean different things. He'd had to learn if they were serious or just testing their voices. Would they be willing to tell him something, or want him to disappear? If he asked something, would they want to help a kid or drive him away? The actions and thoughts of grownups were wrapped up in the sound of their words.

From his first memory, he had wanted to know everything. Getting information from grownups took skill, but he knew he could learn it. He remembered the orphan's home, how his sister had been treated, and how she was sent here and there to work for their keep. Then she had taken him away from the hated place, and he spent time locked in the tiny room by himself. Vast improvement.

In the evenings his sister had played number and letter games with him… as they certainly had nothing else to do. He learned to study her face for the answer to her questions. Was she serious, or was she playing? The small boy, having nothing else to do and no other challenge, learned fast. The things he learned helped him when he finally got to go to school… and to work. He learned quickly that coins were the mark of his success… the validation of his efforts… so he must plan on having more coins.

His sister's praise was his best reward, and he studied on how to earn much more of it. From that, he learned to study faces of others. There was often more to be learned from faces than from uttered words.

He knew, or at least suspected, that a girl as protected as Carlotta, would be damaged in many ways from what she had endured, but was amazed to hear that she wanted to die. Of course that was not what she wanted to do, but it must have seemed the only way out. He must choose his words carefully and not confront her.

Nodding, he responded, "For a fact, Carlotta, that would be one way to go, but that little old stream of water behind the room… I saw it. It wasn't even a river. Why, it isn't any bigger than the one by your Papa's catfish pond. It was just a little stream. Cottonwood Creek, they called it, and a body could jump across it in places." Maybe that was not true, but it sounded good.

He continued, "Now you wouldn't'a seen it, likely, but there's a much better river to drown in down in Oklahoma City. You could'a seen it when you went there to take your test." He struggled for references to her happier life. "Now that river, it's good and deep right now. You could slip and fall in the water. Then, on down stream, your body'd be pulled out, and I could sadly claim it and bring you home."

"NO! You gotta let me stay and not go home."

"Can't do that. I promised to help you in any way I could, and I can't go home without you. I promised my sister and your Papa I'd bring you home. I didn't promise that you'd be alive, and I was of a mind you wouldn't be. Fact is, while I was lookin' for you, three dead bodies showed up in Guthrie. There was a girl with curly red hair, and she killed herself. Another one was a child with long hair and she had been beaten and tossed in some bushes. Another one was strangled and left on the street at night. Then there was the snitch who told me where you were. He'd be number four. He was shot in the neck, and it had to be from Hiram's gun."

After a meaningful pause, he added. "If I'd'a been a few days longer, you might'a been one of the next bodies especially if you gave him any trouble. Then I might'a had a hard time findin' you, but I would have. I wasn't going home without you. I made a promise, and I don't break them."

Carlotta forced herself to nod. "Then we have to go to Oklahoma City to the bigger river. I can't go back home."

Ralph hesitated, then proceeded bravely, "Tell me why not. I deserve an answer. I just spent almost a month of my life lookin' for you, and I shot a fellow's foot off, so I deserve to know. Why can't you go home?"

A sigh. "Cause'a what happened to me. You know that."

"Of course I know that. You were taken against your will, you were locked up, and you were beaten and treated badly. I still don't know why you can't go home."

Long pause. "It was the other things. Things that you don't know."

"Don't be so sure I don't know. Anyway, we can talk about that later." He had sensed from her face it was a losing battle at this moment. If he continued, she might manage to complete her mission without him.

"So if you'll pack up what we need to take, I'll get the horses and buggy, and we'll head out. We can easily make it to the river and get you drowned before night."

With that, he stood and walked out of the little room. His animals neighed a greeting and did a lot of head flinging and harness rattling. They'd apparently had their fill of being locked up.

Sober faced and firm chinned, the girl climbed into the buggy, refusing any help. Settling herself, she stared straight ahead.

It was a silent ride. Ralph decided this was no time to let the argument fester again. He would have to think about it and pick his time and place. He had always welcomed new experiences, but this one was a bit more than he liked.

Another note to the Corners. "…it's going to be a mite longer than I had hoped. Don't worry. I just have to make some decisions, and there's things to see about in the City. Trust me. I'll be doing the best I can, and we WILL be home…."

It was on the day that Carl and Annette received that note that they had a visit from old Mrs. Gray Owl. The old woman appeared at the door, bonnet firmly tied against the spring breeze, and wiry gray hair whipping around the edges.

Annette stared in puzzlement, but Carl explained. "This lady is Mrs. Gray Owl. She came to help when Maudie needed her. She's a friend and a doctor. Won't you come in?"

The old bent woman shook her head. "Won't be comin' in. Just had words to say. Words you need to hear. Girl is safe like the note said. Not well, but safe. You don't worry. She better and better, to be a surprise. Goodbye." With that, she turned and walked away, carrying a basket over her arm and holding to her bonnet with the other, her shawl fringe whipping around her waist.

"Better and better?" Annette wondered, staring at Carl.

He nodded. "Best news we got yet. Even better than Ralph's note. I don't know how she knows things but it's a fact that she does. When she says don't worry, I believe her. All we can do is trust Ralph and wait." With an arm around her, they stood gaining strength from each other.

The rented room in Oklahoma City was very nice. Second floor up and overlooked the river. He had hoped for such a place, and it seemed luck was with him.

"Now, Carlotta, we need food. I could lock you in here while I get it, but I won't. I know you won't run away because you need my help. It's a hard job to kill oneself, and I can make it a lot easier. I promised to do what I could, but I get to take my time about it. Now, you have on that nice dress, so I want you to comb your hair and put on that pretty lacy bonnet. I don't want to be embarrassed when we go to the diner."

Carlotta, trained to be always obedient, did as instructed. She walked silently beside him past the tall glass windows and the new clothes and things that she had seen with Miss Josie and the other girls. Carefully looking straight ahead, she ignored all the finery.

Ralph studied her from the corner of his eye. Good! Things were moving well, but he'd have to be careful.

Wonderful stew. Venison, it seemed like. Come to think on it, he could likely bring down a deer if he tried. His sister would love trying out recipes with it. He forced himself to eat in silence.

Later, reaching the ice cream shop, he turned to go in.

"NO! I can't go there!"

"Why not?"

"He did that. I ate ice cream, and he fooled me."

"Oh, that, huh. Forget it. I paid him back when I shot off his foot. That should erase the bad thoughts of ice cream. Anyway, you don't have to eat any, but you have to wait with me if you want my help."

She stared at the dish of ice cream before her as he leisurely ate his. Finally, she picked up a spoon. Good! A small glimmer of hope. Don't comment, he warned himself. Wait, no matter how hard it is. Wait for the right time.

Back in the room he stationed himself at the window facing the river. "I need to be looking at that water to see where we should do it. I can't be standin' right there with you when it happens, or I might get blamed. We have to find a place where you can pretend to slip in and not be able to swim, and it has to be where I can see you."

"Can't you just shoot me and leave me here in the room?"

"No, they'd find me, and I'd be locked up. I didn't do anything to cause what happened to you, so I shouldn't have to pay. No, the drowning is the best idea."

"Then let's go do it now."

"Can't. I haven't decided on the best place. Besides, I have some business to tend to. I've been thinkin' to expand my route business and offer things like maybe lace and dress material. Maybe jewelry, like necklaces. Thought I'd look around while I'm here for a place to get 'em. You can go with me while I look, or you can stay here. Make up your mind."

It pained him to be so firm with the girl who was hurting so badly, but he sensed that was the only way to handle this.

"Besides, I have to be ready to head on south as soon as I get your dead body. Folks back there'll want to be puttin' it in the ground. Come on, let's go." Ralph drew in a breath of relief when she actually came with him without a word.

Later, back in the room. "You know, Carlotta, there is another answer. I know you're not wantin' to hear about it but our folks back there'll want to know if I suggested it, and I don't lie very good." She was silent, just staring out the window at the rushing water.

"I know what it is you're thinkin' might happen after what you went through. All the scars on you aren't on the outside. Now, if it happened that what you're thinkin' of, was to happen to a married lady, what would be said? Nobody'd have the right to gossip, would they?"

Still watching the river, she retorted, "Can't happen."

"What can't happen? You mean there's a reason you can marry a fellow?"

"There ain't time. Takes time to get married."

"Huh!" He sneered. "Young lady, I could walk down that street for ten blocks and come back with ten fellows that'd marry you in a skinny minute, even knowin' what you been through and that it wasn't none of your fault."

She whirled away from the window and faced him. "And have 'em treat me like that snake! No. I'd rather be drowned."

"Well, now, they could be like him. You ain't givin' me a great lot of time to check 'em out. I'm just tossin' out what could happen. I know you'd rather die. You've been firm about tellin' me that."Enough words for the moment. At least she was thinking.

"I gotta go check on my animals. It's too late to do anything today, anyway, so you take the bed and rest while I'm gone. Shall I lock the door so's nothin' happens to you while I'm gone? Remember, I promised the folks...."

"Yes, lock the door, please." Thoughts of those ten fellows anxious to marry her was a bit frightening.

When Ralph returned, she was soundly sleeping, her lacy bonnet hung over a chair, and her golden hair a halo around her head on the white pillowcase. What a picture. Did he dare to go on with what he thought was the only thing he could do? Or...?

Actually binding her into helplessness all the way home was a bit extreme. But then... She was more hard-headed than she had seemed.

Locking the door again, he walked up the street and down, thinking. Of his many experiences, none matched this one in any way. Of course, living in the same house with her for most of a year gave him a good knowledge of her thought processes. The difference was, at his age twenty-three and her fifteen, there had not been a lot in common between them. Also, his life had been rather rugged, and she was carefully sheltered. A real puzzle. He could only do what he could do.

It was while they ate breakfast in the diner that he dared to bring up the subject again. "Shall it be today that we get on with killing you? We don't have to be in a hurry. We can look for a willin' fellow. What do you think?"

A napkin delicately touched her mouth. A sigh passed her lips. "I always thought there'd be a white dress and veil and music, and that I'd be happy. It's all gone. I've got no place to go to get away from what happened. I know you're just tryin' to help, but there ain't no help to be had. Too late for anything."

Ralph watched. Things were definitely looking up. "Listen to this. We don't have to go straight home. I can send a note and tell 'em we found a lotta things to see here, and that way we could wait around and see if what you are scared of is really going to happen."

Long moment of thought. "Maybe…"

Silence as Ralph forced himself to wait.

"You say that even after what I did there'd be a fellow to marry me no matter what happened?"

"Carlotta, you did NOT do anything. Plenty was done to you, but you did nothing. Remember that. And, yes, there are many fellows in this land of not very many girls who would love to take a chance on you. Even if it was a sure thing that what you're afraid of will really happen, they'd still jump at the chance to have you." He waited and watched her face.

"Of course we're just talkin'. Nothin' we say'll make a bit of difference when you're dead. I'm gonna sure hate tellin' your Papa that you decided not to live. Here he lost his own folks, and he had babies die before they were born." Here he paused to let the words sink in.

"All those babies he wanted, but what he got was only you, and you were more than he ever expected in a daughter. Obedient, beautiful, hard-working. Earning a teaching Certificate in only two years was special, and he was proud of you. But all of that will be gone. He lost your Mama who he loved more than his own life, and now he'll loose his daughter. I know he would want you come home NO MATTER WHAT has happened, and he will try to help you forget it.

"Of course, that means nothing because I promised to let you drown. At least he'll get to have another look at you before we bury you. That way he'll have a last picture in his mind of how beautiful you are."

"I'm not beautiful," she responded, stubbornly.

"Depends on who's lookin', wouldn't you say?"

Silence. The waitress brought the teapot and heated their drink. Carlotta clasped her hands around the warm mug as if to bring life back into herself… as if she imagined the cold river.

Good sign, actually.

"You're sayin' there'd be a fellow to take… whatever happened to me, and maybe say it was…."

"And say it was his? Yes. I can tell you for certain that can happen. Shall we start looking for the fellow? We can't wait around much longer for nothing. I already told the folks we'd be comin' on back soon."

He watched her hand as it moved toward the breadbasket. Would a girl wanting to die bother with another jam and biscuit? It seemed a decision of some kind had been made, and she had accepted it.

He offered, "Do you want to go back to the room before we go down to the river?"

A bite. A slow chewing. A nod.

"Fine. After you finish, we'll go back. Pretty nice room. I might want to take a nap on that bed. It's a good floor back there, but a bit hard. Even harder than the shelf in my van."

"Where would you look?"

"Where would I look for what?"

"The fellow. The one that wouldn't care… that would even…"

Ralph felt his heart pound in response to what was in his mind. Did he dare? Yes. It was now or never.

"Where would I find a fellow who'd marry you knowin' what you been through? Well, if I was to start lookin', first it'd be right here in this café."

Carlotta whirled her head around, gazing. Every table was empty, it being late in the morning. Her eyes turned back to Ralph. He was waiting, his dark eyes watching, his red-brown hair in place. His hands folded before him.

"Not you!"

"Why not me? I know what happened to you. I know for a fact that nothing that happened was your fault. I rescued you. I spent almost a month'a my life doin' it. And I'm NOT your brother. You and I are no more related than my sister and your Papa." Enough said. Time to wait.

"But…?"

"I said I'd do what I could, and this is something I can do. White dress and all."

"NO! No white dress! I don't deserve that. You don't know what happened to me!"

"Now, that'd be up to you. The thing is, I thought girls couldn't wear white dresses because'a what they did. You didn't do a thing. That means you qualify to wear a white dress. That is, if you want to."

"Well, I…."

"We could go now and get the dress. We could get a lot of other things. By the time the sun goes down, you could be a married lady, and whatever happens after that is no business of nobody but us. I promise you this, I will never hurt you, and I will never let anyone else hurt you."

The chosen white dress was not lace as Carlotta had pictured. It was made of white lawn, finely woven and tucked in all the right places. She changed her mind on this because her Papa was not here to see her in the one she had in mind. The one she chose was one she could wear many times. With the white pearl-buttoned shoes that were a perfect fit.

It was not the occasion either of them would have chosen, but at some point, one dealt with what was handed them. The best part was that they two were actually well suited to each other, and the union could have possibly happened anyway even if she had not been abducted. Too bad their first kiss had not happened until after the uniting words had been spoken.

It was again note time. "…Change of plans. Good things can happen, and they must be given a chance to erase some bad things. So sorry I can't say more. Expect another note from me in about two weeks, and we'll be coming home…"

"What's all this about 'good things'?"

"I'm thinkin' we just need to remember Mrs. Gray Owl's words. And wait."

Ralph removed the bedspread to make his pallet on the floor, but Carlotta took it from him. "What might happen could be something… we make happen? Something to say… anyway?"

Ralph had reason to be proud of his new wife's thought process. Bravery above and beyond, and actually not out of character for her. It was her choice. In view of unchangeable facts, she made the best decision available.

The bustling town of Oklahoma City had a lot of things to see and do. Things to be bought and to eat. Things to say to each other. Efforts made to get acquainted in a way they had never imagined, and the efforts proved satisfactory. And it took time… they needed time.

Carlotta even smiled. Maybe a laugh or two. Nothing could happen now that was not expected, or at least known about. A week was spent, and both of them were now eager to get home.

Note time. "…I'm sorry to tell you our good news in this way, but we will be coming back as a pair. DON'T WORRY. More good than bad. When we can talk, you'll know everything that happened, including the fact that when I found that Jake scoundrel, I shot off his foot. Carl, I'd rather have shot off his head, but if I had, I'd have had to stand trial for murder, and then I couldn't get your little girl home until after my jail sentence was served. Don't say anything to anyone until we get there."

A few days later they arrived. Hugs and kisses! No more worries. Four in the household again. Annette was overjoyed, and Carl relieved beyond comprehension.

About a hundred feet west of the house a foundation was stepped off, and during every free moment, Carl and his son-in-law pounded boards. Two rooms to start with, but as Carlotta's waist began to expand, more rooms were planned.

Around the neighborhood, a lot of words were thought of, but none were spoken in the home of the Owens and Carpenters. A lot of questions rested in the minds of the neighbors but not in Mrs. Gray Owl's. She had known already! Months passed, and an early Christmas present arrived.

The parents looked at the new little package and marveled at the brightness of his dark, dark eyes and the thatch of red brown hair completely covering his well-shaped head.

Annette looked at small Daniel Carpenter and then at her brother, smiling her relief and pleasure. As near as she could remember, this tiny squalling bundle of energy was almost exactly like what she had held in her arms as she watched her mother's life fade away. She had been fifteen at the time.

Carl gazed at the noisy bundle with profound relief. A baby! Carlotta's baby! He was born alive and screaming and that was enough for him. A grandson! Imagine! After the horrible month of his daughter's abduction, he had been given a gift for which he was truly grateful. There is indeed a God in heaven.

A baby. A real live baby that needs diapers and food. Oh, merciful God in heaven, thank You. Carl's happiness was more than he thought he could contain.

A small concern tugged at the new family after another visit from Mrs. Gray Owl. She looked at the small newcomer and nodded with satisfaction. Her gnarled fingers reached into a pocket and withdrew a small white feather, no longer than a pinkie finger. With gentleness she placed the white feather on the forehead of the baby… right by the wealth of dark hair.

Looking up at the apprehensive parents and grandparents, she smiled. "For luck and peace. No war. Like our babies, tribal mothers use feather for peace." Shaking her head vigorously, she repeated, "Peace. No killing!"

Then she held up a hand as a signal that she had more to say. "Will be a surprise."

"What kind of surprise?" Ralph demanded.

With another shake of the head, she told him, "Cannot say." With that, she turned and was gone.

Grandpa Carl was first to speak. "I don't think I want a surprise about this baby."

Annette put a gentling hand on his arm. "She didn't say it was bad. We could remember that."

The parents said nothing then, but looked at each other, long and wonderingly. It was that look that they remembered when, at age eight, young Daniel Carpenter received a gift from a long departed third great grandfather. One also named Daniel. He had been a conscripted in the war of 1812 against the old country. There were marks of soil on some pages of the Book, indicating that it had also gone into the conflict that had finally and totally severed the umbilical of their new nation from its motherland.

A gift from the beyond time. A sword, a firearm of ancient design, and a worn copy of the Bible, very expensive at the time it would have been procured. The leather cover had been worn soft with use, and there was family writing on the inside fly leaf. Who could guess what such a gift would do for an eight-year-old boy? They'd have to wait and see.

Josie nodded and then shook her head. An observer of people, she was fascinated by the difference in last year's Level Four class and this year's. She had always encouraged the entire room to take advantage of a morning and afternoon recess for active play of some sort. This year's girls needed no encouragement.

Sometimes organizing games with the younger ones, other times competing among themselves, each group seemed to find its place. She had furnished only an area for play, and no play equipment had graced it. That was before Brad. Having leftover 2X10 planks of lumber, he got the idea of constructing a short stone pillar as a fulcrum for a seesaw.

Interestingly, it was the older girls who took to the larger seesaws, and occasionally one of the boys chose to stand in the center over the fulcrum, thereby directing the activity with his weight. First one foot… then the other.

Johnny Black seemed to be the one who enjoyed it most, and it was his pleasure to have Patricia on one side and Bridie on the other. Their screams, when they were bumped against the ground, were satisfyingly louder than most of the other girls, and their squeals excitingly shrill. The ground bump on one end caused the springy flip on the other end. The game seemed to be an attempt to 'buck' the top one off.

Later an A-frame was constructed with swings for the 5 year olds. The school yard turned out to be a drawing spot for children after school hours.

In addition, it became a meeting place for mothers and younger people, much like the blacksmith shop was the gathering place for the men.

The partnering of Patricia and Bridget came about in a natural way, as the mothers were close. Mrs. O'Grady was of the opinion that girls should be pushed toward an occupation that would keep them eating regularly if they found themselves widowed or abandoned. She was highly in favor of the school and planned for Bridie to attend as long as she could… however she did not trust it entirely.

Women's fingers were naturally made for needles, crochet hooks, and tatting spools thought Mrs. O'Grady. Therefore, her daughter was guided through all forms of joining and decorating fabric. Patricia, being available and a friend, was pushed into the same mold.

Together the girls had marched through straight stitch, lock stitch, and blanket stitch. They became familiar and expert at embroidery and were made to take out any stitch that was not perfect. Mrs. O'Grady was an exacting instructor, as was her friend, Mrs. O'Day. There was the decorative featherstitch that the girls called 'chicken tracts' and the cross-stitch that made fancy chair seats and decorative backs for sofa and chair sets.

The girls then were moved on to handkerchiefs. Ordinary turning under of the edges was not acceptable. The fine threads of the fabric were carefully drawn and the edges softly rolled, hiding the stitches inside the roll. This operation took a special, slender needle, and the girls must work over a table for the safety of the needle. Precious needles must not be dropped. Too hard to find.

These special needles were not only expensive, they were hard to get, having to be ordered from the Montgomery Ward Catalog. Then, there was another operation that required these special needles and that entailed the pulling out of several threads, leaving a ladder-like row across the sides of the hankie. The needles then made a dip, a loop and a twist, and, if done properly, created a decorative edge to the 'ladder'.

Both girls had small boned, dainty hands, and this made them more adept at the fancier side of needle work. As the fall of the year proceeded, Christmas began to enter into the conversation. Presents were, of course, handmade. Anyone with money could buy a gift, but it took time and skill to create one. That added to the value. Giving, as it were, a piece of their life… or more clearly, themselves.

One of the girls mentioned some items their teacher had, and hankies were among them. Bridget commented to her mother that Miss Josie actually had handkerchiefs that were turned under and not rolled.

Whereupon her mother suggested that the girls make a present for their teacher so she would see how well made these dainty necessities could be. Surely she would prefer them to what she had.

The first pair of hankies, one made by each girl, were decorated, one with a fancy, white on white, embroidered 'J' and the other with a ribbon bow design made in perfect satin stitch. Of the next pair, one of the hankies had a double row of the pulled thread ladders and the other a rose embroidered with two shades of pink thread. Of the third pair, one had a tatted edge in thread as delicate as the cobweb lacing one prairie flower to another, while its partner was edged with a triple row of cross-stitch, in white on white, perfectly spaced of course.

So impressed they were by their creations and basking in the praise of their mothers, they designed and created a gift box, folding each item to its best advantage.

Handkerchiefs were a valuable and essential part of a woman's (and girl's) attire. It must be kept delicate and spotless. Keeping it spotless and sweet smelling was a trick, if it was to be used for what it was created. However it might mean that one needed two of them, one for show and the other for actual use.

Josie, no stranger to expensive and well-made articles created for feminine use, opened her gift and stared speechlessly at what lay before her. The girls turned startled and concerned eyes toward each other. Did she not like the gift?

Spreading the six items on her desk, Josie told the girls, "You do not have any idea what these 6 handkerchiefs would cost in New York City. In the first place there would be nowhere to buy them. They are absolutely exquisite. They are much too beautiful to use."

A concerned response came. "Oh, no! You can use them. You just have rinse them out in soap suds and not on the rub board."

Miss Josie nodded. "Thank you, girls. I'll remember to do that. Where did you learn to sew so beautifully?"

Bridgit shrugged. "Our mamas made us learn. Both of us together." A prime example of Irish efficiency.

But when the girls left and walked toward their homes, they had a thought. If Miss Josie liked them so much, and they were so terribly easy to make, why not use them as gifts for other people? And, in addition, would anyone like them well enough to pay money to have them as their own gifts for someone else? Something to think on.

The girls were still very young, and at age eleven, a lot of other interests crowded in. There was a time, however, that they were looking at the fashion magazines that Miss Josie's New York City 'aunt' had sent. Their eyes centered on the hats… and then on each other.

Now, out on the prairie, a hat was a thing of necessity and an attractive one was a thing of value. Not everyone had hair that was tame and obedient, or had time to pamper it if they did, so the application of a hat to hurriedly arranged hair made an instant transformation.

Carrying the thought a bit farther, if one had a hat different from one worn by anyone else, it could be priceless, but where, on the toil-warn, wide-swept prairie, was one to get a hat that was unlike any other?

The two Irish girls were at that time in their final year at the Academy and were helping with the teaching. Both had made a few coins with the sale of handkerchiefs. They stared at each other with an instant and identical thought. Make hats!

It was obvious that someone had created the ones in the picture. Hats didn't just make themselves! Such was the confidence of these girls that if any one could make fancy hats, why couldn't they?

Learning to think from more than one position had been a goal of Josie's. Also, the non-acceptance of something, just because it was currently believed and accepted, was encouraged. As she looked around at the girls (a lot of boys had been held out of school as farm workers), she saw much that she was proud of.

Eve Adams who had been to school before her family came to the Territory, had been in Josie's Level Four class and had also, on her own, volunteered help in practice teaching. She wisely saw that was one way for her future to go and was undoubtedly encouraged by family.

At age twelve, already in possession of a Teaching Certificate, she now had no immediate place to go and spent an amount of time back at the Corners with her classmates, the McLaughlin sisters and the Irish girls. Eva thoroughly believed that just because something had always been done that way, there was no reason for it to continue. Perhaps some other way would be better… at least for her.

That was when she acquired the Lady's Saddle and forsook the use of the small, neat buggy. After consideration, she had decided that, weather permitting, she was just as well off on the back of the horse as on the seat of the buggy.

The Lady's Saddle was, she soon learned, an instrument of torture. It meant that one leg hung down at an odd angle to connect with the stirrup and the other leg was bent at the knee with the sole of the boot turned back and wrapped around the saddle horn. That way it could be tucked modestly under a full skirt. This left the whole body off balance and out of any control of either herself or the unfortunate horse. In addition, only one foot was in a stirrup

It was clear then, to see why most ladies preferred a seat in the buggy. Eva attracted a good deal of attention by riding side-saddle, as it was commonly called, up to the Corners to keep in touch with the rest of the world and pick up the mail, but all the time she was considering what could be done better. It took some serious thought.

True, the side-saddle gave her a wonderful freedom at the end of the trip to where she was going. All she had to do was loop her reins over the hitching rail that fronted every home or place of business. Just as the fellows did. She was free of the buggy and the fact that she would not have to leave her conveyance parked far from the doorstep. Just as the men who rode astride could do.

She had been taught, over the period of greater than a year, that there may be more than one way to accomplish the same thing, and some answers were better for some people than others. Now, if she just had to right kind of clothing… but, of course, she could not wear overalls. And she must somehow cover her legs properly. Her parents would insist on that.

Skirt. Very full skirt? Maybe divided in the back in some minor way such as men's overcoats? That would, naturally, leave her wearing a garment that was strange, after she lighted from the animal. Who would want a very, very full skirt with the fashions become slimmer and more fitting? And she couldn't, of course, ride with legs astride or her dress would be ABOVE her knees. Scandalous!

CHAPTER 9

Another thing about that tortuous side-saddle. With both feet over the same side and still looking straight ahead, the upper body was put in a perpetual twist that could catch a nerve in the vice of a twisted muscle causing unbearable pain. When riding along, however, the legs could be switched and put on the other side of the muscle twist, but the operation involved a serious breech of modesty. The leg had to be lifted up and over the horse's neck and lowered on the other side. Of course, the dress tail never lifted with it. Bare knees, and worse, were visible.

So, now what? Skirts! What to do with skirts! AH, AN IDEA! Two skirts! If she had an overskirt, it wouldn't matter if the skirt of the dress she wore hiked up to her thighs, as her modesty would be fully preserved under the overskirt. The overskirt would be gathered onto a band to be buttoned at the waist and flared out over the rump of the horse behind and up to the animal's neck in front.

This arrangement created a fan effect on either side of the horse, but both legs could be resting in the stirrups as they were intended to. (And as the fellow's did.) That gave the rider balance and also steadied the horse. Both reins would extend back from the cheeks of the horse to the hands of the rider instead of having one of the lines draped over the neck and through the animal's mane.

Problem solved. Eva was fortunate in the parents she was born to, because, after a total viewing from both sides, they agreed that it might work. It was either that, or providing her with a buggy that would put a bit of a strain on the family budget. There was no thought of making her stay at home all the time… that was the surest way to loose her to some fellow who promised freedom.

Word of mouth floated faster than dandelion puffs in the spring. What were the Adams thinking… letting their daughter ride astride a horse like that? Positively scandalous! That is, until they thought it through. What, after all, was immodest about it?

They saw her trot up to the Corners, rein in her animal and slip gracefully to the ground with all activity discretely accomplished under the cover of a black and white gingham checked skirt.

With both feet on the ground, the prim young lady carefully removed and folded the gingham over-skirt and placed it over the roomy, well made saddle of the type reserved only for men.

Eva said nothing, one way or the other. She knew what she wanted to do, and she did it… what did it matter if it had not been done before? What people thought of her was none of her business.

When she reached age fourteen, word was circulated that she possessed a Teaching Certificate and had a genuine, authentic New York education. And it was also circulated that the place her parents had bought was two and a half miles south of the Academy, and that was a rather far piece to travel if a parent wanted a child to be taught.

Reasoning together, they decided that the community did, however, have a 'teacher' living right here in their midst. Maybe a dollar and a half was a lot to pay, but if there was no alternative, it must be considered. Eva's parents were approached, and then Eva, herself. An agreement was reached.

Mama would permit her to have five students, but they must be only girls. She would not permit growing boys in her parlor using the satin covered sofa and loveseat. It had been a hard decision to even let girls use it and certainly no more than five at a time. Of those who were interested, Eva, herself, could choose the ones she wanted to teach, and her 'tuition' would be the standard $1.50 for the month. Both the girl and her parents knew what she was worth, and there would be no deviation from the rules.

It was at that time that the parents of the area got together and agreed to build a building, much on the order of the one at Shady Ridge.Eva's parents, however, being in control of the coveted 'teacher', directed that the building be placed on their property and near enough that they could see the building from their house. They were not going to have her where she might be caught in a sudden prairie fire with no help, or where there might be human invaders. Educated girls were a valued commodity to be protected as was any other thing of value.

It took the best part of two years, but the building went up, and Eva took on a full class. When a lonely soldier from the nearby outpost took a look at the widely fanned, black and white checked skirt covering her horse, it caught his eyes. Look at that! And just rest your eyes on the attractive young lady guiding the animal with one hand and holding a bright red parasol in the other, shading her complexion against the prairie sun.

The young man had joined the military because he thought it would help him make up his mind what to do with his life. Considering that his parents would not be able to help, financially, any effort to get ahead would have to be his. No matter. He could always be a soldier, and a good one.

One look at Eva on her horse, and all thoughts of a military career flew in many directions... much like a bounding coyote landing in a flock of crows. Any girl who would do what that one did was going to be his, no matter how long it took. It didn't take long. Eva's father found him a place behind a mule with his hands on a plow, and the former soldier thought life had treated him well. Possibly better than he deserved.

He could spend an hour here and there at the blacksmith shop at Carlile Corners and stand tall with pride. His beautiful wife was the TEACHER of the SCHOOL at Enterprise, down where the little river turned.

Even while plowing, a part of the book of Proverbs came to him. The last of chapter thirty-one was totally devoted to what would be the highest goal of a virtuous woman... and how her husband could 'stand proud at the city gates because of her.' He could remember his grandmother instilling these virtues into his sisters and that was how he recognized them when he saw them in Miss Eva.

Raymond Canfield spent the better part of a year hauling coal from over the ridge and naturally became acquainted with the care of animals. That was while he was watching the growth of his own pair of Clydesdale foals.

Looking back a few years, this was the way it had added up.

There had been talk that the owner would sell some of the animals, and Raymond lost no time in deciding they were something he should have. When his grandmother had left a sizeable inheritance to him and to his sisters, at that time he had not thought of a thing he wanted except a handful of cookies and someone to fish with.

Now, however, he had different ideas. "What do you think, Pa? Maybe one of those Clydesdales? I'm thinking I'll always want to drive a team...."

The idea was not strange to his father, as he had been expecting such a request. "What I'd do, son, is to see if you can buy a couple'a the young ones off him. That'd give you a chance to train 'em like you wanted 'em and keep driving the other fellow's animals while you do it, so's you'd get more experience."

Even better! Ralph Carpenter actually had two young Clydesdale fillies he'd let go. Consequently, part of a gold coin of Raymond's inheritance went one way across the rutted road and two animals came back.

There they were… black as a lump of coal and shiny as a spring minnow in a sunlit stream. Could anything ever be more beautiful? Yes, there could be. If he just had that other pair, he would loan them to his friends from school who hauled coal with him. Just as soon as he trained them.

Thinking ahead, if Johnny and Willie could get themselves a solid wagon, they could use his animals. The specially made coal wagons were heavy and the rough roads made difficult pulling for the animals. The drivers were forced to let them rest often and catch their breaths. Those Clydesdales, though… Like Ralph had said, they wouldn't win any race, but also, they didn't have to stop and rest.

The more he worked with the animals, the more certainly he knew what he would do. "Pa, there'd be enough money for another pair's those horses and a couple'a really solid wagons, wouldn't there? If I had that, I'd charge for my teams and wagons and for the fellow's time, and I'd own my own business. Could even haul other things, come a good chance. What'd ya think, Pa?"

Pa had already been thinking. "Son, by the time that other pair gets big enough, we should have them wagons located. Could have to bring 'em outta Oklahoma City. You got the money for that and still a bit left. I'm been thinkin' on what'd be best for you, but I ain't got onto it yet. I keep lookin' around a talkin'. Somethin'll turn up."

As a matter of fact, something did turn up. It took a while, but with pa's help, his son, Raymond, had made an excellent deal to furnish all four wagons and animals to the coal company. In this way he was responsible for all maintenance and animal care, and that was a big plus for the coal company. And coins for Raymond.

Stepping forward, again, it was clear that this was the way it should be. What followed later was just as amazing for a young man barely in his teens.

As it happened, a whole section of land came up for sale. It was located across from what was Matt Wilson's land where the old Carlile Corners shop was located.

After McLaughlin had bought that strip for his daughters, he was able to settle a Tack and Saddle shop there. The leather workers also repaired shoes.

Then a well driller came with his spudder wheel and donkeys to keep it moving. The tireless little gray animals walked in circles as the weights lifted and pounded through the prairie soil until they reached water.

The section north the available corner was bought by a miller. He had brought with him from the east, a variety of grinding wheels for every thing from chopped corn to fine flour. Cooks were glad to see him. Mill ground flour and cornmeal were so much better than they could grind at home.

Also, Ralph Carpenter and his traveling van had branched out from only cooking supplies to other notions such as tin cups, hammers, a few nails, and such. He had given his van a coat of black paint covering over his name and renaming it THE ROLLIN' FIVE AND DIME. The new letters were printed in red, outlined with gold. With a wife and son, he found reason to stay closer to home.

When not on the road, he arranged to park it near the COOKIE JAR and the new fabric store on wheels called HANKIES AND HATS. The HATS AND HANKIES van was build by Mr. O'Day for use of his daughter and her friend, Bridgit .

Heading for the blacksmith shop, Sam Canfield sighed, as he often did. The worse trouble with the Territory was the way it scattered family members when they had to make a living. But his Rosalie now had a job she loved… at least until she got married… and it was almost spittin' distance from his house, if the wind was right.

If it was the will of the Almighty that his son could be permanently located right in the center of what could be their town, what more could he want in life? In addition, there would be the pleasure of telling his wife. Thank You, God! As it turned out, it was apparently His will that Sam Canfield get his wish.

When Josie heard that Raymond would beowning the whole quarter section, thanks to the gift from his grandmother, she could only smile with pride. She had no doubt that Raymond would do well. She had seen him joke and tease as though school meant nothing, but he always had his math figures straight and plain. He didn't always work them out the way she would have, but he got the answers. He had created his own 'history of success' that gave him confidence. So important was that history of success.

Failures at an early age were damaging. Josie liked to tell herself that the two years she had taught Raymond had been of value to him and perhaps had pushed him along the way. And that could actually have been true.

Miss Josie had to wait for three years before she saw the sign over the new building across from the COOKIE JAR. A dignified sign that was painted in black and yellow.

CANFIELD GRADING AND EARTHWORKS. Custom Hauling and Dirt Work. It was worth the wait. Coal was still hauled, but a lot of other activity was found that suited the powerful horses.

Old Gray Eagle had since passed on to his reward, but Josie thought how it would have seemed to the old Kiowa elder to see his grandsons dressed in good clothes working at a job that paid every week. He would have been reassured that he had done the right thing when he shortened his own life by overwork and bargaining for his grandson's education. It would have made the old man proud.

Tray Cullen, younger brother to Brad and Janine Cullen had flown through the years at Prairie Academy, easily absorbing what it had to offer. Reading and Grammar excellent and numbers without error. Then... what was to be done with him and his quick-silver movements?

There was a time that his big brother Brad tried to help, but rock laying was just not for him.

For Digby, every other row of stone must be checked to the plumb line, and the bob at the end of the line must not deviate a fraction of an inch. It was not an easy thing to do, as Brad had learned, because individual stones were so irregular. Certainly unsuitable for Tray.

So, on to blacksmithing. Tray was excited at first, but if the melting fire refused to obey his efforts and a shower of sparks from an off-center blow shattered against his bare arm, that was enough for him.

The resulting burn irritated him immensely. Also, the equipment was not the total problem. From ages five, he and Lily had become a unit, and if there was anything not appreciated in a smithy shop, it was a female... not even it she was only eleven. Tray was not interested in being separated from her. At least, all day long.

Next he tried coal hauling. He learned well, and he was capable. In addition, Lily's presence did not deter his ability. The horses, however, could not keep up with his insistence that he outdo every speed record. Coal was heavy, and trips took a while. So what was next?

Old Gaither, his father, finally set his foot down and demanded his son learn the skill of farming until he got his head together for something else. After all, he ate food the same as everyone else, so he could help grow it. Lily helped.

A season in the gardens and fields had begun to get the lad's attention. Heat of the sun and the effort at the upper end of a hoe handle helped. Big brother and father kept him reined in and productive for two whole years to let him think of something he could slow down enough to learn

It was Raymond Canfield who finally hit on the answer. Tray was hired on and was given the position of what might be called a circuit rider representative, or possibly, salesman at large. On a good saddle horse, he would travel the section line roads scouting for places where it seemed the householder might use the services of the dirt slip or the drag-line to dig ponds and cellars or such. He was paid by the jobs he sold, so he learned selling and dealing with strangers, and became almost instantly successful.

He attached a light surrey behind the horse to provide shade for himself and Lily, and set out. Having Lily along gave a semblance of stability to his youth... and his challenged experience with math was a plus. He quickly learned to estimate the hours required for the job, total cost to the customer and often suggestions for the use of the soil removed. His success was such that it was said that he could sell a snowball to an Eskimo. Possibly he could have, but there were no Eskimos in the territory at that time.

When he secured a job, he would then lead Johnny Black and Willie Elk to the site and introduced them. He knew about when the job would be done and would be there to collect the money. Finally, a job was found that suited his talents and Raymond considered him well worth his wage. In advertisement, if nothing else. Young Tray's personality seemed to precede him.

Lily rode beside him clicking her knitting needles or darning socks… whatever needed doing that could be done on the move.

Josie was again pregnant. If she was distressed by the fact, though she had four sons under four years old, no one knew it. Digby seemed to be a natural with small boys, and he made a wonderful grandfather, even though his strength was failing.

In her natural habit of acceptance, Josie assumed another son (or possibly two), would be forthcoming and went about her abbreviated version of teaching, working only with the upper level. Now that her brother and cousin were preparing to leave for New York City to the boarding school, she was easing away from Prairie Academy, considering that she left it in better hands. Likely she had.

When the pregnancy reached its end, the community may have registered a sigh of relief when Josie produced a single, six and a half pound girl. Who could fault her under the circumstances, when she named the child Merytaten Francesca Angelique Evangeline Cullen. Possibly she realized this might be her only chance to use her favorite names. If so, she would have been right, because that child became her only girl.

Brad, when faced with the array of his daughter's names, ended his confusion by calling the child "Mutt" which stuck like a coat of paint onto the fast-moving girl.

As Josie gave up teaching, thereby having more free time, she would need a replacement activity and perhaps expand her social life. It seemed natural that she would move toward Annette Owens, as a 'newcomer', and Carlotta, former student, due to the fact of their sons being of a similar age.

Possibly the girl that Josie finally produced, actually needed the many names she was given, to fortify her in dealing with five boys… her four brothers and little Daniel Carpenter, all six of the children under seven years.

The problem of book education in the Territory still existed in spite of Josie's efforts. Even three miles away from an existing school, if indeed one actually existed, was a bit of a distance for very young children to travel in this new, raw land. Homesteaders seldom had the time to transport their youngsters to and from, and as they became older, the children were drafted into other duties.

The residents of Carlile Corners had opportunities to remember how fortunate they had been to have Josie deposited right there in their midst. Word circulated on the prairie grapevine about the difficulty of the teacher problem. The residents of the separate communities could only be sympathetic with each other. Teachers had a choice, and they mostly chose town schools.

The plight of nearby Shady Ridge was no exception.

This very problem was discussed in the community of Shady Ridge only three miles west from Carlile Corners. It was discussed over the breakfast table, over the cow pasture fence, over coffee in the afternoons, and everywhere that three or more families convened. It hadn't seemed so bad for a while, there being problems of a much greater sort to attend to… like a roof over the head and food to eat.

Then, over the last five years or so, it became embarrassingly obvious that something had to be done to educate their children, and there had been a couple of exploratory journeys to Oklahoma City with strictly negative results.

Oklahoma City had grown too fast and had too many problems lined up ahead of this minor 'tempest in a teapot' happening at a prairie crossroads. But the parents who lived in the 'teapot' thought the tempest rather large.

The thing was, children from eight to ten had no direction. Some of those a bit older could read (passably) and figure numbers (after a fashion) but those younger were totally unexposed, except for sketchy attempts from parents or older siblings. And the fact of the matter was, there was hardly time even for the 'sketchy attempts".

With squared chin and firm lips, a decision must be made. A teacher must be procured and what good teacher would want to come to a place like Shady Ridge? Indeed!

It had become year 1897 already, and it was time for something to be done, for goodness sake! It was clearly time to manage something for the children, or they would grow up totally ignorant of book learning.

The concerned adults had circulated, on the gossip grapevine, the need for a meeting and had offered a convening date. The Browns, living as they did on the community crossroads, took the lead. They had four children (now going on five), and the decision had become paramount in their minds. Chiming in with them were the Colbys, the Martins, the Camerons, and the McGregors (who, themselves had four to contribute).

Two of the men made the trip to the Oklahoma Board of Education and had come back with these precepts:

Yes, Shady Ridge qualified by area and population for an eventual schoolroom, actually a one-room school.

And, yes, along with several hundred other crossroads, they could be put on a waiting list.

Yes, they would eventually get a teacher.

And, yes, the current children might be grown when that happened.

For, after all, the Board could not conscript a teacher, in the way they could a soldier, and send her (or him) out into the hinterland. Teachers must qualify, and those who did were snapped up by the cities and even then, classes were held anywhere seats could be arranged.

The 'scouts' had returned and sadly reported that all the "yes" answers they had received added up to a resounding "no."

John William Brown made the first move. "I got a flat piece's ground out past the garden, and I'll be puttin' up a two roomed cabin, big enough for a starter school. Gonna put it on my own paid-for land, with my material and my labor, and I plan to furnish the food and water for the teacher. That oughtta be some inducement, bein' that the teacher wouldn't have to board, week about, with families who have barely room for themselves."

Next was the question, "How much is that teacher gonna be paid by the Board?"

Answered. "Right now the salary is $376.00 a year."

"What kind of a teacher would we get for that kinda money?"

"Whoever was willin'. It'd be someone likely turned down by a city school board, if they was to be able to get someone better. She, or he, could be anywhere from 14 years old to still breathin'. They's places that are letting a 11-year-old teach 'cause they can't do better. They call 'em 'teachers in training'. Whatever that is."

"Teacher in trainin'? What'd that be?"

"I was expectin' we'd get one already trained. Would that mean the youngens would be trainin' the teacher? Don't make a lotta sense."

"So then what'll we do?"

A lengthy silence occurred, giving Elsa Brown a chance to refill the mugs with steaming coffee... fragrant, expensive and fresh from the pot.

Old Grandma Catlin, with her interest centered on the lump within her granddaughter's stomach, spoke up. "Could be my Miranda could see to her first youngen herself, but we all know there ain't no time after that for book learnin' to be got. A teacher has got to be had. So here's what I got to say. You all know old Gray Eagle, the tribal elder down the road?

"Well, he ain't been sittin' by the road with his pipe no more. He swapped haulin' time with his two grandsons, so they could go over to the Corners to that school under the rock ledge. The old man brags to whoever'll listen that his grandsons are gettin' a New York education, same as his sister's granddaughter, little White Flower. They call her Lily, now." There were nodding heads.

"I heard that, too. Word is, them boys' Pa's wanted 'em to freight coal from over the ridge to Argyle for money. Old Gray Eagle said he'd make a trip every day that he could get outta bed and that the wagon was up to the trip. He'd turn that money over to his sons for them boys to get a year in at the school. He's figgerin' one year'll get 'em up to where Lily is in schoolin'. Said he thought after he done that, his sons were gonna be so proud'a their boys, they'd figger a way for another year."

"That's interestin'. Don't much get past old Gray Eagle's wrinkles."

"That there school under the ledge, it's not a Oklahoma school, is it?"

"Nope, but they got 'em a teacher that was trained in New York, and she's knowin' the latest ways. Word is she's got more education than even a man needs. Parents have been payin' her with help, but they's talk that next year'll cost $1.50 a month for each kid. The New York teacher plans to back off and let them four girls teach while she's there to watch."

"Yeah, and the littlest ones in the school are already being taught by them that's been trained. I'm hearin' nothin' but good. I heard that little Lily Gray Owl reads like a ten year old, and she ain't had but a year. Course, that could be stretchin' it, but I heard it for a fact. Value goin' up like it is, the Corners is plannin' on raisin' themselves to $2.00 a month, if'n that's what it'll take to keep one'a them New York trained girls. They're comin' on a good age."

"Well, can we get one? I can say $1.50 a month'd strain me a bit, but I'd manage. You speck we could figger a way to get one'a them girls?"

"Wouldn't know till we try. We could count noses'a them that's interested right now, and have ourselves another meetin' or two."

"How long you thinkin' it'd take to get the buildin' up, John?"

"Well, it's January now. Oughtta be in business by next September. We'll be that long getting' 'er lined out, even if we can get our name in for a girl. Word gets out there's a teacher to be had, there'll be 20 offers poured in on her."

"You got that right! I got them three girls at my house, and I can see right now they gotta have a chance at everythin' it takes to get that Certificate. Out here in the territory, that'd be one way to keep our girls and them not being called on to marry the first fellow that looks at 'em… just to have a thing to do. I got no loose money a'layin' around, but I'd be up for as much as $2.00 a month it that'd assure a teacher that'd stay, and her not be tempted by a better offer."

Will Martin's jaw was set, and his lips pressed into a firm line of concern. He'd manage somehow for $8.00 a month, and he'd start right now figuring out how it could be done. Maybe hauling coal like Old Gray Eagle. Part time'd do it… likely.

John William Brown motioned Elsie to leave the cookies a minute and join the group. "We're gonna pretend this is like a jury box and see where everybody stands. That'll tell us what we got goin' for us by way'a makin' a offer. I would like a count'a hands on them that could come up with $2.00 a month for each kid, startin' next September."

Several hands went up rapidly and others more slowly as they considered the cost… also the worth. Harlin McGregor was last to ease his calloused palm higher than his shoulder. His Alexander was ten and could drive a team like he was born to it. Harlin rather hoped to have the youngen's help next year, but the boy was his pride and joy and deserved the chance to learn something after missing out for three years.

"Elsie, you been lookin' around? I'm figgerin' that was pretty much the lot of us." With an assent from his wife, she was relieved of her counting duty and permitted to go and bring in the refreshments.

"I'm thinkin' that gives us somethin' to go on. Nuther thing I thinkin', if we was to send over a couple'a our womenfolk, stead'a calloused old men, we could talk with that New York teacher and get some idea…."

"Yeah, and when would it be? Maybe April… or so?"

"Dependin' on when the cabin gets done. I'd think it oughtta be ready when we make a move. We'd want 'er to know we mean business, and no empty promises. And I was plannin' to make that cabin good sized for twenty youngens and maybe more."

Short silence as the men glanced at each other. "How about this," began J.D.Colby. "I'd be willin' to put in a day'a work, or even two if we can get enough others to get that cabin on up."

Bruce Grant cleared his throat. "Count me in. And I got me a wagon not in use and a sixteen year old that'd be fonchin' at the bit to make the trip down to the saw mill to pick up the buildin' material. Should make it in two or three trips, wouldn't ya think?"

John William Brown, figuring he had put enough pressure on his neighbors, accepted a cookie and tried to turn the conversation to the weather. It wouldn't turn.

From the back of the room. "If this here works, that'll shore be a load off my mind."

"I like the idea'a the teacher a'havin' a permanent place and families not havin' to board her fer a week or two. That's worth payin' for. I'd be willin' to send food, if that'd help."

Annabelle Martin spoke up. "One young woman eatin', that'd not even be a mouthfull missed at my house. There's a nuther thing, though, ladies. One girl and 20 or 25 youngens, you can picture that accidents happen, and if there was one of us to sit with her every day, takin' turn about, it'd be about every three or four weeks each for us to have to give up a day. We'd be there if one of 'em got hurt, or sick. We could even read to little 'ens and take 'em outside so's to let her give her attention to the big 'ens on things we may not know about." More nods.

"I could come. I always got darnin' to be done, and I can do that with my eyes shut."

Old Grandma Catlin grinned, toothlessly. "Our youngen ain't gonna be ready for learnin' for a while, but I'd come. Most days I feel right spry, but knittin' socks and mittens is about all I'm good for. Sittin' with youngens is a thing I could do."

Elsie Brown sighed with relief. That had been worrying her, and she knew it had to be brought up sooner or later. Casting no reflection on the ability of the teacher, accidents did happen with children… that was just the way of it. Annabelle could always be counted on to bring up problems that had to have answers.

By the last of March, the building material was on site and being shaped into a large cabin that literally grew up out of the prairie soil fertilized by the sweat of concerned fathers. It turned out to be 40 feet long and 20 feet wide, with a 20 by 30 foot classroom in the front. A huge potbelly stove ruled the enter of the room and was surrounded by work tables and benches.

The last ten feet contained a tiny bedroom with a closet, and there was a miniature kitchen with a wall cupboard and tiny stove to provide heat when needed and food if she chose not to eat with the family.

A working party had met on a sunny Saturday afternoon to finish the last of the shingles. The men had cut cedar logs 14 inches long and brought their hatchets to split shingles for the roof. Shingles went fast but gaiety went even faster. Relief was great that a thing they had dreaded had been taken care of. A job done. A necessity met. That counted big out on the prairie territory.

A small pig turned on the backyard spit manned by small boys. Over the coals, precious potatoes roasted in a pit, and hot bread came out of the ovens. Sawhorses in the yard became tables, children shouted and played, and confidence was high. It didn't take much to make a party.

All except for Annabelle Martin and Elsie Brown. It fell upon them to make the case to the girl who lived about three and a half miles to the east and who was now carefully sewing the dresses she would need.

The girl with the busy needle had learned from Mrs. O'Grady how to lay her patterns… store-bought patterns, they were. She had decided that she should have ten dresses, attractive and serviceable, ones that she could 'suds out' herself in a tub of lye soap bubbles (along with her unmentionables that certainly could not be permitted in the Brown family washtub).

The girl was thirteen, but was due a birthday this summer and was getting taller by the day. At Mrs. O'Grady's suggestion, she allowed for the expansion in certain areas of her physic that would happen in the next couple of years. After all, she hadn't gotten her full growth yet. Tiny, running stitches and solid tie-back knots held the gathers and pleats, and they attached the lace and the buttons firmly in place.

The hem of the ruffle was exactly half way between her knee and her ankle, proper for her age, but there was a lengthening tuck provided. She was sure to grow a bit more. The pulling of a single thread would lower the skirt length a full three inches.

Francine Canfield had treated this year of sewing as she had treated her homework and her lesson plans. She had always prepared carefully and finished ahead of the time required. Being unprepared for any part of her life was a thing not to be considered.

Whatever turn her life took, she would now have attractive dresses for any occasion, and they would be constructed according to New York styles from excellent, imported fabric and New York patterns. They were sure to give her confidence.

She was currently working on dress number six, but there were underclothes yet to construct. She had a whole bolt of fine lawn fabric, light enough for comfort and heavy enough for modesty. A whole bolt would make a lot of pettislips and unmentionables, but that was something she would always need. Best have what it took to make them.

It would take time, but no matter… she would be ready in time. By the time she needed them, everything would be in place and the last thread knot secured.

Josie was relaxing at her desk by the window when there was the crunching of gravel caused by a vehicle entering the yard. A glance toward the driver showed a young boy, ten, maybe? He held the reins guiding the horse pulling a buggy. Two ladies sat in the back of the conveyance.

Josie nodded and smiled. New student, no doubt. Well, they'd have to come back when either Carmelita or Rosalie was here. They would be making the decisions for new students next year. Not her.

A tap at the door. Josie met them with a smile.

Elsie Brown, being a few months older, took the lead. "I'm Elsie Brown, and this is Annabelle Martin. We're thinkin' you might be the Miss Wheeler from New York? The thing is, we're not really sure where to start, but we got a question."

Josie thought she would help. "You're bringing a new student?"

"Uh… er… no, Miss. What we was needin' was to talk about a teacher. We…."

Annabelle picked up the next thought. "It was really Old Gray Eagle that everybody around here knows. He says that he had two grandsons comin' here, and you was trainin' teachers to do the teachin'… we thought…."

Josie took over at the pause. "Well, we have two of our students who have completed their Certification. The boy will be in their class."

Annabelle frowned with puzzlement, then shook her head. "The boy? Oh, that's my boy. We live in Shady Ridge, and we're needin' a teacher'a our own in the worst way. We found out we was at the foot of the line for getting' one. After we listened to Gray Eagle, we had reasons to think that we maybe didn't want to get in line over at the Education Board. Could be somethin' better right here." She hesitated.

Elsie again. "A lot of us got together, and we want somethin' better, and we weren't in the notion to wait for years. We got ourselves rounded up and built a schoolroom with livin' place for the teacher, so's she'd not have to board around. She could eat meals with my bunch or cook on a stove in her cabin. We was thinkin' that'd be a help to get someone."

Then Annabelle, "But we wasn't wantin' just anyone. We wasn't wantin' one that'd stay a year or two till somethin' better came along and then leave us. You said you got only two teachers, and they already have a place. We was hearin' there was four girls that was trained. Them other two… are they… placed…?"

Hmmm, thought Josie. Most interesting that the news of her girls got around, but no real surprise. "To be honest, ladies, there's one of them with some deep family sorrows, and she will not be able to take a position for a time, yet. Two, as I said, are working here. There is another one, though."

Eyes brightened for both ladies. "What'd be our chances'a gettin' her? Can you tell us anything about her?"

"I can, but I can't give an answer. That would be for her folks and Francine, herself, to decide. Miss Francine Canfield will be 14 before September, and she certified with a very high score, as did all the girls. She has spent a year assisting and being trained in teaching methods. She is a young lady who knows her mind and seems to have no trouble with discipline of young boys. She conducts herself like a lady, even at her young age, and would be a good example to your young girls."

The Shady Ridge ladies cast an excited glance toward each other. "That sounds really good! Do you know how much she'd need to take the job with 20 students ten years old and under? Maybe 22 or 23 of 'em, actually."

"Ladies, I can't say what she would do, but Francine knows what she's worth, and she has worked very hard to qualify. There may be one thing in your favor, though. She would like having a living place of her own. She and her siblings have their own rooms at their parent's house. I don't think she is particular about food and may like the option to eat with your family. Here's another thing that may mean something with her family. They will want to advise her, due to her age, and would, of course, prefer her to be close, and not in Argyle or farther away, and she will be expected to return home for the summer months. Of that, I'm sure."

Josie liked these ladies. They seemed to have no allusions that a teacher would put up with whatever they tossed at her. They obviously realized the scarcity of competent teachers. Certified teachers were valuable and for them, one was likely years away. The current children would then be grown and gone. These thoughts marched themselves through Miss Josie's mind as she watched the concerned faces before her.

Interesting that the best compliments laid on her student had come from Old Gray Eagle. Well, he would be in a position to know.

The two boys, grandsons of his, had spent two months at the school this year, and Mrs. Gray Owl had been specific that her brother wanted the boys to learn to 'speak like the newcomers, read their book words and count their own wages when they got a job'. They had pretty much learned that already, and the school now had the promise of their attendance for another year.

Shady Ridge could, actually, be a very good start for Francine and maybe a place where she would like to stay for years. But as to her wages?

"You mentioned the pay for her. Have you discussed what it might be?"

A deep sigh from both ladies. "We have. It'd not be what we'd like, you see, but some of us have several children, and I'm working on my fifth. So we was thinkin' $2.00 a month for each student, and they'd bring a bushel'a cow pats each month and more if they was needed. We was hopin', with the cabin just for her, and all, she'd be thinkin' that was enough to plan on stayin' for a while. One of the Pa's is hopin' his three girls can be taught by a New York teacher long enough so's to Certify… so's they'd have a choice whether to marry, and they'd still be able to take care'a themselves if they was alone."

Annabelle was nodding. "And they's another thing we'd be sayin'. We read that the Board of Education won't let the women teachers be courted or marry, and that'd not bother us a mite."

She continued with a sly grin, "Fact is, if she was to marry a local boy, there'd likely be more reason to stay right there. With youngens comin' on like they are, we'll always need a teacher."

Now it was Josie's turn to smile. "Well, you have a point there. Francine is very attractive and is going to be a beautiful girl in a few years. She'll turn more than a few heads. It might be well if you can get her. Her sister is one of those who is teaching here, and both Canfield sisters are very pretty girls. Also, very serious and talented.

"I hope I haven't said too much because, as I said, I have nothing to do with her decision. I only know that she is highly capable, and if she chooses to take the job, she will do very well. I could say without a hesitation, that the Pa with the three girls could count on his daughters passing the Certification Test with Miss Francine as a teacher. I might add, also, that the girls would earn their grades by hard work, the way Miss Francine did."

CHAPTER 10

With a nod to each other, the two ladies had only to convince the new teacher and her parents, and perhaps they could do that today.

It was later that day that Sam Canfield watched his life's mate as she struggled with her thoughts. Maybe he could help her. Ease her thinking, so to speak.

"Julie? Let's talk on this. I don't like it tearin' you to pieces this a'way."

Julie Canfield turned a helpless look at Sam, her sharer of joys and disappointments… her rock of stability. With a sigh, she picked up the egg-gathering basket and headed to the henhouse… and here it was, still the middle of the day. Much too early to be thinking on gathering eggs. It'd not be likely that talking would help her too much.

But Sam followed her anyway, right into the alien territory of nests and floating feathers. Real men did not tend to chickens. He ducked through the low doorway into the musty smell of manure and nest straw.

"Julie, honey, you gotta talk so's I can give them ladies a good answer that we both agree on."

Julie's graying head lowered as she reached under the hen. Nothing yet. Straightening, she slumped her shoulders with mental weariness. "I wasn't thinkin' it'd be yet. Her bein' only 13 oughtta give us another year."

Sam braced his shoulders. It wasn't easy for him either, but he had to do what was right for his daughter. "Julie, honey, our little girl will be 14 in ten days. I counted 'em. I know it hadn't oughtta be so soon, but it is. The fact is, we was knowin' when our two little girls was born that they'd be lost to someone and movin' somewhere else when they married. Sometimes sons are lost, but the girls… most always. The Good Lord was kind and let Rosalie be contented to be a half a mile down the road. If it works out, she could stay around here a long time."

He paused, and swallowed the lump in his throat. He had to get these words just right. There were things that were hard to prepare for, but this one had suddenly dropped in their lap, and it must be settled.

Julie leaned against the nest boxes and turned her face to him.

He continued, "This here that happened, it was a bit more sudden-like than we might'a wanted but the fact is, that girl was gonna go somewhere. She weren't settin' in the house hooked onto that needle and thread for nothin', and she spent 2 years'a study and a whole year'a practice. She's comin' up on the age expected for a beginnin' teacher. If we take the idea in hand and look at it, what was we expectin' if it wasn't for her to go to where we let 'er be trained for?"

Another sigh from the disturbed woman as she wrestled with her thought. "What you're sayin', it's all true, but…."

"I know. But think on it from this angle. Shady Ridge, that's a heap sight closer'n Oklahoma City… or even Argyle, for that matter. And here's the thing that'll comfort us… those ladies from Shady Ridge said the community'd be happy if she was to marry someone close and maybe stay. That'd never happen if she was to take a job with the Board of Learnin' over in the city.

"If she went to Shady Ridge, she'd pretty nearly be the boss of herself, and you know how our Francine is. She knows how she wants things to be, and she's mostly right in her idea. Seems like them folks want her so bad they'd do almost anything for her, and they come here beggin', hat in hand you might say. Think on that… beggin' for our little girl to come do for them what she wants to do already?

"Now, you know we gotta agree on this, and if this all goes against you, I'll say 'no'. You know that. But here comes what'd happen next. We could keep 'er from goin' there, just three miles down the road, and when she takes a notion, she'll go somewhere, and it may be 20 miles or maybe 50 miles."

Julie stood a little straighter, and Sam knew he was on the right track.

"Nuther thing. When there's a baby, you'll get a chance to see the little'n grow up. Chances are. I'm thinkin' if she wants to keep on teachin', she'll be needin' help with the youngen when sneezin' and a runny nose happens, and what'll she do if she's 20 miles away? And measles… the little fellow'd have to go somewhere that wasn't a room full'a other youngens. We're sure to be needed."

Julie turned and took two eggs from a nest box that had no hen at work. Sam knew it was time to stop. Being needed was the most important of his statements, and he had said it.

"Think I'll run down to the Corner. Might stop in on old Gaither and see how his son is makin' on. That old man loves to talk about his son. You needin' a thing I can pick up for you when I check on the mail hook?"

"I reckon not. You get on out then, but get yerself back for milkin' 'afore supper. I'll be needin' some for the gravy."

Sam nodded and ducked back out the door of the henhouse. Julie stepped to the door and called after him, "I'm thinkin' on somethin' we gotta do tomorrow. We're gonna go down to the Academy and speak to Miss Josie. That'd set my mind to ease, one way or the other."

Sam nodded and continued toward the road to the blacksmith shop. The fellows living at the Corners had long needed a place like the blacksmith shop. It made a wonderful escape… a refuge for men, and it was also a natural gathering place for news from all directions. Old Gaither Cullen was quite a one for keeping up the gossip. Worser'n an old woman… and Sam chuckled.

The next afternoon the students had left for the day, and Josie had settled back to do a bit of thinking. There was so much to think about. For everyone. Sam and Julie Canfield would do the most of it, and it wouldn't be easy. This kind of thinking was scary.

She was not surprised to see the man and woman as they walked toward the schoolroom. In actual fact, she had expected them and opened the door as they approached.

The woman began, "Fine weather we're havin', ain't we?" That was the way it started. Weather first and business later. It was a way of saying that the visit did not entail an emergency.

"Yes, indeed. Lovely. Won't you come in?"

As they stepped through the door, Josie was handed a cloth sack. "Had a few extra eggs. Hoped you could find'a use for 'em."

Josie took the gift with thanks, knowing it was given as an opening for conversation.

Sam took over. "Had us a visit from the folks from over west. Heard words that sort'a took us back a spell with surprise. Didn't hardly expect that…."

At that juncture, Julie could wait no longer. "We just got us one question, and we knowd you'd tell us the truth. It's about our Francine. Now we know you got 'er ready to do her job, but you gotta say this to us. Would you think she was grown up enough to know what to do with a room full'a youngens? The way she is, it wouldn't do for her to come up against a thing she couldn't handle, and her bein' so young. Just tell us… fer sure… what you think?"

Two pairs of eyes were trained on Josie's face… eyes that looked at her from under a beginning network of fine lines from work in the sun, a lifetime of worries, and now a concern for their daughter. Josie thought a moment.

"Mr. and Mrs. Canfield, if Francine was my own daughter, or sister, I wouldn't give one thought to Francine having a situation she could not handle. If you decide that it would be the right thing for her, you might be making a very good decision. I would safely say that I consider your Francine is as ready as any 14 year old, and much more ready than most. She has had two whole years of hard work with her books and another year working with children as a teacher. She passed her Certification with high marks. I have watched her very closely, and there was never a time that she had trouble and didn't know what to do or a time that she was not able to teach what was required.

"As far as her safety is concerned, that community wants her so badly that they would never, never let a thing happen to her. She would be living within sight of the Brown's house and encouraged to eat her meals with them. She would have her own permanent room, and that would be something that Francine would value. I'm sure you could never find a place that was more suited to Francine, and I know that if you were ever needed, their fastest horse and rider would let you know."

She ended with a reassuring smile and received satisfied nods from her visitors.

"One more thing I might say. If you have fully decided to let her go, and if she wants to go, it would be kind of you to let the people at Shady Ridge know about it right away. Here's the reason. They are GOING to start school in September even if they have to use mothers and older children at the beginning. They will be looking for a teacher until they find someone, but Francine is clearly the one they want. So if you could let them know...?"

And that is the way it happened to cause Francine to shine up her worn shoes and put on dress number three. She had just completed dress number seven and was looking forward to the next three outfits, which she had decided would be skirt and shirtwaist combinations.

Mrs. O'Grady had encouraged her in that direction, explaining that skirts grew with young girls as they became taller and that shirtwaists could expand in selected areas. When that could not be done, they could be replaced much more easily than an entire dress. Francine had listened carefully, and within her own mind could see that styles for shirtwaists changed more often, as well.

So it was that she and her parents traveled three miles to the west for a visit. They were treated to coffee and cake and given a tour of the new schoolhouse in Shady Ridge. It was a cheerful thing to see the freshly painted sign bravely stating: SHADY RIDGE ACADEMY.

The almost 14-year-old girl glanced about the classroom, still smelling of new lumber, checked out the size of the closet and examined the small stove.

Annabelle Martin offered, "Now, Miss Francine, we can put in a bed...?"

Whereupon Francine reassured them. "No, thank you. I'll bring the one from my room. What about school books?"

Mrs. Elsie Brown hesitantly fielded that question. Money for lesson books and a library was in scarce (to non-existent) supply. "Well, that was a thing we haven't decided on. We was not knowin' what to get, actually. We was thinkin' you'd be able to help us decide on that? Maybe on what we'd need to start up with?"

Francine nodded, agreeable. "That's all right. Don't bother about the books. I'll bring them when I come to move in. Next August." She had hoped that would be the way of it and was supremely relieved.

The Canfields left two happy ladies with wide grins. Success! Wasn't it wonderful, after all their work and talking and planning? Once and a while things worked out, and thanks be given to the One above for His favors.

On the journey home, Francine's mother hesitantly asked, "Honey, how're you feelin' now?"

After her usual thoughtful hesitation, she calmly answered, "Pretty much how I expected to feel. I know I'm ready."

Such confidence was scary to her mother. She sounded so much like Sam had when he had announced that he planned to make a run for property in the Territory. She had asked him, "Do you think you can?"

The answer was, "I feel very confident. I know I'm ready." And he had been.

The last week in August, Francine loaded her books aboard her 'lady's buggy' and hitched her somewhat shaggy Conamara Irish horse between the doubletrees. She had insisted that Jeff teach her how to keep the animal gentled while she worked the bridal and harness. She could not bear to be dependent on help from others if there was any to avoid it. A sign of weakness for sure.

She stopped in front of the new building, and a thrill of excitement passed over her... head to feet. Spread above the door was a banner, WELCOME MISS FRANCINE. Following the excitement was a comfortable feeling of coming home to a place where she had never lived.

She used her key in the Yale lock and entered the empty room. Echos. Smells of new lumbar. Shiny windows. Bookcases along each of the sidewalls. Tables with attached benches like at Miss Josie's school. Perfect.

Hers. She nodded to herself. "I feel very confident. I know I'm ready to do this alone."

A NOTE FROM THE NARRATOR

(Researched and written by historian Merytaten Franchesca Angelique Evangeline Cullen Carpenter)

I know a lot was said about the Teacher's Certification Test, and there may be a few who might wonder what it consisted of. I know the horrible requirements of a Board of Education teacher have already been shared, but I have more.

Miss Josie made certain she kept a copy, just because she is careful about everything concerning education. Oklahoma being still a Territory, the actual test used was the one from Kansas. Here is a copy.

EXAMINATION GRADUATION QUESTIONS OF SALINE COUNTY KANSAS April 13, 1858. J.W. Armstrong, County Superintendent

READING AND PENMANSHIP: The examination will be oral, and the Penmanship of Applicants will be graded from the manuscript.

GRAMMAR (Time, one hour)

1. Give nine rules for the use of Capital Letters.

2. Name the Parts of Speech and define those that have no modifications.

3. Define Verse, Stanza, and Paragraph.

4. What are the Principal Parts of a verb? Give Principal Parts of do, lie, lay, and run.

5. Define Case, illustrate each Case.

6. What is Punctuation? Give rules for principal marks of Punctuation.

7. – 10. Write a composition of about 150 words and show therein that you understand the practical use of the rules of grammar.

ARITHMATIC (1.25 hours)

1. Name and define the Fundamental Rules of Arithmetic.

2. A wagon box is 2 ft deep, 10 ft long, and 3 ft wide. How many bushels of wheat will it hold?

3. If a load of wheat weighs 3942 lbs, what is it worth at 50 cts/bushel, deduction 1050 lbs for tare?

4. District No. 33 had a valuation of $35,000. What is the necessary levy to carry on a school seven months at $50.00 per month and have $104 for incidentals?

5. Find cost of 6720 lbs coal at $6.00 per ton.

6. Find the interest on $512.60 for 8 months and 18 days at 7 percent.

7. What is the cost of 40 boards 12 inches wide and 19 feet long at $20.00 per meter?

8. Find bank discount on $300 for 90 days (no grace) at 10 percent.

9. What is the cost of a square farm at $15 per acre, the distance around which is 640 rods?

10. Write a Bank Check, a Promissory Note, and a Receipt.

U. S. HISTORY (45 minutes)

1. Give the epochs into which U. S. history is divided.

2. Give an account of the discovery of America by Columbus.

3. Relate the causes and results of the Revolutionary War.

4. Show the territorial growth of the United States.

5. Tell what you can of the history of (Oklahoma Territory).

6. Describe three of the most prominent battles of the Rebellion.

7. Who were the following: Morse, Whitney, Fulton, Bell, Lincoln, Pen, and Howe?

8. Name events connected with the following dates: 1607, 1620, 1800, 1849, 1865.

ORTHOGRAPHY (Time, one hour)

1. What is meant by the following: Alphabet, phonetic, orthography, etymology, and syllabication?

2. What are elementary sounds? How classified?

3. What are the following, and give examples of each: Trigraph, subvocals, diphthong, cognate letters, linguals?

4. Give four substitutes for the carat 'u'.

5. Give two rules for spelling, with final 'e'. Name two exceptions to each rule.

6. Define the following prefixes and use in connection with a word: Bi, dis, mis, pre, semi, post, inter, mono, sup.

7. Give two uses of silent letters in spelling, illustrate each.

8. Mark diacritically and divide into syllables the following, and name the sign that indicates the sound. Card, ball, mercy, sir, off, cell, rise, blood, fare, last.

9. Use the following correctly in sentences, cite, site, sight, fane fain, feign, vane vain vein, raze, raise, rays.

10. Write 10 words frequently mispronounced and indicate pronunciation by use of diacritical marks and by syllabication.

GEOGRAPHY (Time, one hour)

1. What is climate? Upon what does climate depend?

2. How do you account for the extremes in climate in (Oklahoma Territory)?

3. Of what use are rivers? Of what use is the ocean?

4. Name and describe the following: Monrovia, Odessa, Denver, Manitoba, Hecla, Yukon, St Helena, Juan Fermandex, Aspinall and Orinoco.

5. Describe the mountains of North America.

6. Name and locate the principal trade centers of the U. S.

7. Name all the republics of Europe and give capital of each.

8. Why is the Atlantic Coast colder than the Pacific in the same latitude?

9. Describe the process by which the water of the ocean returns to the sources of rivers.

10. Describe the movements of the earth. Give inclination of the earth.

THE END

So that's the test. I'm not including the answers to the test questions because if you have been reading so far, then you know them all.

I'm sure you know that there would come a time that my Uncle Jefferson Wilson would quit looking at the gray and charcoal horses and started looking at Aunt Janine. There wasn't much way he could have helped it. There she was, just over the fence from his horses on most days. And a fact was, Aunt Janine liked looking at him.

They built a nice rock house a lot like Josie's, but they didn't have the beautiful Cinderella carriage in their yard, and they didn't have the two beautiful horses trimming the grass around the school. Instead of the horses, Uncle Jeff had a couple of sheep. He said they did a better job, and he got to have lamp chops sometimes.

My mom, Miss Josie, was relieved when her daughter was born. After she had Aaron and Adam, and then James and John, she was expecting to get another male double. Patterns do tend to continue, don't they?

It was only one girl, but there were those smart mouthed people like her papa, Brad, who said there really was two of her, both were just in one body. Old joke, but Papa Brad didn't know it, or care if he did.

Anyway, the girl got all the names Josie had been saving up for her daughters. She was named Merytaten Francesca Angelique

Evangeline Cullen, but papa couldn't seem to remember what came first, so he called her Mutt. That name sort of stuck to her until she became wife of the local minister. It didn't seem appropriate, somehow, after that.

I might mention, though there will be more later, that Josie kept all of Miss Francine's rhymes. After a while there were a whole folder full, because Francine started just slipping a copy to her every time she wrote one. Even after Francine had her own school, there were more of them. Miss Francine just thought that way... in rhymes.

Josie was as proud as a peacock when she thought of Francine's poems and Carmelita's stories. She was proud of Rosalie's help to make her cousin Carmelita's life so full, as that was what Rosalie wanted to do, anyway. Those two young ladies needed each other like two halves of a peach, and it was the two of them who taught Miss Josie's own daughter everything the girl learned at Prairie Academy.

Miss Josie was also proud of Carlotta for a totally different reason. When Josie heard the account of Carlotta abduction, which came out piece by piece over the next months, she was very proud of the girl who found the inner strength to hold her head up high and survive the degradation she had experienced. She hoped that the Academy had helped to give her a sense of confidence and worth, as she would have been a distinct loss to Carlile Corners if she had been left to carry out her stated intentions.

I am really glad, too, as Carlotta became my loved mother-in-law. She taught me an acceptance that I might never have learned without her, as I had no idea that the "surprise" promised by Mrs. Gray Owl when she saw the infant Daniel, was the gift of the wonderful, special Bible. Also, I could never have guessed the effect that Book would have on my own life.

Josie liked to think of the girls in her first two classes at the Prairie Academy as her "Belles." She wanted to think that she had a good part of what had set her "belles" to ringing, and she knew the world would appreciate the melody. I could understand that, of course, but to me they were still BLOSSOMS IN THE

GRASS. Each generation has their own viewpoint, and I was the one commissioned to create the chronology, so I get to chose the titles.

Miss Josie was also right about Eva Adams, because the young lady took a school about three miles south of the Corners. All in all, there had been more than 12 new teachers added to the prairie, counting those taught by the graduates of Prairie Academy and Shady Ridge Academy. That knowledge had always been important to her, a tangent result that validated her efforts.

New people came into the Territory constantly. Older folks gave over to the younger ones. Some who were from cities found the ruggedness of the prairie more than they were ready to absorb so they left.

There were those who lost an important family member and were forced to go "back east" to family. A mother lost in childbirth was a prime example, such as the Sutter family who had to leave the rock ledge house that Josie had purchased.

Others never intended to stay past the five-year proving up requirement. They were ready to trade five years of labor and time for a good price later. These quarter sections sold well because house, fence and water would be immediately available.

More hooks were applied to the wall in the small shop of Carlile Corners. The mail address to General Delivery, Argyle, Oklahoma Territory, with the note, "in care of Carlile Corners" had become a well-used address.

The old lady who maintained the shop, Miz Carlile, dozed her way through the day. Her money jar sat on the counter, and coffee or tea was warm on the potbelly. A cookie jar fed the hungry.

The wall sported a row of hooks with a small clip attached to hold letters. A shelf below was handy for packages, such as the ones containing orders from the Montgomery Ward Catalog. At least once a week, most of the Territory residents checked in, hoping for the all-too-infrequent letters.

An important incident occurred at that corner. It had been two years after their last year at the Academy, and the important test that proclaimed them able and qualified to teach children, ages twelve and under, that the McLaughlin sisters stopped by to check their mail hook, and maybe meet someone to chat with.

On that day, Kristy was almost fourteen, and Gwinnie had celebrated her thirteenth birthday. Miz Carlile was leaned back as usual in her comfortable rocker, the one whose cushions had been pressed into the exact reverse shape of her lumpy body. The tea was still warm, and there were still several coins in her jar.

Gwinnie spoke as usual and received no answer. Something was wrong, because the old woman never missed an opportunity to greet a customer. On checking closer, the girls realized old Miz Carlile would no longer be greeting customers on this earth.

Wide-eyed, the girls stared at each other. Someone had to do something, and it seemed they were elected as that one, or two as the case turned out. Kristie hurried to the door and stared out, silently begging for someone to be in sight.

There was. Old Mrs. Gray Owl was wrapped in her shawl against the brisk breeze and was stepping along with a lively gait. The frightened girl hurried with pounding feet to meet the old Kiowa doctor.

"It's Miz Carlile! She…"

"Hush, child. I know. I stay here you go tell mama."

The girls lost no time obeying and soon a gathering of neighbors crowded into the small building and began to make decisions. No relatives of the old woman had ever been mentioned.

Matthew Wilson, uncle to Josie, stepped forward. With no family of the old lady aboard, and at that time being the owner of the land under the building, he would be the logical next in charge.

Brad Cullen had the lumber available and a box was hastily put together. The ladies sorted through the small back room for suitable clothing for her last ride and farewell celebration, and a horseman was sent to notify close neighbors.

The McLaughlin sisters watched the flurry of activity, and at the same instant looked at each other with a question in their eyes. With the sudden sharing of knowledge that the girls had always had, they nodded agreement on what must be done.

Cornering their father, Kristie whispered, "The mail, Papa. Someone has to stay with the mail."

As they had often done in matters like this, Kristie spoke first to get the parental attention, and her sister was ready with either reinforcement or a suggested solution. Before their father could respond, Gwinnie whispered with a sad shake of her head, "Papa, we gotta stay here, Kristie and me. We gotta keep the door open and take care'a the money jar."

Kristie nodded, and followed up with, "See how Mister Wilson's wagon is coming with the box? You fellows could go help, and we'll take care of everything here."

Gerald McLaughlin ran a quick thought through his mind. His little daughters...? But then, if they could qualify to teach school, why couldn't they take care of this important place of business until something could be decided?

He looked at each of his attractive daughters noting their eager and expectant eyes, and agreed... as the girls had known he would. "Yes, you girls must stay, and we'll figure something before night."

Gwinnie's turn. A rapid shake of the head. "Papa! You men'll be busy. We know how to lock the door." They hadn't actually looked into that, but how hard could it be?

Then Kristie. "Tell Mama we'll need a few more cookies. We want to be here when someone brings the mail out from Argyle. I think there's a law or something about that, isn't there?"

By morning the girls had their plan solidified and complete. Papa would buy the corner of land where the shop stood and they would run the business. Someone would have to, and who could be better than a pair of young ladies who had passed the all-important Teacher's Certification test?

The girls knew there would be much more to it and a lot more that Papa would need to do, but it could wait. One thing at a time, and they needed to have their argument in order. This way, however, they would have their "feet in the door," so to speak.

The burying of Miz Carlile would give them a couple of days, or maybe three, and by that time they would have everything put together in their minds and in the best verbal form. It would cover what they wanted to do and what they wanted their pa to do.

It was actually something that Miss Josie had stressed. Think a problem through and put your thoughts in logical order. Hadn't they done it many times?

Matt Wilson was glad enough to be relieved of that half-mile strip. He didn't need it anyway. Two of his sons had taken over the Hastings place, Jeff had bought half of Josie's land, and his own baby, Darrel, would come back from New York City as a solicitor (lawyer), not a farmer.

Within months, Josie had reason to wear a proud smile as she walked only a short way farther for her mail. The new building was considerably bigger, much sturdier and a very great lot cleaner. The same neat mail hooks and shelf were there, but also there were two rows of them to accommodate expected newcomers.

A freshly painted sign announced that the building was THE COOKIE JAR, and variety of cookies were offered. Also soup or beans.

Clever, actually, Josie decided. Could it be that her plan of making her students create their own problems, have given birth to this idea? And how many more good ideas would follow? She'd wait with anticipation and watch.

Also, had the Certification Test given the girls been what had created in them the courage to venture into this business? Or even the very idea of owning their own business?

Gradually THE COOKIE JAR became a meeting place for young people with time and a few pennies to spend. Young men from the military outpost discovered the JAR as it came to be known, and their presence attracted young ladies who, in turn, attracted more of them.

There were several marriages that resulted in the loss of a girl when the young man went home after his enlistment, but there were just as many gains with the young men decided to stay and find a way to tie themselves to this new land.

Francine Canfield had such a good way with words. Just walking through the grass of the territory, she had noticed that the minute specks of bright colors almost hiding in the green spears, were readily found by the bees and butterflies.

She had penned, BLOSSOMS IN THE GRASS, and passed a copy to Miss Josie, as she had been instructed to do.

Josephine Wheeler Cullen read the poem with interest.

She saw Carmelita and Rosalie solidly tied to the Prairie Academy and doing well. Patricia O'Day and Bridget O'Grady with their needles, were becoming more proficient and skilled by the day, and expanding into more areas of needlework creation. Kristallyn and Gwendollyn McLaughlin were in business taking care of the mail and selling food, along with their sparkling personalities.

Francine Canfield, the poet, would be managing the school at Shady Ridge and Eve Adams had a school in process of being built, and it was only three miles south. At Enterprise, it would be

Even America Forrester had her own unique success story, but there is no room for it here. It will come up in detail in COOKIES, HATS AND HANKIES.

Eight young ladies in the process of making the first marks of their own life and none had yet reached age sixteen. They would marry, of course, but only when they wanted to… not of necessity.

If they were not the colorful blossoms in the grass of the prairie, what else could they be called? The mere sight of these exceptional young ladies was enough to comfort Josie's mind that she had indeed done what had to be done. But what about these girls was exceptional, and would others have been just as confident… given the same gift of education? It would bear thinking on.

A bit more about the Blossoms. The idea of Miss Josie's that the level four class would write an autobiography as their final examination in Grammar and Punctuation seemed to be such a good one that she continued as long as she taught.

Even after she turned it over to Carmelita and Rosalie, it was a good idea, so they continued it. Josie continued to show an active interest in the plan and was known to review later essays.

The two young teachers who replaced Miss Josie tried very hard not to pick favorites, but it was difficult. It was several years later that another Blossom appeared in the grass of the prairie, and the new teachers were quick to hand it over to Miss Josie to read.

Josie had not taught the girl, but she was aware of the time her family came to the Corners, as that was when the grist mill arrived. That, in itself, was a memorable occasion. The first daughter of them family, Bernice Bramwell, was four at the time, and her essay was penned six years later.

It began:

"The small girl's name was Bernice, but she was always called Neecie. She remembered a few things about being young, but her biggest memory was when she was four.

"Papa and Mama talked a lot and seemed happy, and then not happy, about something that was going to happen. It was like something good was going to happen, but it might be coming at the wrong time.

"Papa spent his days with his wheels. They looked like huge cookies, and they went around and around on top of each other when the little horses pulled them. They crunched and ground up stuff that people made bread out of. But now it seemed they were going to have to move the cookies.

"The cookies were very heavy, and Papa had to have help to roll them onto his wagon, and when he had half of them on his wagon, he went away for a lot of days. When he came back, he still had the big horses and the wagon, but the cookies were gone, and then he put the rest of the cookies on the wagon.

"That was when he got another wagon and loaded it with things from their house and a lot of quilts and pillows. They told Neecie that she and Reenie would be going for a ride. A very long ride. Reenie was too little to listen, but Neecie listened and thought a lot about it.

"Neecie's Mama had bad feet. They were fat and red, and they hurt when she stood up. She was eating a lot. The girl thought it was because she didn't feel good. Then she got fat in the tummy, but she still didn't feel good. When she sat down, she put her feet on another chair, so they wouldn't ache. When she needed something that she couldn't reach, she asked Neecie to get it for her.

"Then when everything was in the other wagon, the Papa watched Mama climb up onto the driver seat, and he looked worried, and he shook his head sadly. Neecie thought Mama looked good in the seat, because it was wide and she could put her feet up. The Mama told Papa, 'Don't worry because the horses will follow you. I won't even have to drive them.' Papa looked like he wasn't sure that would happen.

"But then there was a day that Papa helped Mama get in the wagon and lifted Neecie and Reenie in with her. He had a long rope, and he tied it around Reenie's tummy and tied the other end to the leg of Mama's bench.

"Reenie was little and couldn't talk, so she sat there and patty-caked. Neecie watched everything that was happening, so she would know what to do next. The Mama said 'Neecie, you'll have to play with your sister a lot because I have to sit up here and drive the horses. I want you to bring the sack of diapers over here, so I can reach them when we have to change Reenie.'

"That was easy, so Neecie brought the diapers. Then she handed Reenie a piece of biscuit so she wouldn't squeal.

"Papa still looked worried, but Mama told him to get started so they could get there. So Papa stepped into the front wagon and yelled at the horses. Mama said 'Git up' and the other horses followed. Mama was right about that.

"Reenie ate the biscuit and went to sleep, but when she woke up, she was cranky and the Mama said, 'Neecie, play with your sister and try to keep her quiet.'

"Neecie tried, but Reenie liked to squeal, and it made Mama sad, and she cried sometimes and rubbed her feet and legs, but the red did not go away and her legs got big and round. Neecie really wanted to go to the back of the wagon and watch the little horses that followed us. They all had ropes on their necks, and they followed along behind like they were in hurry to keep up with us.

"Neecie got really tired of riding and trying to make Reenie be quiet so Mama wouldn't cry. She wondered if they would ever get to the place where Papa wanted to go. They stopped at night and slept in the back wagon. Papa fed the horses, Mama tried to feed everyone, and then they went riding again.

"One of the days Mama felt really bad, and her face was wet. Neecie was so sad she crawled to the back of the wagon and looked out because she couldn't help Mama, and Reenie tried to crawl after her. The rope stopped her, but she kept fussing and trying to crawl out of the rope. Then she got really mad and screamed, and Mama said 'NEECIE, do something for your sister!'

"That was when Neecie saw that Reenie had untied the rope and was crawling to the back of the wagon with her. Neece called out and said, 'Mama, look at Reenie! She's trying to crawl away.'

"Mama said 'No, she can't. You have to play with her, so she won't squeal.'

"By then Reenie had crawled almost all the way, and if Neecie grabbed her around her tummy, she just screamed louder. Mama said 'SHUT HER UP, NEECIE.'

"Neecie tried to, but she couldn't. Reenie reached the back end board and pulled up on her legs to look out. There were so many pillows, she was wobbly on her legs, and so was Neecie. Reenie's diaper was soggy and was slipping down, but she didn't care. She just squealed and waved at the six little horses.

"Neecie put her arm around her, but she pulled it off and screamed. Then she leaned over to get away from Neecie's arm, and her feet came up and her tummy was rocking on the end board.

"Neecie caught both legs and tried to pull her back, but too much of her was already over the board, so she was too heavy. Neecie got a hold onto the diaper that was soggy and tried to pull her back, but the diaper started slipping down on her legs. That was when Reecie tipped over, and her feet came came all the way up.

"Neecie grabbed her leg right by her foot and hung on and yelled, 'MAMA! MAMA!' Mama said 'Hush, Neecie. I can't come back there to you. You have to be a big girl and hush.'

"Neecie was then leaning over the end board, and holding Reenie with one hand on her foot and one hand on her diaper. Reenie was upside down with her dress hanging down over her head, and she was waving her arms and screaming. Neecie looked down at the ground just below Reenie's hands, and it was rocky, and the little horses were right behind and would step all over her if she fell.

"Neecie felt her hand slipping because Reenie was wet and slick, and her diaper had come all the way down to her knees. She was kicking so bad that Neecie couldn't hold the other foot. Then Neecie screamed again, and said 'MAMA! MAMA! MAMA! MAMA!'

"Finally Mama said, 'ALL RIGHT! I'M COMING.'

"Mama put her sore feet over the back of the bench and saw Neecie with her feet waving, and she didn't see Reenie at all. She screamed, 'HOLD ON, NEECIE!' She tried to come to help, but pillows got in the way and she fell and bumped her head.

"One of Neecie's feet caught under a bench, and she stopped slipping, but Reenie was almost on the ground. Neecie's hand was cramped, and her fingers hurt. She knew Reenie was going to fall under the feet of the little horses.

"Finally Mama got there and leaned over, but she was fat in the tummy and couldn't reach all the way down to Reenie. Then Reenie kicked again, and Neecie got the other foot in her other hand.

"Mama said, 'Hold on, Neecie!' And then she began to pull Neecie back in the wagon. When Neecie's both feet were on the wagon floor, Mama could reach Reenie's diaper, and then her leg. Together, they pulled her back up over the end board and Mama lifted her down.

CHAPTER 11

She pulled Reenie into her lap, and Neecie didn't want her to do that, because then her dress would be soggy, but Mama was mad at Reenie and didn't listen. She looked her and said, 'Katerina Bramwell! You're going to be the death of me yet.'

"Reenie just looked at her and patty-caked on her face and squealed. But Neecie looked at Mama to see if the death had started yet. She didn't look different, but her face was very red. Then she started to cry, and Neecie was scared that she was crying because the death had started.

"That's when Neecie crawled over everything and got to Mama's driving bench. She screamed as loud as she could 'PAPA! PAPA! PAPA!' The big horses pulling the wagon turned to look at Neecie, and she must have said for them to stop, because they did.

"In a minute, Papa yelled, 'Whoa!' and the other horses stopped. Papa jumped out of the wagon and ran back. He grabbed up Neecie and carried her to the back of the wagon where Mama sat and held Reenie and cried while Reenie patty-caked on her head and squealed.

"Mama tried to tell Papa what happened, but she couldn't for crying. Papa crawled in the wagon and found the diapers. Reenie really needed one, so Papa put it on her.

"Finally he could understand what Mama was saying, and he said, 'You mean Reenie fell out the back, and Neecie caught her and held on until you got here? But she's only four! She's too little to do that.'

"The Mama said, 'But she did, I tell you.'

"Papa put down Reenie's soggy diaper and reached for Neecie. He pulled her into his lap, and scooted over close to Mama, and hugged them both. Reenie patty-caked on the Papa's arm and squealed and Mama started to cry again.

"Papa looked at her and said, 'Do you think it's time?'

"Mama nodded, and Neecie thought Mama would fix something to eat, but that wasn't it. Papa just took a deep breath and let it out in a long, tired sigh.

"About that time another wagon came down the road, and it stopped to see if they could help Papa. They said they lived just down the road, and maybe Mama would like to come in and rest a minute. But Papa said she needed to do more than rest. He said he thought it was her time and the man said, 'Oh, that! Just pull on up a little piece to the house.'

"Neecie wanted to cry because it was Mama's time for death to start, but she didn't cry. If she was crying, she might not hear if someone needed her to help.

"Papa drove Mama's horses, and Neecie stayed with Mama and tried to see if the death had started, and if maybe she could stop it. She couldn't really tell, because she had never seen death before.

"The people from the other wagon had a nice house and the Papa and Mama stayed all night with them. They gave Reenie a bottle of milk and let Neecie play with toys and their little boy. Mama was so tired, she laid down and cried a lot.

"When it was dark, they made a bed for Neecie, but Mama still cried, and Neecie thought the death was starting, and she wanted to help Mama, but the Papa wouldn't let her.

"Sometime in the night, someone brought a baby girl to the Mama, and it made her happy, and she didn't cry anymore. Someone said it was likely that the fall did it, but Neecie had fallen down a lot of times, and bumped her head sometimes, and nobody brought her a baby. Maybe she'd ask someone how that worked. She'd wait until sometime when there wasn't so much going on.

"Then Papa and the man left and took the big round cookies away. Neecie stayed and played with the little boy. It was a lot of days later that the Papa came back on a horse without the wagon or the man. He loaded Mama and his three girls on the wagon that pulled the six little horses. They rode for two days and came to a house where they stopped. It was a really good house, and the Mama laughed and sang. Her feet turned pink when the red went away. Her fat belly went away, too.

"When we looked around at the new house, the rest of the big cookies were there, and the man took a horse and left to go back to the little boy. Neecie stayed at the good house.

"The Papa rolled the cookies in place and hooked on the six little horses, so they would turn around and around. Then he was happy and he whistled and sang, but he got awfully tired.

"Sometimes he hugged Neecie too tight and told her she was such a strong little girl to save her sister's life. Neecie just smiled and didn't say anything. She didn't see how she had a choice with Reenie hanging down in front of the little horses. Nobody would let her fall, especially her sister, but Neecie kept remembering how bad her hands hurt.

"Neecie did a lot of things after that, and if they all were written down, there might not be enough paper in the world. Mama still had trouble with her feet, but they didn't get fat and red, and Reenie didn't like to help the Mama, even after she got to be 4 and 5 years old. Little Marietta was fun, but she made a lot of diapers that had to be washed and hung on the line.

"Papa got so tired, Neecie tried to help him, but Papa said, 'Never, never, never are you going to work around these grinding plates, or take care of the donkeys. You're a girl and you're not strong enough.'

"She asked him, 'If I was a boy, would I be stronger?'

"He looked at her, and finally he said, 'We'll never know, will we?'

"Neecie thought about that for a long time. She really didn't like for things to happen, or not happen, that she didn't know about. That was why she tried to listen to Papa and Mama when they were just talking. She liked to be really close but out of sight, playing with her doll or something, so she could hear. That was when they started talking about something called school, and how wonderful it would be for Neecie.

"Neecie thought... 'They are going to send me away? Why? I am a good girl, and I take care of Reenie, so she doesn't get in the road, or get lost in the tall grass. I hang diapers on the low line, and sweep the carpet, and I stay away from the feet of the little horses like Papa said. Why would they send me away?'

"She decided that she would watch closely, and when they started to take her away, she would hide. She spent a lot of time looking for a place to be hidden where Papa and Mama couldn't find her.

"But they tricked her. Papa took her for a walk and bought her a cookie, and then he took her across the road where a lot of children were. The children looked at her and smiled, and some of the girls waved their fingers. A beautiful lady showed her a place to sit at a little table and let her look at a book. If this was school, Neecie wanted to come every day... and sure enough, it was school. She came every day that she was not really, really sick. School was wonderfully fun!

"Nothing very special happened until Neecie was nine years old, and that's when a boy came to their house. He was not as big as Papa, but he was bigger than Neecie. Papa talked with him and showed him the big cookies that he called grinding plates. The boy seemed really nice and didn't get mad when when her little sister patted his leg with sticky fingers. He just smiled at her.

"The boy turned levers and twisted handles and he fastened the little horses into their places. He watched the cookie plates go around and emptied the little buckets of flour. He did a lot of things that Papa did, and Papa was happy. That was good, and Neecie was glad he was there.

"One thing was scary, though. When the day was over, he unfastened all six of the little horses and took all their ropes and walked to the barn. All the little horses followed him like puppy dogs, but she thought they might start running, and they had so many feet that they might mash him into pieces. If that happened, then Papa wouldn't have someone to help him.

"Neecia thought she would watch until he got to the barn, so if they tried to walk over him, she could yell and make them stop. She peeked through the logs of the barn and watched while the boy fed them and brushed the dirt and flour off their backs. Then he locked them in their pens with a lot of dry hay.

"The boy didn't seem afraid, but she always watched him go to the barn if she wasn't doing something else. She wanted the boy to stay and make Papa happy.

"She started noticing how much he liked to eat, and when Mama made a platter of eggs for breakfast, Neecie always set the platter by his plate to make sure he got all he wanted first. After a while she started putting three eggs on his plate before the blessing was asked, just to make sure he got them. He didn't say anything to her, but he smiled a lot. He talked with Papa a lot, too.

"After about a year, Neecie asked Mama how to make the boiled pudding with raisins because the boy named Homer liked it so much. She liked his name, too, because it sounded like "home" and she wanted him to be sure to stay at her home.

"It was when Neecie was eleven that Homer was sitting on the bench under the trees, watching the cookie plates go around that she came to sit beside him. After a while, when he didn't get up and leave, she asked him if he thought she should stay in school another year. Miss Carmelita and Miss Rosalie thought she should, but Mama needed a lot of help on things that Neecie could do.

"Homer thought a minute, and said she should do what her Mama thought she should do. Neecie nodded, but stayed on the bench beside him.

"Then he said, 'Neecie, I said the wrong thing. If the teachers think you should stay for another year, I think you should. You are a girl who wants to know everything, so you can help it happen if you think it should. If you don't like it, you always want to make it not happen. The teachers are smart, and they must think it's good for you to be that way.'

"Then he picked up Neecie's hand and turned it, palm side up, and said, 'You have nice, strong hands, but you don't need blisters and bumps on them. Your hands need books, chalk, and rulers.' He waited a minute and added, 'Neecie, I wouldn't have said all that, but you asked me, and I know you wouldn't ask if you didn't really want to know what I thought. I want you to be ready to do what you want to do, and you like school so you should go.'

"That gave Neecie a lot to think about, and she told Mama that the teachers wanted her to stay in school another year. She told Mama that she really wanted to, but she knew there was a lot to do at home.

"Then it was a few weeks later that Papa and Mama called her to them, and they all sat down to talk. Papa said, 'Do you really, really want to stay in school another year? If you got to do that, would you think it was something very special, like a gift?'

"Neecie was surprised, but she knew she must tell the truth. 'Yes, Papa, it would be the nicest present I could ever think of having.'

"Papa smiled at Mama and Mama smiled back. Papa said, 'Well, your Mama and I have talked a lot since you were four years old. We thought that sometime there would be something very special we could do for a very brave little girl who hurt her hands holding to her little sister and keeping her from dropping under the feet of the horses. We thought when that happened, we would be happy to give her the special thing she wanted if we possibly could. So have you decided this would be your present?'

"Neecie felt her mouth start to smile, and her arms flew around Papa's neck and then around Mama's neck, and she giggled and laughed and said she was so, so happy she might burst. Then she hugged them both again.

"When she saw Homer when he was not working with the cookie plates, she whispered 'I get to stay in school!'

"Then Homer smiled at her, and she noticed that he had the nicest smile in the whole world, and that was good, because he had the most handsome face in the world, and he was stronger than any boy she ever saw. She knew right then that she would do everything she could to keep him at her house forever.

"That pretty much covers the memory of Neecie's life up to now."

Miss Rosalie read Bernice Bramwell's essay and stared out the window for 3 whole minutes, and then she read it to Miss Carmelita. After that, the two ladies looked at each other and nodded their heads. It was written much as they had expected.

Bernice (Neecie) had appeared at the Prairie Academy at 6 years old... a solid-built youngster with a short dutch-bob of her black hair. Large black eyes peered out from under her bangs.

She attacked her lessons with notable seriousness for a 6 year old and demanded specific directions for every assignment. She did not like to be wrong or to be surprised. She was a pupil who would be hard to forget, but was such a pleasure to teach.

Next, the teachers shared the essay with Miss Josie, who had never had Neecie as a pupil, but had chances to observe her. The incident of saving her little sister had a total ring of truth to those who knew Neecie.

Being happy when Homer Forrester was hired... it pleased her as it was help for her beloved Papa. She assigned herself the duty of keeping him safe and healthy, so he would continue to be of help. She must have gradually come to realize that there was more to him than smiles and muscles.

When the important decision was to be made, she went to him first, hoping for advice. The encounter seemed much like a brother-sister relationship as he tossed off the first comment, turning the responsibility back to her mother.

But then, he obviously cared enough about her, personally, to tell her what he really thought and to add what he really wanted for her. That last statement was more like words from a valued friend, than a brother's bit of advice. His answer indicated that he had thought the matter through and had an opinion, even before he was asked.

The three ladies decided that, as being BLOSSOMS IN THE GRASS, Miss Neecie had certainly staked out her own place. As the next years passed, she opened out, petal by petal, into a full blown prairie daisy, well able to withstand the sun and wind of the rough territory.

Therefore, I, as the narrator, decided to put her here, though her time was a number of years later. More of Neecie will be noted and her future actions will fit with the information in her essay. Everything about Neecie fit together like a glove, which was the way she intended.

For a composite of the prairie girl who would turn into a solid, capable lady, well able to be teacher and principle of her own school room, Miss Bernice Bramwell would be high on the list. Her almost perfect Certification Examination also bore this out, and Neecie would have had it no other way.

In closing, I might comment again on the difficulty of putting a Chronology in logical order without repetitions. The fact is, a lot of things happen at the same time in a community, and that entails a few back-tracks and the resultant repetitions. Bear with me, and we'll cover it all. Or at least enough facts to tie it all together.

The neighboring community of SHADY RIDGE was so closely involved with the Corners, it has to have its own place. That is where you will meet Miss Francine Canfield again.

Hang on for the SHAPING OF SHADY RIDGE, we're almost there!

-BONUS EXCERPT-

VOLUME SEVEN

The Ozark Mountains Historical Fiction Series

MISSISSIPPI CENTRAL

THISTLES IN THE WIND

JOANN KLUSMEYER

MISSISSIPPI CENTRAL

1

The Findley family was in direct line of the right-of-way for the locomotive tracks for the Mississippi Central railway. Their sparse farm was located on the flat plain leading to the Tuscalera River. They would have to be moved. Trouble was, the owner of the land and the father of seven children was hard to deal with. It seemed an injury (or something) had happened, and his thoughts came out a bit twisted. It was pathetic and unfortunate, but the railroad was going to take the land, and there was that family to consider.

The oldest girl, Josephine, seemed to be the one to deal with, but her father wouldn't permit it. He was a wood cutter by trade, but there were no trees on his land that could be cut. He worked pitifully hard on land belonging to others who wanted it cleared, and his oldest son was drafted to help,

There were the children to consider, so what was to be done? They had no recourse but to avail themselves of the skill on a negotiator. The land would be taken, but the owner could not understand how the railroad got access to his land. It didn't make sense to him. Perhaps the negotiator could help.

It all started with the Mississippi Central, a busy little locomotive that plowed through Mississippi until it reached the big river. There it stopped suddenly, and any movement west was done by ferry, and then by horse drawn wagons and motor lorries.

Obviously, not much business happened that way. Now, if that track was made to pick up on the other side of the river, they could do away with the wagons and have contact the capital city of Arkansas, called Little Rock, and also a lot of lesser towns on the way.

Of course everyone knew that northern Arkansas was quite mountainous and unwieldy for building a railroad, but the southern part of the state was relatively flat and ideal for rice production.

Also, the Rock Island Line came down from Kansas straight to Texas, but there was a spur line over to a small town called Jacksonville. If the rail line left the river and went as far as it could on the flat land, perhaps, somehow, a connection could be made for the Mississippi Central to hook onto the Jacksonville spur.

A lot of the mountainous portion was practically uninhabited, as there were rock ledges and bluffs to contend with. But now the wise heads got together and decided it was possible. A lot of the land could be gotten practically free, and the owners of the rest of the land would just have to contend with it. Either take the price offered, or be evicted, and evictions were really bad press for the railroad owners.

A wide strip of trees must be taken from the railway right of way, and that made a lot of wood that was downed and must be cleared, but usually there were homeowners who came and cut it up for their home use.

The decision was made and the connection began in Jacksonville heading southeast to be met by the extension of the Mississippi Central.

This event made a lot of conversation in the small towns along the way, as to whether it would be good or bad, but it would make changes all along the right-of-way. In time, the small town of River Bend came into their sights. There the usual mountains to contend with, but there was also a very wide and rushing river to cross, and to get a permit from the state, they must install a wide, four lane bridge of steel with treated wood pilings to hold it up.

They had circled the end of one mountain range, being required to buy an eighty farm hanging on the side of the mountain. That farm was made up of bluffs and ledges of old rotting lava and solid gray boulders the size of a small house. If they bought that farm, they could use a narrow valley and escape a much worse section.

After that, the next land to be acquired was owned by a family with seven children and a man who cut wood for a living. He sold the wood to the residents of the little town, and seemed, somehow, to eke out a living.

The owner was a hard headed fellow, and didn't seem to see the value of the money paid, and insisted it was his land, and he was staying on it. Of course that was not going to happen, but the railroad hated evictions. They left such bad feelings, but they had a negotiator named Jonathan Snowden, a clever Scotsman from a family that was acquainted with mountains and volcanic hills.

Jonathan would be sent to iron out this little problem before the loggers who were cutting the right-of-way got close. Maybe a deal could be worked out for wood to sell, but that would be Jonathan's problem.

Mr. Jonathan Snowden, 25 years old, arrived unceremoniously on horseback. He tied his horse to the rickety hitching post and knocked on the door. Pa answered. Not good.

Josephine, age 17, was bent over the washboard with the stomper beating the dirt from the overalls of the wood cutter father and brother. Her ma, Ettie, was turning the handle of the wringer that transferred the washed clothes from the soapy water to the rinse tubs.

Ettie, in a concerned hoarse whisper, said, "Josie, get on in there and get where you can listen. You know Pa can't put two and two together nomore."

Josie nodded, dried her hands, and left. Her ma was a little bit wrong. Pa could put two and two together, but he could never understand a transaction, and ever since the accident, he thought everyone was 'out to get him.'

Josie eased into the room with a dust cloth. She wished to avoid an introduction, so she crossed the room and wiped the cloth on the glass of the window. It could stand a bit of cleaning, anyway, but who had time… and energy?

Mr. Snowden must have been clued in on pa, because he was using a soft voice and starting with reason. Yes, it was a raw deal, and a lot of people were upset about having to move. The railway made it as easy as possible, and even helped to find a place for them, and also provided help in moving their livestock and household possessions.

Pa wasn't having any of it. The fact was, he wasn't understanding what was said, or realizing the inevitability of it. Josephine and her ma couldn't see how they could lose on any deal made, as what they had was next to nothing. Wouldn't even grow a good garden. Winter rains on the mountain overflowed from the tributary and kept the ground soggy. Couldn't even leave turnips in the ground the way they should be kept, they rotted. Couldn't have a root cellar, it filled up with water.

Finally Mr. Snowdon gave up and walked back out to his horse. Josephine slipped out the back of the house and signaled to the negotiator, "Sir, are you permitted to talk with me?"

Jonathan looked toward the voice. "I can talk with anyone who'll talk with me. Would that be you?"

"Yes, sir. "My name is Josephine. I listened while you talked. Where would you find a place for us?"

"Josephine, my name is Jonathan. Do you have an idea of where he would consent to go? It would be dreadful to have the sheriff have to physically move him, but it will happen if we can't come to an agreement. The railroad line is coming right though where your house stands. I could have showed him the schematic, but I didn't think he'd look at it."

The girl nodded. "Yeah, and likely wouldn't understand it if he did. He didn't used to be this way, and he knows he ain't what he used to be and it makes 'im mad at everyone. I don't hardly think he could stand it to live in a town, and he couldn't cut wood, and that's all he can do now." She stared helplessly at the negotiator who stared helplessly back.

"Tell you what, Miss Josephine. I'll do some thinking. You've helped a lot in tellin' me about 'im, and I'll do some thinkin' and get back to you. Would there be a way to see you, without him along?"

"Sure could. Him and my brother go cut wood of a mornin' and get back for dinner about 2 o'clock. Till then it's just me and ma, and the little'ns. If you can give us an idea, maybe ma and me… well, we can try."

Jonathan nodded. "I can surely do that. Would tomorrow be good?"

"Any time you can come."

"Look for me tomorrow about mid morning." And he took the reins from the hitching post and swung aboard the horse. Josephine watched until he was just a spot on the horizon.

She went back to the laundry, and ma was wringing clothes out of the rinse water. It was a hard job alone, so Josephine took the wheel and turned while her ma fed the clothing into the rollers of the wringer.

Her ma looked her with a question in her eyes, and Josephine told her, "He's gonna come back tomorrow when it's just you and me. He's gonna see what he can do,"

"What'd that be…?"

"Don't know, ma. We'll see tomorrow."

TOMORROW MORNING

Jonathan was apprehensive as he entered the shack on the flood plain of the Tuscalusa. He was not particularly fond of this duty, but he knew it had to be done, and his success told him he was likely the best for the job.

He came in a buggy this time, as, if he was successful with his negotiation, he might need it.

Josephine and her ma were in the kitchen, which had a window toward the front of the shack, and they were glancing every minute or so, mentally crossing their fingers. This problem could get messy. Years ago there'd be no trouble with pa, and he'd see what had to be done and make the best of it, but his injury made him apprehensive, and extremely paranoid.

And when the buggy approached, they decided that must be him. Drying their hands and brushing down their dresses in an attempt to be presentable, they met him at the door.

Jonathan carried a roll of paper, and Josephine was immediately uplifted. He had something. A cross of fingers helped her to be hopeful.

He began, "I know you must be wondering if I had an idea, so I'll start right in. I did have one thing, and I hope it will be good for Mr. Findley."

He spread out what seemed like a hand-drawn map of the immediate area. There was the river and the marked out area of the right-of-way. There was a block representing the shack and an outline of a fence just on the other side of the river.

"What we have here is a Schematic, showing the projected path of the Mississippi Central and the surrounding area. Here where the marker is we have an abandoned farm. Your neighbor across the river could have just deeded a slice of land to the railroad, but he stubbornly held out for a total sale. He was getting older and wanted a place in town that was flat because he was tired of climbing.

"We arranged that for him, and the place is empty. It originally contained 100 acres, but 13 acres are in the right-of-way, leaving 87 acres, mostly up and down. It's impossible to show that on this drawing, but there is a bluff here and also up here, but the land is not soggy and has an excellent turf of grass. The former owner dynamited an edge of the bluffs to create a way to climb to the top.

"The whole area is fenced with the exception of that bordering the right-of-way. The place has a house in good condition, somewhat larger than this one, and it has a garden space that seemed to be productive. There is an all-weather spring and a roomy cellar. The shed could use some repair but is usable and quite roomy."

He paused to let the ladies try to imagine what he had said, and then he added, addressing Josephine, "There is now a number of goats in the top enclosure that the former owner used for food,

221

and they go with the place. If you think this might be a possibility for your family, I am ready to take you there. Would there be someone to stay with the children.

Josephine gave a look at her ma, who looked back and nodded. "Mister, them youngen can take care'a themselves."

Then Jonathan, "So you are ready to go look at it?"

Josephine answered for her. "Yes, sir, Mr. Jonathan. We'd like to go right now."

While the ladies sat on the back seat of the buggy, Jonathan drove across the rickety bridge that the railroad would turn into a wider bridge, braced with iron girders. He urged the horses to climb the hill to the first flat area. There, behind a grove of oaks and a few catalpas, was the house.

It stood tall and solid against the mountainside. It could use a coat of paint, but still looked strong and attractive. A rosebush was blooming in the yard, and a part-collie dog came out to meet them, wagging his bushy tail.

Jonathan said, "That dog refused to leave, so they just left him here. I imaging he is friends with the goats, and he seems well fed, so he must take care of himself."

He pulled up to the front porch and tied the horses to the hitching post prepared for that purpose. He could almost feel the anticipation of the ladies. Even from the outside, they could see it was miles better than the one down on the flood plain.

He produced a key, and they entered. Josephine turned and looked at all sides of the front room. "Look, ma, at these windows. I can see the river and the road and when the leaves turn colors, it's gonna be like a bouquet!"

Ma was silent, but nodded. They passed through the house and out to the shed. It had a southern exposure, against the north wind, and had a fenced corral. Josephine added, "Our cow'd really like this… and the horses, too, and look at all that grass!"

Jonathan smiled inwardly. It seemed all was well. "Would you like to climb up to the next level?"

They would, and also to top level. On top there were a lot of trees, and all were neatly trimmed to a height of about

6 feet. There were six long-haired white goats and several kids, bouncing around in their play. Jonathan wondered if he should say something, or should he let the goats do the selling. He paused and watched ma's face.

"You say them goats go along with the deal?"

"Sure do. There's room here for cows and horses, and I was told the goats take care of themselves, along with the dog, and I think they called the dog, Bowser. Sometimes animals form friendships like that. He may think he's protecting the goats"

Josephine stood on the edge of the top bluff and looked out over the land. She breathed in a deep breath of the breeze that was flowing up from the river.

"Mr. Jonathan, if we was to agree to the trade, how much money would it take to have this place?" That was important to know before she let herself get her hopes up.

Jonathan could never have heard words he liked better. "Miss Findley, there would be no money required. It would be an even trade. In addition to that, the railroad would move you free. They would send a van with fellows to do it. And they'd bring your animals, as well.

"You can plainly see the value of this place, and the railroad is willing to make an except in this case, and not put this place up for sale. The thing is, the decision must be made quickly. If Mr. Findley insisted on money, the value would not be nearly enough to buy this place, you can see, but the railroad is willing to do this for your family, so this difficulty can be over in a short time."

Josephine wanted assurance. "You sayin' we wouldn't need to pay any money, and we could just move in?"

"That's what I'm saying, but I might remind you. The state taxes on this place will be more than your house on the flood plain, thought I don't know how much. If you decide to do this, you'll know what the taxes will be. If you've seen everything you want to see, we'll go down and let you ladies talk about it."

They were silent on the down hill trip. Jonathan knew they were thinging what would be best with pa. He mustn't be let to say 'no' too quick, as he would not be likely to change his mind.

When Jonathan was driving away, ma turned to her daughter. "Josie, honey, you set your head to how to tell you pa. I couldn't do it. He'd see how much I liked it and he'd say 'no' thinkin' there was a trick in there somewheres."

Josephine was not surprised at the assignment. She was already thinking. She'd need to approach the subject round about so he'd not say 'no' until he listened to everything.

Ma had Josephine kill a chicken, and she had made huge kettle dumplings. There wasn't much meat, with so many diners, but there was fat from the chickens scratching on the wet soil for insects. The fat helped with the flavor, and pa liked dumplings... so warm and filling, and reminded him of his ma.

He was resting on the porch when Josephine brought him a cup of peppermint tea. While the tea had steeped, she thought, "I'll have to lift up them peppermints plants and take 'em to the hill." In her mind, she had already moved.

She gave him the tea and sat on the edge of the porch leaning back on a pillar, just like she had nothing better to do. Actually, she didn't, because this was the most important thing she ever did in her life, and she had to do it right.

"Pa, do you like goats?"

Pa thought a bit. "Used to," he finally said. "Your grandmum had a way'a fixin' 'em that us boys really liked. Thought one time I'd like to have 'em, but there weren't no place for 'em here."

Josephine waited a minute. "Today I saw some that were right pretty. Had long hair and the little fella's bouncin' around like rubber balls."

"What was you doin' out where you'd see goats?"

Josephine was ready. "Ma needed something from the Mercantile." True, as ma always needed something from the Merantile. That didn't mean she was going to get it.

"Fella that had the goats was givin' um away. Course, they had to stay with the place, and it was really good for goats. It was all up and down, and the goats were up top. Right pretty they were."

That had Pa attention. "He was givin' 'em away free?"

"Yeah, but they had to stay with the property. He wasn't lettin' em be took off, because they liked it there so much. You know what, Pa? Goats can trim trees. They stand up on their hind legs and reach up as far as they can for leaves. Can you beat that!"

"Yep. Seen that myself. Why'd the fella with the goats want to sell his place?"

"Gettin' old, he was. Bad knees... at least that's what I heard. Didn't see 'im, myself."

"Who's takin'care'a the goats?"

This was going good. Pa was interested.

Josephine answered, "Nobody, I reckon. Seemed there was a part-collie dog that was left with 'em, and the dog thought he was in charge."

Pa nodded. "Seen that, too. Them collie's... their good to have."

"Could be he'll not be alone very long. It's a good place with a house and shed, and it's up for sale or trade. I sure did like it." She stood and straightened her dress. "If you're through, I'll take you cup. I gotta get busy."

He handed the cup to her, and asked, "When you get time, you could bring me another cup'a that tea."

"I'll do it now." And she was gone. She smiled at the walls and doorway. The conversation was going better than if she had scripted it. Pa could still think, it just took him longer, and he was inclined to mix up the important parts of it. He must not be told too much.

Ma was waiting in the kitchen with a question in her face. Josephine told her, "Looks good, Ma. I didn't tell him about the railroad. He'll think about it, and I'll say more tomorrow."

Ma sat down heavily. She was in the last months of pregnancy, and it had been a hard, discouraging time. She was not up to it, physically, and they certainly couldn't afford another mouth to feed, but the mouth was coming, and the baby was certainly not to blame.

225

Josephine and Ma spent an anxious day, and Pa was again on the porch, relaxing from a hard day, and was preparing to go to bed.

Josephine brought the tea, and turned to go, and he stopped her. "You said them goats was up for trade?" Not that he had anything to trade, but the existence of the animals intrigued him.

Josephine drew in a concerned breath. It was dangerous to tell Pa what he could and couldn't do, but it was necessary this time. "No, Pa. It was the land with the nice house that was for trade. You wouldn't want a place that was so up and down."

She made a move to go, and he told her, "Sit down here, girl. You don't know what I'd want!"

She sat, practically at his feet. "That's right, Pa. I shouldn't'a been talkin'. It was just somethin' that I saw, them bein' so pretty and white against the grass and trees."

"Where at is this place?"

"Not far. A body could almost see it if they had a telescope."

"You think that fellow'd want to trade for somethin' like we got?"

"I don't know, Pa. I didn't talk with 'im, but I heard he didn't want no hills to climb on bad knees."

The silence hung heavily, disturbed only by a flock of gulls headed for the river. Should she… or shouldn't she. But she might have risk it. "Pa, I didn't ask much, not knowin' how you felt, or if you even liked goats. I think some folks don't like 'im. Wisht I knew how your Ma fixed 'im."

"Why would you care? We ain't got goats"

"I know, Pa. I just thought I might have goats some day. If I did, I'd like white long hair like them I saw on the bluff."

"Well, I gotta work, but if you'd locate that fella and asked, I might be interested. Couldn't handle much in the difference, if he wanted what we got. I'm thinkin' maybe mountain air'd be good for your Ma."

Josephine forced herself to not ruin this by being in a hurry. "Sure, Pa. I can find some time. Could be a while to track 'im down, and maybe it'd be gone by then." She knew perfectly well that Mr. Jonathan was expected tomorrow, hoping for an answer. This looked good, but there was another dangerous thing she must say.

"I don't know, Pa. That land bein' part'a the right-a-way, it'll be the railroad that has to ok the deal. That fella that was here, I don't know, Pa. Maybe he'd help, but he didn't say he would. I didn't get to talk to 'im that evenin' he was here. Maybe the fellas workin' on the right-a-way'll know how to reach 'im."

"Well, tell your Ma you gotta check it out. I'm done in. I got'a hit the hay." He handed her the tea cup and left through the door. She sat still for a moment savoring the success. Maybe it could get done before Ma's time came.

As she lay awake, she mulled over in her mind the shape of the hillside house. There seemed to be five rooms, and they were big rooms. There's be one for the boys and another for the girls, and one for Pa and Ma.

After that there would be a room for the kitchen and one for the parlor. What does a person do with a parlor? Not that they had furniture for a parlor! But it would nice to have an empty room on rainy days that the little ones were home from school. The school would be a little farther, but that could be taken care of later.

The thing, now, was to get the move done before Ma… Well, it was going to be a hassle but well worth the effort, if it worked. If this fell through, she thought she just couldn't stand it.

Spring water, it had, and it came flowing down inside a pipe all the way to the back door. Pure luxury. For sure!

She finally went to sleep. With a family of seven children, soon to be eight, life was nothing but work and problems. Some nights she was too tired to sleep. Maybe they could put a big tub in the shed and heat water for a bath. It seemed like a bath in a tum would help her sleep, and the wash cloth and wash pan just didn't get it.

JONATHAN CAME

His was apprehensive. He would have made the trip in a saddle, but the ladies might want to see the place again… hopefully the pa would be at work. He was.

Josephine listened as he told what the next steps would be. Her eyes shone with anticipation. She told him, "Even if the trade was even-steven, Pa'll likely want to make some change just to show he was in charge. I thought maybe you could put up a fence along the right-a-way between the goats and the train."

"Uh, the goats are fenced in, but I can to tell you this. We would be putting up a fence anyway. It's in the contract."

Josephine frowned, "But don't let him know. He'll want to think he got sometin' extra. I didn't tell 'im that there's be help movin' in. That'll mean a lot to'im."

Jonathan nodded. Understandable, from one in the shape of her father. There is often that paranoia when one is disabled.

He suggested, "I think I have a way to work this out. If you are sure of his answer, you and I can make the trip into town to make the transfer. Considering the health of your mother and the number of your siblings, I feel that the property should be in your father's name, and your name. It might be you taking care of your mother, if I don't miss my guess."

Josephine agreed. "Yeah, she had too many of us. Most of her life has been pregnant. Oh, I didn't mean to say that to you!"

"Think nothing of it. We'll take care of this. Shall we wait for your father for his signature? I will be signing for the railway, and believe me, you're doing the right thing. It was just a lucky chance that place was available. It is worth twice the price of this one, but the railway is glad to avoid the delay."

"Mr. Jonathan, you saw him. My pa won't even know his name was required. My ma needs to know what I'm doin'. I can tell my ma, and we can go now." Josephine's heart beat so hard it hurt her chest. The whote deal could be completed today! Then ma can be comforted that it's done.

At the bank where the transfer was made, there was no problem with Josephine signing for her father. The entire town knew the shape he was in.

THE MOVE

Pa came in exhausted as usual. Duncan, sixteen years old, worked with him and said he worked like a demon that was tryin' to escape the flames of perdition. He even had to be made to stop for lunch.

Duncan said, one time, that it seemed that Pa had been assigned a certain amount of work to do, and he was afraid he wouldn't get it done. He and Josephine were to think of that, later.

And he came home with hardly the energy to wash up for supper. Then he always sat on the front porch for a while. No matter how cold or wet, he sat on the porch a while before he went to bed. Said he really loved a porch, and never had one as a boy. So today he settled himself in the chair.

Josephine sat herself at his feet and leaned against his knees. "Pa, a wonderful thing happened today."

"Today…?"

"Yes, and you're gonna be glad. The house is all taken care of, and I knew you'd want somethin' extra, so I said we'd have to have a fence 'tween us and train track on account'a the little 'ens. They agreed to it 'cause they really want this place. And another thing you're gonna like. They'll do all the movin'. Strong fellas'll be her to load on the furniture, and they'll take the extra horses and the cow. Hard as you work, you shouldn't have to do that, and I fixed it all up for you. the same way you did things for me when I was little."

- END OF EXCERPT -

ADDITIONAL BOOK SERIES BY JOANN KLUSMEYER

The Great I Am Bible Story Series for Kids
6 books

The Young Pioneers Adventure Series for Kids
5 books

The Wentworth Triplets Mystery Series for Young Teens
3 books

Footsteps in the Canyon Adventure Series for Young Teens
4 books

Burnt Tree Junction Historical Fiction Series for Adults
6 books

Ozark Mountains Historical Fiction Series for Adults
7 books

Taming the Wilderness Historical Fiction Series for Adults
4 books

The Sheltering Stones Historical Fiction Series for Adults
5 books

The Trilogy of Wishbone Hollow Historicial Fiction Series for Adults
3 books